Crazy
for Your
L❤VE

Crazy for Your Love

New York Times Bestselling Author

LEXI RYAN

Cover and cover image © 2019 by Sara Eirew

Print ISBN
ISBN-13: 978-1-940832-23-4
ISBN-10: 1-940832-23-3
Interior designed and formatted by

E.M. TIPPETTS
BOOK DESIGNS

emtippettsbookdesigns.com

Other Books by
LEXI RYAN

The Boys of Jackson Harbor

The Wrong Kind of Love (Ethan's story)

Straight Up Love (Jake's story)

Dirty, Reckless Love (Levi's story)

Wrapped in Love (Brayden's story)

Crazy for Your Love (Carter's story)

If It's Only Love (Shay's story) – coming September 2019

The Blackhawk Boys

Spinning Out (Arrow's story)

Rushing In (Chris's story)

Going Under (Sebastian's story)

Falling Hard (Keegan's story)

In Too Deep (Mason's story)

LOVE UNBOUND: Four series, one small town, lots of happy endings

Splintered Hearts (A Love Unbound Series)

Unbreak Me (Maggie's story)

Stolen Wishes: A Wish I May Prequel Novella (Will and Cally's prequel)

Wish I May (Will and Cally's novel)

Or read them together in the omnibus edition, *Splintered Hearts: The New Hope Trilogy*

Here and Now (A Love Unbound Series)
Lost in Me (Hanna's story begins)
Fall to You (Hanna's story continues)
All for This (Hanna's story concludes)
Or read them together in the omnibus edition, *Here and Now:*
The Complete Series

Reckless and Real (A Love Unbound Series)
Something Wild (Liz and Sam's story begins)
Something Reckless (Liz and Sam's story continues)
Something Real (Liz and Sam's story concludes)
Or read them together in the omnibus edition, *Reckless and*
Real: The Complete Series

Mended Hearts (A Love Unbound Series)
Playing with Fire (Nix's story)
Holding Her Close (Janelle and Cade's story)

Other Works by
LEXI RYAN

Hot Contemporary Romance
Text Appeal
Accidental Sex Goddess

Decadence Creek (Short and Sexy Romance)
Just One Night
Just the Way You Are

ABOUT
Crazy for Your LOVE

From **New York Times** *bestseller Lexi Ryan comes a sexy friends-to-lovers romance. A family wedding with a fake boyfriend, meddling parents, and an obsessive ex . . . What could go wrong?*

The only thing worse than being single at my sister's wedding is finding out that my ex will be there too. Not just any ex—the guy everyone expected me to marry, the man I came to Jackson Harbor to escape.

Now I need a date, and fast. Enter Carter Jackson—the firefighter who's dealing with an unwanted five minutes of fame ever since a shirtless photo of him saving a puppy went viral. He's warding off propositions left and right, and he needs a fake relationship as much as I do.

Sweet and sexy, Carter is completely off-limits. See, I have a rule. A no-heartache rule. Not only is Carter my friend and a known heartbreaker, but his job as a firefighter puts him in danger daily, and that's something I just can't handle.

The commitment between us might be pretend, but the passion all too real. As crazy as it makes me, I have to keep Carter at an arm's length. Even that might not be enough to spare my heart.

Crazy for Your Love is the fifth book in The Boys of Jackson Harbor series. All books in this series can be read as standalones!

For Rhonda, my editor, my friend

Chapter ONE

TEAGAN

He's *nervous*. Carter Jackson, Jackson Harbor's most eligible bachelor, viral internet sensation, and the face of female fantasies all over the country, is *nervous*.

"If you keep pacing, you'll wear a hole in the floor," I say from my perch behind the curtain.

Carter stops and spins to face me, those midnight-dark eyes narrowing. "You have to get me out of this."

I bite back my smile. I shouldn't laugh. It's not nice. But my hot friend's predicament has been a laughter gold mine for me during the last month. Tonight is the first annual Jackson Harbor Brews for Shoes benefit dinner and bachelor auction. Two months ago, Carter agreed to be auctioned off for a good cause. At the time, it seemed like nothing. He was one of many firefighters who agreed to sell themselves for an evening of wining and dining. But one month ago, everything changed, and now the Jackson Brews Banquet Center is packed to capacity with crazy, screaming women from all over the country, ready to rip each other's hair out to get the winning bid.

"*Hero, hero, hero!*" The chanting gets louder and louder.

"You want me to sneak you out the back?" I ask, grinning. "Save you from the scary rich women?"

His eyes are wide as he strides toward me. "Think you can?"

To say Carter is a ladies' man is a serious understatement—he's the biggest player I know. So why is he scared to let some women bid for a night of his company? I try not to laugh. I *try*, but it's just ridiculous. A snort slips out anyway, and then my laughter follows.

Carter scowls at me. "I hate you."

I hold up a hand. "Sorry. No, really. I get it." I inch the curtain open and peer out onto the stage, where Molly McKinley is quieting the crowd and segueing into her speech about the good the Shoe Bus will do for the children of Jackson Harbor and surrounding communities. Beyond the stage is a sea of women, many pushing around each other to get closer to the front. "They do all look a little . . . intense."

Sighing, Carter drags a hand through his dark hair. It does nothing to ebb that rumpled, fresh-out-of-bed look he has going on. I wouldn't admit it if someone paid me to, but I totally understand why women lose their minds over this guy. He's hot. *So hot.* "They're nuts."

On Labor Day weekend, Carter rescued a golden retriever puppy trapped beneath the trampoline float at the public beach. Some well-meaning bystander snapped a picture of him striding out of the water—bare-chested, his jaw set with determination, the sopping-wet pup curled in his arms. The Jackson Harbor Fire Department posted the image on their social media, and in the following forty-eight hours, Carter's world exploded. The image went viral, and he became the face of every sexy firefighter fantasy out there. Carter did a couple of TV interviews, deciding to use his fifteen minutes of fame to speak to the public about life jackets and water safety, but his fifteen minutes lasted longer and stretched further than anyone expected. Suddenly, Jackson Harbor wasn't only teeming with tourists here for the beach, but with women who made the trip for the scenery of the JHFD variety. Then when word got out that Carter was one of the bachelors up for auction tonight, Carter fever picked up anew, with tickets for the event selling out within five minutes of going live.

"You should have backed out when Molly gave you the choice." I squeeze his arm through his suit jacket. "She would have understood."

"I thought it would die down by now," he grumbles. "There are men and women literally risking their lives saving people every day, and all these ladies are losing their minds because I performed a puppy rescue that my niece probably could have managed."

My amusement fizzles away when I see the frustration in his eyes. As easy as it is to laugh about how any single guy would want the attention thrown his way the past month, the reality has been an endless invasion of his privacy at best. I slide off my stool and straighten his jacket. "I'm sure most of the women out there are completely normal. I doubt many of them plan to chain you in their basement."

"Somehow, that's not reassuring."

Ava Jackson, Carter's sister-in-law and one of my best friends, pokes her head through the door backstage, her new dark bob swaying around her jawline. "You're up first, Carter. Are you ready?"

There's something close to terror in Carter's eyes. He's six foot two, two hundred-some pounds of solid muscle, and he's truly afraid of these desperate single women. "Ready," Carter says without taking his eyes off me.

"You'll be fine," I whisper.

"I hope you're right."

"And if the lady who wins you turns out to be a serial killer, wave me down. I'll be here all night."

"You *do* owe me a favor."

I frown. "I do?"

He folds his arms. "Remember the night you mauled me in Jackson Brews and made me pretend to be your boyfriend?"

Right. That. My cheeks blaze with the reminder. "I already said I'd help."

Out front, the music begins to play—Carter's cue—then Molly says, "Now, to kick off the night, the man you've been waiting for, Jackson Harbor's most eligible bachelor, Carter Jackson!"

"They're waiting." I wink at him.

Carter rolls his shoulders back and pushes through the curtain. I blink as he transforms himself with a smirk and a cocky swagger. He looks at home on that stage, as if doing this is *his* fantasy.

"We'll start the bidding at one hundred dollars," Molly says. She beams at the crowd, a picture-perfect emcee with her fitted pink dress suit and sleek platinum hair. "Friendly reminder, ladies, your bid entitles you to the pleasure of Carter's company for the evening, nothing more. This is a family event."

As the crowd laughs at her warning, I jog to the access door to take the back hallway around to the banquet room. I was only in the back to tease Carter, and I'll be in the way if I stay through the whole auction. By the time I enter, a throng of women have pushed themselves to the front, and bidding has reached fifteen hundred dollars.

"Fifteen hundred dollars for a couple of hours with my brother?" Shay asks, stepping up beside me. The lone Jackson sister is dressed like me tonight—little black dress, her dark hair pulled up. "Damn. Maybe he should leave the fire department behind and be a male escort."

I laugh, shaking my head as the women talk over each other with their bids. Carter is *smoking hot,* and if he weren't a friend, I'm pretty sure I'd happily empty my bank account for a night of looking at that face and getting to feel his body pressed to mine.

"Two thousand dollars to the woman in the pretty red dress," Molly says.

Carter struts across the stage and stops by Molly, who's updating the bids as fast as her mouth can say the words. He scans the crowd and then stops when his gaze lands on me.

"Excuse me," he says into the microphone. His sexy baritone reverberates throughout the room, and the women at the front lose their shit, throwing their arms up and surging toward the stage like he's some sort of rock star.

"Marry me, Carter Jackson!" someone shrieks from the mass of bodies.

Carter chuckles into the microphone and gently takes it from Molly's hand. "Hey, everybody."

More screams of adoration. More desperate shrieks proclaiming love.

"There are no words for this level of insanity," Shay says.

I grin. "No kidding."

"I'm sorry to interrupt the bidding, Molly," Carter says with a bashful grin toward the banquet's emcee. "I have something I need to do."

"Four thousand dollars," someone shouts, and the crowd laughs.

Carter draws in a deep breath. "Wow. Ladies, I'm humbled. I truly am. But I'm going to ask if we can do something a little unconventional tonight."

"What is he doing?" Shay asks.

"I have no idea," I mutter, even as dread curls in my stomach. Is he going to call in that favor *now*?

"When I agreed to do this bachelor auction, I was a single man looking to meet a beautiful woman, but a lot has changed since I signed up to stand on this stage tonight." The crowd laughs. "I started seeing someone. We've kept it a secret until tonight, but I have to confess, in the past two months, I've fallen in love."

"He's *what*?" Shay says as the crowd reacts with a chorus of *aww* and a few gasps of protest.

"Would the beautiful Teagan Chopra come on stage, please?"

He didn't.

Shay snaps her head to me, her eyes wide. "You're seeing Carter?"

6

"I . . ."

One by one, the members of the crowd turn away from the stage with whispers of *"Who is she?" "Where?" "He has a girlfriend?" "I thought this was a singles auction?"*

"Teagan?" He crooks a finger at me and flashes that lopsided smile that makes even *my* knees go a little weak.

My cheeks blaze. To all the world, Carter is smiling at his girlfriend, but I know him well enough to see the truth in his eyes. *"You owe me,"* that smile says. *"Don't let me down."*

My journey from the back of the room to the stage is miserable. Thousands of eyes are on me—judging, speculating, criticizing—and the whispers feel like razor blades to my flimsy confidence. If this is Carter's way of calling in a favor, I'll be sure to never ask anything of him again.

When I step onto the stage, he takes my hand and grins. "Isn't she beautiful?" he asks the crowd, and he's treated to agreeable, if reluctant, applause.

I lift onto my toes so I can whisper in his ear. "I'm gonna kill you."

He gives me that signature Carter Jackson cocky grin, and I'm sure the whole damn crowd thinks I whispered some dirty promise. He brings the mic back up. "Since I wouldn't feel right letting someone bid on me when there's only one woman I want to spend my night with, I'm going to bid on myself."

I snort, and he flashes me a look.

"Molly, I'm proud to donate five thousand dollars to the Shoe Bus in exchange for spending my evening dancing with the woman I love." He squeezes my hand tighter, as if he's afraid I'm going to run away. To be fair, if I weren't so paralyzed by shock,

I might. He pauses dramatically and turns to face me, and the crowd is really into it now and cheers loudly. I spot a few angry faces pushing toward the exits, but he's laying it on thick enough that most people are smiling. "What do you say, Teagan?" he asks so softly that the mic almost doesn't pick it up. "Would you spend your night with the man who can't keep his eyes off you?"

"You're killing me," I say, and the mic picks it up, making the crowd laugh.

Grinning, he passes the mic back to Molly and pulls me into his arms. I have no choice but to let him. Okay, I do have a choice. I could snatch that mic out of Molly's hands and tell everyone that he's a big, fat liar who *is*, in fact, single as a Pringle. But if I do that, tonight's fundraiser might go all to hell, and as irritated as I am with Carter right now, I like him too much to sacrifice him to an angry mob of lust-crazed women.

And you do owe him, the little voice in my brain chides.

Fine. One very public night with Carter Jackson in exchange for him pretending he was my boyfriend for five minutes last year. *Totally fair.*

The band smoothly transitions into Etta James's "At Last," and Carter leads me into a dance onstage. I'm well aware of the heat of his body against mine. The smell of his aftershave fills my head and makes me forget this is Carter, my friend, *not* some guy who's going to take me home and ravish me.

"Thank you for the incredibly generous donation, Carter," Molly says as the song plays. "And thank you everyone for coming tonight, and of course a huge thanks to our sponsor, Jackson Brews. Don't fret, ladies. Carter's only the first of many bachelors ready to wine and dine you tonight. Stick around for your chance to bid on more men from the Jackson Harbor Fire Department, followed by dinner, dancing, and door prizes!"

"I cannot believe you used me to get out of this," I growl in his ear. "Who knew you'd be so afraid of some handsy women?"

He chuckles and runs his big palms down the sides of my sexiest little black dress. A hot shiver races up my spine. "I thought it was genius. Thank you for playing along."

I pull back enough to scowl at him. "You owe me so big."

"How do you figure? You were returning a favor, remember?"

"I had to get onstage in front of hundreds of people."

The band plays the closing chords of the song.

"Thank you," says their vocalist. "And thank you to the beautiful couple on stage. You two look amazing together. Don't they?"

The audience applauds.

"See what I mean?" I mutter. "This is hell."

"Teagan, shut up and kiss me."

CARTER

I think I just stunned Teagan speechless, but now I have her in my arms.

Teagan Chopra. Teagan, who's all mouth-watering curves and wicked humor. Teagan, who's best friends with my brothers' women and has become a fixture in my life.

Teagan, who's friend-zoned me so many times that I vowed

9

to stop fantasizing about her. But the moment she looks up at me with those big, dark eyes, I know my embargo on Teagan fantasies has been shot all to hell.

Truth be told, I've wanted to kiss Teagan Chopra for a long time now. Like, *years*. And, sure, I would've picked a different place than at a fancy-ass fundraiser in front of hundreds of people for our first time, but as I dip my head and touch my lips to hers, I decide I don't care. I don't care where we are or how long I had to wait.

"Carter," she whispers against my lips. But the crowd roars its approval, and she gives a subtle shake of her head and a sigh of surrender. She slips her hand behind my neck, and her long fingers thread into my hair as she brings her lips to mine.

Her mouth is soft and sweet. I grip her hips, pulling her body against mine. I'm aware of every inch of her—every curve and plane, every hitch in her breath.

"That's more like it," the vocalist says. The band starts into Ed Sheeran's "Thinking Out Loud," and someone pulls the curtain on the front of the stage, shielding us from the stares of the crowd and leaving us in darkness.

I keep her close for a beat, trailing my knuckles up her side and down again.

She trembles before stepping back, fingers to her lips. Even in the near darkness behind the curtain, I can see the worry on her face, and I don't like it. "I haven't had enough to drink for this."

Damn. I don't know what I expected to see or what I expected her to say, but her words hit me in the gut. I do my best to cover with humor. "Come on, I can't be *that* bad at kissing."

10

Her laughter breaks the tension. This is Teagan. Of course she's not going to make a big deal out of a kiss. "If only you were, Carter. If only you were."

As Molly introduces the next bachelor, I take Teagan's arm and lead her through the service hallway so we can return to the party. "Was that a compliment?"

"Maybe." She sighs. "Or maybe it's been too long for me, and I've forgotten what it feels like."

We stop at the double doors that lead into the Jackson Brews banquet room. "Any other physical sensations I can help you remember?"

She smacks me in the stomach with the back of her hand. "You are *shameless*."

I turn up my palms. "What? I'm just offering."

"Real selfless of you, Carter Jackson," she says, but she's still smiling, so I call it a win.

"Let me get you a drink. The least I can do." Taking her hand, I lead her back into the fray and to the bar, where my brother Jake is flipping bottles in his best *Cocktail* impression, to the delight of the small crowd gathered there. "What are you drinking tonight?"

"I think I need a martini." Her grin is apologetic, the whole *it's not you, it's me* thing.

I push down my disappointment. I didn't think my fake grand gesture would be the beginning of something for us, but I hate feeling like my arm is the last place she wants to spend her night. "Sure thing. You can go ahead to the table, and I'll meet you there."

"After seeing those women throw a fit about losing their

chance with you, I don't think you should get too far from me." She tugs me closer and cuts her gaze to the cocktail table a few feet from us. Two women sip on pink cocktails and leer at me. They're beautiful, but "barely legal" isn't my thing.

"You're going to be my bodyguard now?"

She surreptitiously glances their way again before nodding. "I could totally take them."

"I don't doubt it."

"And you're my bodyguard too," she says. "I don't want to be alone when your family corners me for explanations."

"They won't. Not tonight, at least." The fundraiser is too important to Jackson Brews and to Molly for my siblings or mother to risk bad press by exposing my very public lie. And anyway, they know how nuts it's been this last month, so they might not be surprised that I couldn't go through with the auction—even if they don't fully understand why.

"I can hold my own for a few minutes." I point to the sweetheart table at the front, reserved for me and my date. "Standing in those heels can't be comfortable."

"They're completely wicked." Teagan shrugs. "But who can resist a strappy, glittery heel?"

Who, indeed? I recognize this pair as her go-to for fancier dresses. They make her legs look amazing and have inspired more than a few fantasies I'd rather not admit. Fantasies I've typically pushed out of my mind, but that refuse to go now that I know what she tastes like . . . now that I can hardly think about anything but tasting her again.

"I'm a pro, Carter. I can stand in these all night long."

"What else can you do in them?" I ask.

She jabs me with her elbow. "Don't you wish you knew."

I show my palms, all innocence. "I was asking about *dancing*."

She snorts. "Sure you were."

"That was quite a show," Jake says as we step up to the bar, but he's studying me as if he's trying to figure out if maybe we do have a secret romance.

"He needed a big, strong woman to protect him," Teagan says, winking at me.

I lean over the bar so only Jake can hear. "You have no idea how scary some of those ladies are."

It's true. For the past few weeks, I've even been avoiding Jackson Brews and the tourists who've been frequenting my family's bar in search of me. About a week after the picture went viral, I took home a woman who turned out to be a reporter here for the scoop on "the hot firefighter." After that, I couldn't risk it.

"He's lucky I owed him a favor," Teagan tells Jake. "It's only a matter of time before my mother hears about this and calls me to ask about our wedding plans."

"I hope you don't think I'm putting out before the wedding," I tell her, folding my arms. "I'm not that kind of boy."

This draws a loud snort from Jake. "That was one hell of a nice donation you gave to the Shoe Bus. I had no idea firefighters made such good money."

"It's the money from those damn interviews." I don't accept them anymore, but right after the picture of me and the pup went viral, I let my chief talk me into doing a couple of TV appearances. I used the opportunity to spread the word about water safety. Turns out I hated it, and it only made my weird fifteen minutes of fame last longer. I don't tell him that it feels wrong to keep the money. Or that I hate all this attention in the first place.

Jake's eyes narrow on me, but he nods. "It's just money, right?"

"Exactly."

"Are you two drinking tonight?"

Teagan grins. "We didn't stand in this line for *water*."

Chapter TWO

CARTER

Ten grand—that's how much the bachelor auction brings in for the Shoe Bus, fifteen counting my donation. The guys from my station are going to be cocky sonsofbitches for *weeks* after how much money they each brought in, but that's the least of my worries. Between the rest of the auction and dinner, something changes between me and Teagan. I get us more drinks between courses, but the easy laughter fades away the longer we sit at the table with everyone staring at us.

After our plates are cleared, Teagan finally looks at me. "Why'd you do it? Why not spend your night with one of the ladies who came to charm you?"

I'm sure it seems unreasonable. After all, I'm no stranger to beautiful women, and I'm not exactly shy. "I could see how the night was going to unfold. I'd have to recount the story and then have them sing my praises for something anyone would've done—anyone *could've* done."

She cocks her head to the side and studies me. "Not *anyone*, Carter."

I shrug. "I hate them acting like I'm a hero when in the scheme of things . . ." I grimace, unwilling to finish that sentence. *In the scheme of things, I'm a fucked-up failure. In the scheme of things, I'm just lucky, and the real hero of the JHFD died in a warehouse fire in April.*

"Well, it wasn't so bad," she says. "And now we're even. Right?"

"Right." I'm ready to tell her we can make excuses and get out of here, but the young women who were leering at me earlier descend on our table.

The first extends a hand to Teagan, flipping her straight honey hair over one shoulder. "Hi, I'm Jennifer. I wanted to meet the woman special enough to claim the heart of such an amazing guy."

Teagan shakes the offered hand. "Nice to meet you." She chases the words with a long pull from her martini that suggests otherwise.

"How do you two know each other?" Jennifer asks.

"We've been friends for a long time," I say, watching Teagan, who's staring at her martini so intently that I'm pretty sure she's preparing to write an ode in its honor. "It took me a long time to find the courage to tell her how I feel."

Jennifer presses her palm to her chest, her jaw dropping. "Oh. My. God. That is *so sweet*." She looks at her friend and squeals. "They were *friends*. And he's been into her *forever*, and just recently found the courage to do something about it."

Wow. I didn't know I needed a translator.

"Oh my God. *So sweet,*" the second woman says.

"You are so lucky," the girls tell Teagan in unison.

Teagan coughs on a gulp of martini, then nods as she wipes her mouth with the back of her hand. "So lucky."

"We're disappointed, of course," the first woman says. "We drove eight hours for a chance to bid on Carter."

"Heartbroken, really." The second one drags her gaze over me. I try not to squirm, but it's an effort.

"But we love *love,* don't we, Brit?"

"Totally," Brit says. "Love is our favorite."

"Right," Teagan says. "I mean, who doesn't?"

"Right?" Jennifer says.

I reach across the table for Teagan's hand. I'm probably going to burn in hell for this, but it might be worth it to get that tortured *we all know this is fake, would someone kill me now* look off her face. "It turned out Teagan had been harboring feelings for me the whole time too." Her gaze snaps up to meet mine. Good. At least she's looking at something other than her drink. "I'll never forget the day you showed me all those journals where you wrote me secret love notes."

Teagan's eyes narrow. Her jaw hardens, and the corner of her eye twitches. "Excuse me?"

Nodding, I turn to the girls. "She wrote one every day for a whole year. Some of them were a little . . . odd." I turn back to her and tilt my head. "I never thought I'd meet a woman who's actually turned on by watching me drink *beer.*"

Brit smiles. "*I'd* watch you drink beer."

Teagan ignores her. "My love notes were nothing compared to your little collection from my trash." She turns to the girls. "He saved old napkins and water bottles I drank from. Even little bits of my hair."

The girls cover their mouths and take a few steps back.

I choke back a laugh, determined to keep a straight face. "You make it sound creepy."

"We have to go," Brit says. "But congrats to you two."

"Yeah," Jennifer says. "You're a totally . . . special couple." They walk away, and I can barely make out Brit telling her friend that they dodged a bullet. Teagan drains her drink as we watch them go.

"Little bits of your hair?" I ask. "Am I in love with you or planning to murder you and store your corpse in my freezer?"

"I've known guys with creepier tendencies," she says. Standing, she holds out a hand to me and motions toward the crowded dance floor. "Come on. If we sit here, more women are going to want to talk. You dance, don't you?"

"I think I have to if I want to save my reputation. I'm lucky those women aren't local, or I'd never get another date."

I don't have much time to dwell on that thought. Teagan loops her hands behind my neck and rolls her hips to the song's quick beat, and I can't think of anything but her.

I'm stunned by the sudden press of her body into mine, and at first I'm not sure what to do with my hands. Sliding them behind her neck seems too junior high, but if they're in her hair, I know I'll be too tempted to tilt her face up so I can kiss her again. If I put them on her waist, they're bound to roam south to cup the curves her little black dress shows off so well.

"You started this," she whispers into my ear. "You'd better dance with me like it's real, no matter how much you're regretting it right now."

I grunt in surprise. Regret is the furthest thing from my mind. "I didn't want to scare you away," I say, wrapping my arms around her waist to rest my hands at the small of her back.

"I'm still here, aren't I?" She looks up into my eyes, and I wonder what's going on in that head of hers. She turned so quiet and awkward over dinner. I thought it was because everyone was staring at us, but . . . maybe there was more to it.

Am I crazy to hope that she's as attracted to me as I am to her? That she's thought about it—fantasized about it—like I have?

I lean my forehead against hers but keep my eyes open so I can watch her as we dance. When the music transitions into Christina Perri's "A Thousand Years," Teagan leans her head against my chest and sighs.

"You like this song?" I ask quietly.

She pulls away enough to look up and meet my eyes. "I just *love* love. Love is my favorite." She giggle-snorts so loud that half a dozen people turn to stare, and I stare too. Teagan's beautiful, but it's always been her quick humor and open personality that have drawn me to her. I don't care if this is fake. I'm going to enjoy every minute of this night.

I lose track of the drinks we have, the dances we share, and the women she politely sends away when they try to cut in. I imprint these moments on my mind—Teagan's smiles, the brush of her hands across my back, the way she leans her head against my shoulder when the music turns slow.

When the party's wrapping up and the guests are trickling

out, she says, "I'm glad I wasn't planning to drive."

"Come with me for a minute?"

She studies my face for a beat. Is she thinking the same thing I am—as desperate to give into this chemistry as I am? She swallows hard, then nods.

I lead her out of the banquet room, down the hall, and into the vacant office by my brother's. I press her against the wall. "I'm not ready for tonight to end." My voice comes out husky, all the desire I feel tangled into those few words. I could blame the alcohol, but this buzz in my veins is more about her nearness than the beer I consumed.

"Me neither," she says, her gaze dropping to my mouth. I don't need any more invitation.

I kiss her.

TEAGAN

This isn't the kiss from the stage—it's not a kiss that's gentle or asking permission. This kiss is hard. Demanding. Insistent. It's the kind of kiss a girl dreams about, where desire is written in every nip of the teeth and slant of the mouth, where the chemistry is so potent that it has a taste of its own.

Keeping me pinned between the wall and his hard body, Carter strokes a hand down my arm and positions a thigh between mine. "You look so damn beautiful tonight."

I pull back and stare into his dark eyes. My whole body is

buzzing. I'm tipsy from irresponsible amounts of vodka, sure, but I'm drunk on *him*—his touches, his smiles, his whispered jokes in my ear, his body pressed to mine. "You think so?"

Insecurity nagged at me all through dinner. I watched those women staring at him and kept thinking he should have let one of them bid on him. His brothers might give him shit for his revolving door of women, but Carter deserves a little fun. And a lot of happiness. One little kiss onstage had me wishing he could find both with me—despite our friendship, despite my own rules for pushing him away any time his flirting turned too intense.

"I thought so from the minute you walked in the door. I love looking at you in this dress. And those sexy shoes . . ." He swallows, his eyes dipping to the swell of my cleavage. "Dancing with you like that was killing me."

"Me too," I admit, and the room spins a little because I *want* this. His words, his mouth, his touch . . . *him*. "This is crazy."

"Then tell me to stop," he says, even as his hands skim up and down my sides.

"I don't want you to."

He groans in satisfaction. "Good, because I've been dying to do this . . ." He reaches for the hem of my skirt, tugging it up to give his hands access to my skin.

"Just that?" I ask.

He nips my neck, his mouth trailing up and down—kissing, sucking, biting. Hot bolts of pleasure arc down my spine and have me arching closer. "All of this," he murmurs. "I'm not done yet."

I encourage him with a low hum of approval. I love the feel of his rough fingertips over my hipbones, relish the scrape of his callouses across sensitive skin as he traces the satin waistband of my panties. His lazy fingers that send shivers down my arms and make my knees weak.

I pull his shirt free from his dress pants and fumble with the buttons. Three buttons in, impatience has me abandoning my task. I slide my hands under his shirt, needing the feel of his skin, needing to get closer.

He sucks my earlobe between his teeth, and I gasp. I rock my hips forward in pleasure, but he shifts his stance, denying me the friction I need. Before I can protest, he cups me between my legs. His fingers dance across the satin in light, teasing strokes. He growls. "You're wet."

I shift my hips, chasing his teasing touch. "You're observant."

He chuckles against my ear and finally gives me the pressure I'm dying for, rubbing my clit. Once. Twice. Three times.

"*Please.*" The word rips from my throat. I don't care about anything but the feel of his hand between my legs and the need that's growing bigger and bigger within me, erasing everything else that I am and replacing it with need. *Please, please, please.*

Slipping his fingers beneath the scrap of fabric, he grazes his knuckles right down my center and across my clit. He circles a finger right where I'm aching and most desperate for him.

"Carter," I beg. This is a fantasy. A waking dream. The alcohol in my blood makes everything hazy, but I can't blame it for this attraction between us. I've spent years pretending it's not there. Pretending we're nothing more than friends who know how to make each other laugh.

When he plunges a finger inside me, I'm already wound so tight that I think I might come immediately. All my focus, my energy, my *need* narrows to that one spot, and my body clenches.

"Hold on," he murmurs between licks up my neck. "I've got you."

He's slow, torturously slow, pumping in and out of me in deliberate strokes that are the antithesis to the frenzy in my blood. His thumb scrapes over my clit as his finger gradually drives deeper and deeper.

Some modest part of my mind worries I should slow the thrust of my hips against his hand or quiet the wanton pleas slipping from my lips. I ignore it and beg him to move faster. I tell him how good it feels, how close I am to coming on his hand, and *oh God please, yes, like that, please.*

Carter.

When I can't hold back anymore, he presses his thumb to my clit with the perfect pressure and slides a second finger in. Deep. Stretching me. Pushing me over the edge the moment his mouth opens over mine.

And I fall apart.

CARTER

I can't stop tasting her. Touching her. I trail more kisses up the side of her neck as she comes down from her orgasm. She shudders in my arms, and I want to make her come again and again. I want to drink her desperate moans, let them fill my head until they block out the rest of the world.

Her hands are up my shirt, one on my back, the other on

my stomach, stroking lazily, her fingertips dipping beneath the waistband of my dress pants with each pass. It's all I can do not to thrust into her touch, to guide her hand to my aching cock and feel her there.

But I don't want this to be a quickie in a vacant office. I've wanted her for too long to settle for that. "Come home with me."

"What?" Her eyes are unfocused, heavy—from the alcohol or the pleasure? Maybe both.

"Come home with me. Spend the night with me."

I see the fog clear, and she stiffens in my arms. She pulls her hands out from under my shirt and shakes her head. "I shouldn't. I mean, we . . . shouldn't. I'm sorry, I . . ." She searches my face. "Carter, we're friends, and if I go home with you . . ."

I wait, giving her time to finish that thought and willing myself to see it as a bad idea. But I can't. Right now, that's all I want. Teagan in my bed, in my shower, under me, over me, in front of me. I squeeze my eyes shut as the images roll through my mind, as thrilling as they are tormenting. "It's your call," I say, but I want to beg. I need her in a way I can't explain.

Her eyes search my face. "I'm scared of what happens if I do."

And I'm scared of what happens if you don't. But I nod. Even if I want her more than I can remember ever wanting anything, I won't push. "I'll get a cab. Let me see you to your door, at least."

"You don't need to do that. Molly is driving me home." She presses her palms to my chest, gently urging me back, then steps out from between me and the wall. "She's probably wondering where I am."

Tell Molly your plans have changed. Fuck the consequences, and go home with me.

I swallow the words. I recognize regret when I see it, and right now, it's all over her face. That's not what I want to be to her—a regret or a mistake. This isn't about her plans, and I'm not the guy who gets pushy when the end of a night doesn't go his way.

"I'm sorry." Even her voice sounds shaky. "The booze and that dancing . . . I got carried away."

I should let her go, but I cup her face in my hand and stroke my thumb along her jaw. "Promise me you won't go home and freak out about this?"

She nods, but we both know she already is.

I force a smile, for her benefit or mine, I'm not sure. "We'll talk tomorrow."

"Tomorrow," she says, the word as broken as I fear our friendship just became.

Chapter THREE

CARTER

Something's not right. It's too hot. I thought this was contained. There's static on my portable, then Gordak's voice. "New activity in the southwest quadrant. Pull out, boys."

I gesture to Max and wave toward the door. He's on the line only a couple of feet in front of me, but the smoke is so damn thick that I can barely make out his silhouette. "Come on!"

In together. Out together.

"There are kids on the second floor," Max says.

"I said, pull the fuck out," Gordak growls. "You can't see what I can see, boys."

I tug on Max's arm. We're all guilty of pushing the rules of engagement when kids are involved, but if Gordak says to pull out, we've gotta do it.

"Fine," Max mutters, turning. He nudges me forward, urging

me to lead the way, and I follow the rope line we've strung up and follow it to the exit. When I glance behind me to make sure he's close, Max isn't there. The heat is suffocating. I take a step back into the depths of the warehouse, but the rafters groan in protest. A warning.

"Mayday!" I shout into my portable.

I know what comes next. I lift my eyes to the ceiling and watch as it comes down on me. Suddenly, I'm in the navy-blue suit I wore to my father's funeral, and my mother is clinging to my arm.

"He was so proud of you, Carter," she says, right before the ceiling collapses and everything around me goes up in smoke.

I wake up with aching lungs and the taste of ash in my mouth. My throat is raw, and my heart is racing. Across the room, my alarm clock screeches from beside my bed. I'm in the middle of my bedroom floor, and my blankets are scattered around the room, as if I tore apart the bed in my sleep. I'm guessing I did. This isn't the first time.

I push myself off the floor and walk across the room to shut off the alarm. My vision's still blurry from sleep, and my hands are shaking from the nightmare I can feel as vividly as if someone set fire to my room while I was out cold.

Sleeping through my alarm is new, but the dreams aren't. I live a fucked-up variation of the night at the warehouse every time I close my eyes. This morning wasn't the first time my subconscious mixed that night with the day of my father's funeral.

"They were both traumatic for you," my friend Bethany said when I told her about my recurring nightmare. "Your subconscious is trying to sort through the pain and guilt that come with trauma and loss."

It made sense to me, so I haven't talked about it since. Talking doesn't change anything anyway.

I pad to the kitchen to turn on the coffee pot before heading to the shower. I was going to hit the gym first thing, but all I want now is to wash away the damn dream.

I stand under the spray with closed eyes, willing the water to work its magic—wake me up and wash the illusion of smoke from my nose. I lean my forehead against the wall and focus on my breath. It's over. It's done. I can't go back.

Can't go back. Can't go back.

Maybe I should be glad Teagan didn't come home with me last night. I wouldn't want her to see me scrambling on my bedroom floor in the dark, crawling from a fire that burned the First Avenue warehouse to the ground months ago but has never fully left my mind.

But maybe that's why I invited her. For six months, I've walked around broken but pretending to be okay. When she was in my arms, the taste of her skin on my tongue, I felt whole again. For those moments, I could forget my failings. I could . . . *be.*

I almost called Myla when I got home. She's always happy to come by and distract me, and she never pushes to sleep over. But I couldn't. Not when I wanted Teagan. Not when a few hours with her made my other relationships feel . . . cheap.

I turn off the shower and grab my towel, drying off quickly before throwing on a pair of jeans, a tank, and a long-sleeve University of Michigan T-shirt.

When I go to the kitchen, my phone blinks at me from its spot on the charger. I grab it while pouring my coffee, expecting a text from one of the girls or a message from Shay demanding to know what's going on between Teagan and me.

Sure enough, there are three texts from Shay, and another from Levi. I scroll past those and spill my coffee when I see there was a text from Isaiah at three a.m. Just over two hours ago.

"Shit." I shove the pot back onto the burner and grab a paper towel to clean up my mess.

> *Isaiah: Don't freak out. I was in a car accident last night. I'm in the hospital but I'm okay. I might be in trouble though.*

I tap the screen to call him but stop myself. One thing I've learned in the past few months is that Isaiah will spill his heart out over a text, but he freezes up about the same topic over the phone and in person.

Exhaling slowly, I reply to the text.

> *Me: What's your room number? I'll be there in twenty.*

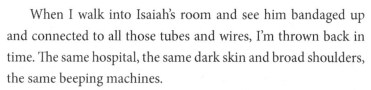

When I walk into Isaiah's room and see him bandaged up and connected to all those tubes and wires, I'm thrown back in time. The same hospital, the same dark skin and broad shoulders, the same beeping machines.

No. Not the same. There's no ventilator pumping up and down here, no machine forcing his lungs to do the work they won't do on their own.

Tears sting the back of my eyes, and I tilt my face toward the ceiling to hold them back.

"Hold it together," Marta says.

I was so distracted by the machines and my own memories that I didn't even notice Isaiah's grandmother sitting in the corner. I clear my throat. "Yes, ma'am."

"He's gonna be okay." Marta's voice is crackly on the best of days, but this morning she sounds even older than her seventy-five years. She might be hunched over her cane, and her ebony skin might be more wrinkled than smooth, but only an idiot would miss the shrewdness in those wise, dark eyes. "This might look like Max, but it's not the same. Isaiah will be okay."

"And what about you?" I ask.

"I've been better, as you can imagine." Tears slowly trail down her cheeks. "I try to do right by this boy, but I . . ." She takes a ragged breath.

"You're doing just fine."

She shakes her head. "He drank half a case of beer before getting behind the wheel."

"Five," Isaiah says, his voice rough, his head lolling to the side. "Five beers."

I draw in my own ragged breath and realize I didn't expect him to be conscious—ridiculous, since he texted me himself and asked me to come. Maybe Marta's right and my mind had already entwined his fate with his father's. *Not the same.*

"I'll go get coffee downstairs so you two can talk," she says. "But he's doped up pretty good, so don't be surprised if he starts talking nonsense."

I offer my hand, helping her stand from the chair. "I can hang out for a while. Why don't you go home and get a shower, maybe take a nap in your own bed?"

"You're sure?"

"Absolutely."

"You're a good boy, Carter Jackson." She squeezes my shoulder. "Isaiah, I'll be back in a couple of hours."

"I'm sorry, Grandma," Isaiah says. He forces his eyes open, but they only float shut again.

"You can apologize once you're better," she says. "That'll be the only way I'll accept it." She hoists her purse up on her shoulder and gives me a nod before using her cane to help her out of the room. She leans into it more than usual today. Her arthritis is flaring up again.

I lower myself into a chair, still too shaken by the sight of Isaiah like this to trust my legs.

"They said I broke my femur," he whispers. "And a couple of ribs."

I nod, not that he can see me. He can't seem to keep his eyes open. I want to ask him what on earth he thought he was doing, getting behind the wheel after drinking, and why the *fuck* he was drinking in the first place. Instead, I say, "You're strong. You're gonna get through this."

"Carter?"

"Yeah, buddy?"

"Don't tell my dad. Okay?"

I know he's confused—delirious from the meds and the trauma. But the words are like a blow to the chest.

I won't tell his dad. I can't. Because his dad is dead, and if I

31

were the hero everyone claims I am, he wouldn't be.

TEAGAN

There's a knock on my door way too early on Sunday morning. I groan as I roll over in bed and look at the clock. It's just after eight a.m.

I pull a pillow over my head. What kind of sadistic asshole thinks this is an appropriate hour to wake me up on my day off?

"If you don't answer this door, I'm going to assume it's because you're in my brother's bed, and I'll gossip with the girls about it at breakfast!"

Shay's warning has me bolting upright and flying toward the front door.

On my way, I grab my robe from the hook in the bathroom and shove my arms into the sleeves. I don't bother to tie it as I stomp toward the door. If Shay doesn't want to see me in my boy-short "Can't Touch This" undies, a tank top, and no bra, then she shouldn't be pulling me out of bed with threats of Jackson family gossip.

I unlock the door and open it, scowling. "What do you want?"

"Cute panties." She grins and folds her arms. "But you don't look like you spent your night getting ravished."

"Because I didn't." She's all sweaty and in shorts and a T-shirt so thin that I can see her blue sports bra through it. My scowl deepens. "Have you already worked out? Do you know how early it is? Don't you ever sleep in? What is wrong with you?"

Completely unfazed by the bite in my tone, she pushes past me and into my house. "I ran here. Because, as you know, it's Sunday, which means I'm having brunch with the family later." She plops down on my couch and arches a brow. "A brunch at which you're likely to be the main topic of conversation if you don't show your face."

It's not uncommon for me to go to the Jackson family brunch. In the four years since I moved here, the Jacksons have become my surrogate family of sorts. They're the kind of people who are more *inclusive* than exclusive, so they make it easy for a single girl like me to have a place that feels like home. But that's on days when I didn't just have a hot make-out session with one of the Jackson brothers.

I shake my head. "I can't go today."

"And why is that, may I ask?"

Because things happened between Carter and me last night, and it was supposed to be nothing, but it felt . . . like something.

I need to stay away from him for long enough for the buzz in my blood to fade. Since the thought of those dark eyes and that arrogant smile has my stomach doing Olympic-level gymnastics, I think it's fair to say I'm not there yet. A girl doesn't simply forget getting finger-fucked senseless by Carter Jackson, let alone forget it in less than twelve hours. "I need to clean the house."

Shay looks around, obviously not buying it. "Your floor is still gleaming from the housekeeper. Try again."

I shrug. "Maybe I don't want to go."

"You don't want to because you're avoiding him, or because

you're avoiding us?"

I snort. "Can't it be both?"

"You two looked awfully cozy last night."

I sigh. "It was . . . He was only . . ."

"Yeah, yeah, I know. He told me when I saw him in the parking lot after. It was all *pretend*."

Oh, this sneaky bitch. I glare at her. "If you saw him leaving alone, then you *knew* I wasn't in his bed this morning."

"I didn't know *for sure*. You could have gone to his place after having Molly drop you off here. Trust me, I've jumped through bigger hoops to keep my own rendezvous secret from my family."

I arch a brow. "Do tell."

"Oh no. You're not getting off the hook that easy. We're talking about you and Carter right now."

I pad to the other side of the island that separates my kitchen from my living and dining area. I'm still struggling to keep my eyes open. This morning—this *conversation*—calls for coffee. "You're overthinking this," I mutter. "I promise you, there's no secret relationship you've been missing out on."

"But you *weren't* just pretending. I saw you two dancing. Any closer, and I'd be asking if you used protection."

I yank out the carafe and shove it under the faucet. "Don't start with the matchmaker stuff."

"If you insist," she says with a sigh.

I pour the water into the back of the pot, grind beans, and dump them into the filter while she toys with her phone. When I flip the pot on, she wanders into the kitchen, still staring at the screen.

"Here," she says, handing me her phone. "You might need to

know about this."

My stomach drops. On her screen is a picture of me dancing in Carter's arms, his forehead touching mine as I smile up at him, his arms wrapped around me and holding me close. We look . . . deliriously smitten. The headline above it reads, "Foxy Fireman's Charity Auction Takes Unexpected Romantic Turn."

I look at Shay, who's smirking like she played her trump card. "Is this local?"

"*That* is. The local paper got the picture, but it was picked up by some tiny online gossip pages. You're lucky Carter fever has mostly died down, or this would be everywhere. People love their puppy-rescuing firefighter, and they love a good romance."

"Shit."

"Surely you both knew this could happen when he called you up on that stage."

"I never imagined he'd do it, honestly, and once he did, I was too shocked to think that far ahead." But I'm thinking ahead now. Specifically, about the call I'm bound to get from my mother and sister the second they see the article.

There's another knock on the door. Shay looks toward the sound, then to me.

"Teagan?" Carter's voice is low, cautious. "Are you awake?"

Shay snorts. "Just an act, huh? Who exactly are you two acting for this morning?"

I swallow hard. We *were* pretending, but sometimes pretend leads to something more. In this case, his hand between my legs and the best orgasm I've had in years. I bite my lip at the memory. *Damn.*

Another knock. "Teagan?"

"She's coming!" Shay calls, flashing a wicked grin at me as if she knows I was considering ignoring him.

"Seriously?" I ask. "I'm blaming you if I don't make it back to bed this morning."

Her grin spreads wider, and mischief dances in her eyes. "Isn't that up to Carter?"

I let out a low growl. "Get out of here, brat."

She takes a step toward the door then stops, pointing at me. "By the way, you might want to do something about that love bite on your neck before you leave the house."

I throw a kitchen towel at her. "Go."

She winks, but then her face goes serious. "Don't break his heart, okay? I know he's a bit of a player, but he's sensitive under that tough-guy façade. You're my best friend, but he's my brother, and I'd hate to have to punch you in the babymaker." And with that, she opens the front door and breezes out past her brother.

Carter's brows shoot into his hairline. "Bye, sis!"

"Bye," she says over her shoulder, already jogging away.

Carter walks through my barely there foyer to the living room. My house—which is pretty small to begin with—shrinks around us, and I swallow. I'm still half-asleep and am nearly bowled over by a surge of memory and lust as I take him in. Carter. In my house. Steps from my bed.

Oh, hell, I'm in trouble.

Chapter FOUR

TEAGAN

*C*arter hasn't shaved today, and his cheeks are scruffier than usual, making him exude even more testosterone and sex appeal than normal. His long-sleeve T-shirt is molded over his chest and shoulders, and when he shoves his hands into his pockets, his jeans dip dangerously low on his hips and expose the waistband of his boxers.

A shiver runs through me as I remember the feel of him—hands roaming, his hard body pressed against me, hot breath on my neck. Every cell between my thighs and my navel is suddenly doing its best Oliver Twist impression: *"Please, sir, I want some more."*

"Is it okay that I'm here?" he asks cautiously.

Probably best to play it cool. "Why wouldn't it be?"

He studies me for a beat before slowly shutting the door, as if he was considering leaving it open. Maybe he should so we both have an easy escape from what promises to be an awkward conversation.

"Coffee?"

"Yeah."

I pour us each a cup from the fresh pot and doctor mine with cream, stirring thoroughly as an excuse to avoid his eyes. When I can't delay it anymore, I cross the kitchen to the other side of the island and hand him his coffee. I still can't look him in the eye, so I keep my gaze on his chest. *Coward.*

I frown at the Jackson Harbor Hospital pediatrics visitor sticker on his shirt. "Who's in the hospital?"

He glances down, following my gaze. "Oh, shit." He peels it off, crumples it, and tucks it into his pocket. "A . . . friend of mine was in an accident."

"Is he okay?"

Carter pinches the bridge of his nose. "Yeah. Doped up on pain meds at the moment. Lucky as fuck, if I'm honest, but he'll be okay."

"Good. That's my unit, so let me know if there's anything I can do to help."

"Thanks." He takes a breath. "What was Shay doing here?"

"You know, trying to get the scoop on what happened between us last night and threatening to do me bodily harm if I break your heart."

He grunts. "I thought it was your brothers who were supposed to threaten *me.*"

"I don't have any brothers, so I guess you lucked out."

He shrugs, as if he wouldn't mind, or maybe he's distracted.

He seems . . . off. "Regardless, I'm sorry she's butting in. I'll talk to her."

I wave a hand. "She's my best friend. I'd be worried if she *wasn't* trying to pry the details out of me." I wince, realizing we've landed right on the conversation I was hoping to put off until . . . never. "Not that I admitted anything, but the hickey you left behind probably did the confessing for me."

He squeezes the back of his neck and grimaces. Awkwardness threatens to creep back into the room.

Now's as good a time as any. "About last night," I say, at the same time as he says, "I'm sorry if things moved too fast."

I blow out a long breath. "It's not that, Carter. It's . . . you're my friend."

He takes a seat at the table. "And you're mine. I'm not interested in *changing* that." His eyes wrinkle at the corners, and he laughs, some of that uncharacteristic tension leaving his shoulders. "But if those panties are supposed to keep me from thinking about last night, I have to tell you, they're failing spectacularly."

When that self-assured gaze of his dips again, I remember I'm not wearing pants. Sleep must still have ahold of my brain for me to forget that quickly. I yank my robe closed and tie it tight, embarrassment licking flames up my neck and into my cheeks.

His gaze lingers below my waist for a beat, as if he can see right through the terrycloth. "Should've kept my mouth shut."

"So you could stare at my crotch over coffee? That's mature."

"Never claimed to be." He winks at me. "Are we really going to pretend that what happened last night could happen between two friends who aren't attracted to each other?"

I snort. "I'm *plenty* attracted to you."

"Wow." He grins.

"What?"

"You surprised me, that's all."

"Come on." I take the seat across from him. "You have enough of an ego to know you're attractive. Enough to know *I* find you attractive."

He shakes his head. "Oh, I know you do." *Cocky sonofabitch.* "It's not that. It's just . . . I didn't expect you to admit it."

"What's the point in denying it now?"

His gaze drops to my mouth, and I'm there all over again—in the office, pressed against the wall, his mouth at my ear. Would it be so bad to have a repeat performance before we have this conversation? If the damage has been done, is it much worse if I drag him into my bedroom to finish what we started before we officially declare it a mistake and say *never again*?

I swallow. *Be strong, Teagan.* "But we're just friends. Regardless of that attraction. Last night was an anomaly and never would have happened if we hadn't been . . . pretending."

He scratches his stubble. "So you hadn't thought about it before I kissed you onstage? Not once?"

"I didn't say that. I'm saying I'm not going to think about it again."

His grin widens. "I'm gonna call bullshit on that."

"What? Why?"

"You're thinking about it as much as I am. I can see it in your eyes and your pink cheeks . . ." His gaze trails over my face, and his voice softens. "And the way you're looking at me."

"Fine. I'm *thinking* about it, but that doesn't mean I want it."

Another smirk. "Sure. If you say so."

I growl. "Okay, so I want to do it again." *And more. As soon as possible, please.* "But that doesn't mean it's a good idea." I fold my arms and shoot him my best scowl. "It would be *really* helpful if you'd stop looking all hot and self-assured. I'm trying really hard not to let my hoo-ha call the shots right now."

He coughs and raises a hand, one brow arched. "Can I be team *hoo-ha*?"

I can't believe I just used Ellie's favorite word for her female anatomy. My friends are a terrible influence. Or maybe I can't think straight in Carter's presence now that I know what it's like to have him—

I rub my temples, trying to stop that line of thinking. "Carter, I'm serious."

He leans back in his chair. "So am I."

Panic starts to claw at me, like growing points of pressure on my ribcage. What if I screwed up everything last night? What if this becomes a *thing* between us, and we can never go back to how we were?

My thoughts must be written all over my face, because his grin falls away. He exhales heavily and ducks his head. "Can I be completely honest with you?"

"I hope you will."

"The whole drive from the hospital, I told myself I wanted to check on you." He wraps his hands around his coffee and looks up at me through thick, dark lashes most women would pay a premium for. "But the second I walked in the door, I knew that wasn't what brought me here. I want to finish what we started."

I bite my lip and whimper. "You're killing me."

"And when you look at me like that, all I want to do is seduce you into ignoring your better judgment."

That! my traitorous body cries. *Yes, let's do that!*

"But I get it," he continues. "We're friends, and as tempting as I find you—as tempting as I've *always* found you—if adding sex to our friendship is out of the question for you, this conversation is over. I want you, but I'm not enough of an idiot to ruin this just to take you to bed."

My brain stumbles on *as tempting as I've always found you* before landing on *adding sex to our friendship.* Is that an option? Does that *ever* work? Crap on a cracker. I've known Carter for four years, and I've never had to exert so much self-control for something as simple as *not* straddling his lap.

"Tell me what you're thinking." His voice is low, a husky rumble that bypasses my brain and speaks directly to the parts of my anatomy I'd rather exclude from this conversation.

I'm thinking I want you too. I'm thinking we could be naked and in my bed in less than sixty seconds. "I'm thinking you should leave," I blurt, pushing the words past the other *really bad ideas* on the tip of my tongue.

He blinks at me, then nods as he pushes out of his chair. "Sure. I understand."

Jumping up, I catch his arm. I can feel the heat of his skin through the cotton of his shirt sleeve. "I've never done this."

His eyes go wide. "Wow. I thought . . . Seriously?"

"Not sex, you idiot. The whole friends-with-benefits thing. I'm not sure I'm made that way."

He's quiet for a long beat. "If you need more than that from me, Tea, I—"

I press my fingers to his lips and shake my head before he can say anything else. I'm *not* hoping for more. More is out of the question for me with someone like Carter. But even so, I don't want to hear that he doesn't want anything either. I know it'll feel like rejection—even if that makes me a hypocrite. "I don't want more, but I don't know if . . ."

I drop my hand from his mouth and lift onto my toes to press my lips to his. I want to know if it'll feel like it did last night, and the second our mouths touch, I have my answer. Electric need zips through me. I loop my arms behind his neck, planning to take the kiss deeper.

He doesn't let me. With a hand on either of my wrists, he pulls my arms away and steps back, his eyes dark. "I'll go. You think. If we do this, it needs to be a decision, not an accident."

I nod and watch him leave, but I stand there for a solid five minutes, considering running after him.

CARTER

I drive around for a bit after leaving Teagan's, trying to get my thoughts in order before facing my siblings and their well-intended, overly intrusive questions. I shouldn't be disappointed by our conversation—by her caution—not when Teagan's being the voice of reason that could very well save our friendship. But I am. I'm not sure I've ever wanted anything as much as I want to prove those sexy cotton panties wrong. *Can't touch this.* I'm competitive at heart, and her damn *underwear* was issuing a challenge I was dying to win.

Before I walked in her door and saw her in those ridiculous panties, her long legs on full display and her nipples visible through her cotton shirt, I'd had myself convinced I was only there to talk her down from her panic. I'd apologize that we got carried away and maybe laugh with her over coffee to reassure us both that nothing about our friendship was broken. But my visit with Isaiah left me raw, pulled memories too close to the surface that I prefer to keep buried deep. One look at her messy morning hair and I knew the perfect cure for my aching heart.

I still want her, consequences be damned, and her kiss today could have so easily become something more. Does she want that? Would it be a mistake?

By the time I park in front of Brayden's, I've had a chance to cool off and am ready to face my family. I'm a little late, so the sound of our weekly brunch chaos meets me at the door. The clatter of dishes is the musical accompaniment to my family's laughter and conversation.

Every Sunday, the whole Jackson crew, plus or minus a few regular guests, meets at my childhood home for brunch. Brayden lives in the old house with his fiancée, Molly, and her son, Noah. He moved in years ago, when Mom relocated to Ethan's to help take care of my niece. At the time, none of us were ready to see Mom sell the house that holds all our childhood memories . . . and all our memories of our father. Brayden held down the fort until it was clear Mom wouldn't be able to move back in. He officially bought it from her last summer. Legally, it might be Brayden's, but I don't think any of us will ever stop thinking of it as *our* home.

I follow my nose to the kitchen and find everyone's beaten me here. Ethan's feeding Nic a piece of fruit, his eyes focused on her mouth in a way that makes me look away fast. Ava and Jake are cooing over their infant daughter while Lilly bickers with Noah. Molly and Brayden are at the kitchen table, looking at spreadsheets on his laptop—workaholics getting one more fix before the meal. At the counter, Ellie and Levi are pouring mimosas and laughing together over some whispered secret. Mom is handing out plates, encouraging everyone to eat up, and Shay is monitoring the coffee.

Typical Sunday.

Most of my adult life, the sight of this place—*these people*—has filled me with indescribable gratitude that soothes my soul and washes away any angst from the previous week. But lately, it's been different. Maybe because all my brothers have fallen in love, and I've felt a little lonely. But it's more likely because ever since Max died, I haven't felt like I belong here. As if I'm playing at a life I don't deserve to be living and any minute, someone is going to yank it away.

"It's the man of the year," my youngest brother, Levi, says, lifting his mimosa in the air as if to toast to me.

His girlfriend, Ellie, nudges him in the side. "Don't be a dick."

"Language!" my niece, Lilly, scolds, sounding just like my mom.

"Thank you," Mom tells her granddaughter.

"You'd think these boys were raised in a barn," Lilly says, parroting another one of Mom's favorite expressions.

Lilly's stepmom, Nic, bites back a laugh. "That was quite a

show you put on last night," she says, studying me. Nic's known Teagan longer than the rest of us. They went to college together, and in a roundabout way, Teagan's the reason Nic moved here to take the job as Lilly's nanny. If anyone knows for sure how Teagan feels about last night, it's Nic. But by the way she's studying me, I can tell even she is wondering how much of an act it was. Wondering what happened between us after we danced together.

I turn to Shay, and my need for caffeine must be all over my face, because she shoves a steaming mug in my hands before I can ask. This is the third pot of coffee I've been in contact with this morning, but I've yet to manage more than a few sips.

"I smelled the stuff Teagan was making," she says. "You should teach her how to make it my way."

"No one can make it your way," I murmur. A groan of appreciation slips from my lips as I take my first sip. "And I mean that."

"You were at Teagan's this morning?" Jake asks.

"Mind your own business." Ava scowls at him and adjusts my new niece on her hip. Five-month-old Lauren shoves her fist in her mouth and happily gnaws on it with her gums. Long streams of slobber trail from her mouth. Lauren has a head of thick, dark hair, blue eyes, and the most adorable baby giggle I've heard in my life.

Jake rolls his eyes at his wife. "You want to know more than I do, so don't give me that holier-than-thou glare."

Shay snorts into her coffee. "We *all* want to know, but they're not telling."

Things were finally starting to get predictable around here with everyone settled down. Nic and Ethan are married, as are

46

Jake and Ava. Levi and Ellie are living together, and Molly and Brayden are engaged and planning a spring wedding. My little display with Teagan is blood in the water, and they're a bunch of gossip-hungry sharks.

"Come get some food," Mom says, sliding a plate into my free hand.

"Can't wait," I say. I lean down and kiss her forehead.

This morning's exchange with Teagan must have worked magic, because I feel hungry for once. I spoon eggs and bacon on my plate and follow everyone to the dining room, taking a seat between Shay and Lilly.

I've spent enough time with Dr. Google to know my lack of appetite is one of the many symptoms of *survivor guilt*. Knowing the cause doesn't make it any easier to chew and swallow when everything tastes like ash on my tongue and turns to lead in my stomach. The month after they pulled the plug on Max's vent, I lost fifteen pounds, and I could see the worry in everyone's eyes when they looked at me. I've managed to hold steady since, but not without a struggle.

"It's like we're not even here," Shay says, and I snap my head up and realize everyone's staring at me.

Did someone ask a question? I was lost in my thoughts. I've been working on that too, and getting better lately. Seeing Isaiah this morning drew me into a bad place.

And flirting with Teagan pulled you out of it.

"I asked how Teagan is this morning," Mom says. "You two made a very handsome couple last night." Of course. Because the expected conversation wouldn't be awkward enough without my mother chiming in.

"She's fine." I shove a forkful of egg into my mouth and chew to avoid having to say more.

Shay grunts. "It was all *pretend,* Mom." She doesn't sound like she believes it.

"I feel so bad," Molly says at the other end of the table. "If I'd realized how much you didn't want to be auctioned off, I never would have asked you to do it."

I shrug. Truth be told, I feel like an ass for essentially backing out. I should have let the richest woman in the room get her night with me, but I saw Teagan standing there, and I knew the only way I was going to make it through was if she was there to keep me laughing. If I had to listen to some woman wax poetic about my "bravery," I might have had a total breakdown. My family has been through enough in the last decade. They don't need to worry about the middle son losing it. "I hope I didn't cost you too much," I tell Molly.

"Well, your donation was more than generous, and I can tell you for certain we wouldn't have made half as much without you there. The other bachelors went for more than expected, and we did great in the silent auction thanks to the numbers you brought in."

"Our local *hero,*" Levi croons.

I take a pull of my coffee, trying to swallow back the bile surging in my throat. "Don't call me that."

Ethan and Brayden exchange a look. I focus on my plate. I don't want to see the worry on their faces. I don't want to see how well or how badly I've done hiding what a mess I've been.

"That picture of you and Teagan was in the paper," Lilly says. "Are you gonna get married?"

Ethan chokes on his coffee, and Nic says, "*Lill.*"

"They're just friends, sweetie," Shay says. "Uncle Carter isn't nearly cute enough for a girl as smart and cool as Teagan."

"True story." I nod. "I'm lucky she even danced with me."

"But my friend Jasper said his mom was there, and she said you and Teagan are having a secret love relationship," Lilly says.

"We're not," I say gently.

"But she showed him a video of you on the stage and said you kissed Teagan in front of everyone. With *slobber.*"

"Eww! Slobber!" Noah says, wrinkling his nose.

Ethan frowns at his daughter. "When did you see Jasper?"

"He texted me this morning," she says.

Red creeps up Ethan's neck. "You're exchanging texts with a *boy*? You talked about kissing and slobber?"

"Um, *yeah,* I'm *eight.*"

"That phone is a privilege, Lilly. If—"

"We can talk about it later." Nic puts her hand on top of Ethan's and squeezes until he looks at her. I can practically see his horror receding as he meets his wife's eyes. Lilly's lucky Nic came along. If it weren't for Nic, Ethan might have put Lilly in a bubble by now.

"I'm more curious about what happened when everyone *wasn't* looking," Levi says, only to be elbowed by Ellie again. "What?"

"Seriously?" she says.

"Everyone's thinking it."

Ellie shakes her head. "That doesn't make it okay to say out loud."

Molly clears her throat. "I took Teagan home last night. If

that, uh, clears up any questions."

Levi shakes his head at me, truly distraught. "You are such a shitty closer."

"Language!" Noah says, and Lilly gives him a nod of approval.

Jake shoots me a look. He's at the bar enough to know my old reputation doesn't hold true. I used to be incredibly picky about who I'd take home. I used to be more interested in a relationship than an evening of fun. But since Max died, my female *friends* have been my favorite escape from the hellish churn of memories that wait for me in the quiet moments. I'm still selective and want nothing to do with women who hold me up as some sort of idol, but I "close" just fine. Not with Teagan, but maybe that's for the best.

"What's a closer?" Lilly asks.

Ethan chokes on his coffee again, and I cringe.

"Yeah, Uncle Levi," Shay says, propping her chin on her hands. "What's a closer?"

Ethan scowls at our youngest brother, daring him to say something inappropriate to his daughter.

Levi keeps a completely straight face as he looks Lilly in the eye and says, "It's the person who cleans up the bar and locks up at the end of the night. And if they do a bad job, it makes more work for whoever opens the next day."

"Oh." Lilly nods, as if this makes sense, but after a beat, she frowns. "But what does that have to do with where Aunt Teagan slept last night?"

Jake coughs, and my mother's glare sweeps across the table like wildfire, wiping the amusement off the faces of all her children.

"I tried, Mom," Levi mutters, ducking his head.

"I'm waiting," Lilly says.

"It's adult stuff," Nic tells her softly.

"Like what you and Daddy do when you send me to Aunt Shay's?"

Nic and Ethan simultaneously shoot Shay a glare.

She holds up her hands. "I didn't tell her that."

Lauren fusses in Ava's lap, and Jake sweeps the baby into his arms. "Well, baby needs a diaper change, so I'll see you all later."

Chapter FIVE

TEAGAN

When my phone rings, I know it's my mother before I even look at the screen. Anyone else's mom might have missed the news, but my mom has been reading the *Jackson Harbor Gazette* online every morning for the last month—as if obsessively watching the news and weather here might allow her to actually control it during my sister's wedding next weekend.

She learned about Carter fever from the local paper and has asked me about him before.

How well do I know him? *A whole lot better after last night.*

Did he really save that puppy? *Yes. But please don't bring it up if you ever meet him.*

Is it true that it was all a publicity stunt because he wants his own reality TV show? *Absolutely not.*

I'm not surprised when I see her name on the screen, but I'm also not ready for this call. While I don't want to lie to my mother, explaining to her that Carter and I worked together to deceive a roomful of people sounds even less appealing. *Something else you should have considered when he called you up on that stage.*

I plaster a smile on my face—because she's got some weird mom voodoo that I swear allows her to determine my facial expression over the phone—and swipe my screen to accept the call. "Hi, Mom!"

"I cannot believe you didn't tell me you were dating Carter Jackson."

I cringe. I guess we're starting with guilt today. *Okay then.*

"All the times we've talked about him, you never thought to mention you two are involved and *getting serious*?"

"It's . . . complicated." I flinch and silently reprimand myself for the evasion. If I was planning to be honest with her, this isn't the best way to start. But the half lie is already out there, and . . . I'm a coward. What am I supposed to say? *Mom, we're not dating, but we are considering elevating our friendship from casually flirtatious to fuck buddies?* My conservative mother would *love* that. She would cry, fret, and pray for me. My father would offer to cut off Carter's balls. "I didn't want you to get your hopes up in case nothing came of it."

"Consider my feelings, will you? My daughter is in love, and she didn't even tell me. Never mind the logistical nightmare of you keeping this secret."

"No one said I was *in love*." I pause a beat as the rest of her objection registers. "What logistical nightmare?"

"Well, whether or not you're using the L-word yet, I assume he's coming to the wedding. We can't have additional guests showing up unannounced."

The wedding. Shit. "Oh, no. He's not—"

"Don't even worry! It's already taken care of. I've talked to Saanvi. We're making adjustments. We want him there."

"Carter has to work." *I hope.*

Mom makes a sound I recognize as disapproval. The grunt-sniff combo was practically the soundtrack of my teenage years. "Your sister will only get married once. If this boy is serious about you, he will be there."

"It's not his fault. He was scheduled to work before he and I got serious." *Another lie.* I shrink into my chair and rub my forehead. If I were a smarter person, I'd have let her call go to voicemail and gotten my story straight before calling her back.

"Well, at least he's a good man. Have you talked to Rich about this?"

My body locks up at the mention of his name. Rich Nasser was once the love of my life. Then, four years ago, he became someone I needed to escape and the reason I moved away from my hometown. "Why would I talk to Rich?"

"Teagan, you know he still loves you. He asks after you all the time, and . . . I always thought you two would eventually find your way back to each other. He deserves to hear this news from *you*, not through the grapevine."

I clench my teeth so hard my jaw clicks. "It's been years, Mom."

"Even so."

Sighing, I try to redirect the conversation. "How are the plans coming? I'm excited to see everyone for the wedding."

It works, and Mom launches into a ten-minute monologue

detailing the latest plans, excitement, and hiccups for my little sister's destination wedding—the destination being Jackson Harbor, of all places.

I like hearing about Saanvi's wedding and the buzz of excitement in Mom's voice when she talks about the plans for the extended celebration. In three days, my family will descend on Jackson Harbor and spend a long weekend celebrating together and enjoying the excuse to have a bit of a family reunion. I smile as Mom talks about menus, decorations, and minor family dramas that have sprouted up and thrown a wrench into the details of her plans.

"Oh, and have you driven by the Hayhurst mansion?" she asks. "They've been sending me pictures of how the gardens look with the leaves turned, and it's going to be perfect."

The Hayhurst mansion was turned into a bed and breakfast thirty years ago, but Mom rented out the entire place for the wedding so everyone would have a place to stay and could be together. Even though I live less than ten minutes away, I'm expected to take a room at the mansion too, but I don't mind. I want to be close to Saanvi during her special weekend.

The longer Mom talks, the more my anxiety over my lie lessens. When she arrives for the wedding, I'll tell her Carter and I broke up. My lie won't matter, because it'll be like nothing ever happened.

Then Mom drops the bomb. "Of course, I'll have to reconsider sleeping arrangements now that Carter will be there."

"Carter doesn't need to stay with us."

"Don't be silly. He's family now. But the only available bed is in the room with Rich, so—"

"Rich is coming?" I practically shout into the phone.

"Of course he is. He's family too, regardless of whether or not you two get back together."

I haven't seen Rich since he showed up at Jackson Brews a year ago. That night, the sight of him freaked me out so much that I made Carter act like he was my boyfriend—the favor I was returning when he called me up on stage last night. *Why didn't anyone tell me he was coming to the wedding?*

"I'm afraid asking Rich to share a room with Carter will make them both uncomfortable," Mom says.

I shake my head, still trying to wrap my mind around the news that Rich will be under the same roof as me and my whole family. I open my mouth to repeat that Carter won't be staying at the mansion, then close it. Suddenly, I want him there. How much would it hurt to extend our deceit for one more week?

CARTER

Unknown Number: Guess what? I'm going to be in town again soon. I went shopping yesterday and was hoping you could check out my purchases. I can't decide if I like the black lace or the red satin more. ;)

I frown at the text as I finish wiping down the dining room table. I'm not sure who it's from. The number isn't saved in my phone, but that doesn't necessarily mean it's a misdial either.

Even if I've changed my standards, I'm not completely indiscriminate with my bedroom partners. With rare exception, I keep my activities limited to a few local friends I can trust to be discreet and who know our nights together are casual fun and nothing more. Friends who know not to talk to me about that hero shit. But I talk to those women regularly, and they're saved in my phone. *This* must be one of the exceptions.

I scrub a hand over my face. When did I become an ass who categorizes his bedroom partners into *regulars* and *exceptions*? And what would Teagan think of me getting a text like this from a number I don't recognize?

Before I can figure out how to reply to the mystery number, another text comes through. This one's from Bethany, a former firefighter I worked with for five years before she started a new career as a nurse.

> Bethany: I saw the paper. I didn't know you were seeing Teagan. Please tell me she knows about me. I don't have the energy for drama in my life, but especially not at work.

At least I can be honest with Beth. The only reason we started hanging out again was because I needed to talk to someone who could understand what I was going through after Max died. But it turned out I didn't actually want to talk, and neither did she. We're both busy, but we get together a few times a month to . . . not talk.

"Everything okay?" Shay asks.

I shove my phone into my pocket and shrug. "Sure. Why?"

"You've been scrubbing the same spot on the table for two minutes now."

I shake my head and turn to the laundry room. "I'm just distracted," I say over my shoulder, but she follows me.

"About Teagan? Was that text from her?"

"No, it was from . . ." I wave it away and plop the dishrag into the washing machine. I'm one thousand percent sure I don't want to discuss my sex life with my little sister. "Did you know there's an article in the paper about me and Teagan?"

She chuckles. "One of your side pieces unhappy about your little performance?"

I step around her. "Forget I asked."

Shay laughs. Nothing amuses her as much as watching her brothers have love-life angst.

"Carter, Shay," Brayden calls from the top of the basement stairs. "We're going to watch the game. Join us?"

"I'll be down in a few," I reply.

Shay follows him, and I slip out back to get some fresh air. The neighbor is burning leaves and yard waste in his firepit, and the smell reminds me of my childhood somehow—weekends with my family at the cabin, and fires by the lake.

It's sunny and cool, with a crisp breeze that rustles through the dry leaves on the trees. I sit in one of Brayden's cushioned patio chairs and unlock my phone.

I've missed a text from Teagan.

Teagan: Can you meet me at Jackson Brews tonight?

I grin. I don't want to wait until tonight. And I don't want to meet her in a public place.

> Me: *You sure this isn't a conversation we should have at your place? Or mine?*
> Teagan: *The bar, Carter. Meet me at the bar at seven.*
> Carter: *As you wish.*

For the best, I remind myself. Teagan deserves better than a guy carrying around a freight-ton of baggage.

So why did I go straight to flirtation mode the second I walked in her door this morning? Why I am ignoring the texts from Bethany—not to mention some unknown number—and praying Teagan will want to "talk" in private?

Guilt nags at me, so I reply to Bethany.

> Me: *You don't need to worry about any drama. I'll be at the hospital tomorrow. Maybe we can talk then. I'll catch you up.*

I reread the mystery text and decide not to reply—for all I know, it's a wrong number. Instead, I tuck my phone back into my pocket and tilt my face toward the sky, closing my eyes. I need a few minutes alone before I can face my family again.

One of the worst things about being so fucked up is the guilt. The guilt of wanting to crawl out of my skin when I spend time with the people I love. The guilt of so desperately wanting to be free of their questions and concerned glances, and wishing I could be anywhere else. Before this summer, I'd never missed Jackson Sunday brunch without a damn good reason, but since the warehouse fire, I've come up with more excuses to skip than I want to admit. I used to relish our jibing and poking at each other. After Max died, it became something I had to endure. Even small talk was painful. Somedays it still is.

The back door clicks, and I know my moment of solitude has come to an end. Pushing away the instinct to bolt, I make myself stay still.

"Do you want to talk about it?"

My eyes fly open, and I see Jake standing in front of me, hands tucked into his pockets, his head cocked to the side like I'm some puzzle he's trying to figure out. For a moment, I can't breathe. *They all know.* They can see right through me into the mess I've become.

My palms are sweaty against my thighs, and I have to look away from my brother's too-perceptive gaze because, no, I don't want to talk about it. I don't even want to admit there's an *it* to talk about.

"You know we don't mean to upset you," Jake says. "It's just fun to tease you about Teagan."

Oh, hell. My breath whooshes out in a rush. He's not talking about the warehouse. He's not talking about Max or my nightmares, or me avoiding my family. He's talking about Teagan. About last night.

My relief is like the cool breeze that brushes the leaves off the trees and lets them start over. I'd love that—to have everything wiped away so I could start fresh, so I could feel like the person I was before I lost my best friend.

"What happened between you two last night?" Jake asks.

I shrug. "It really wasn't anything."

"You like her," he says. "You've always liked her."

Yeah. And if I'd heard her moans in my ear and had my hand between her legs before my life burned to ash in the warehouse fire, I'd have fought like hell to turn the chemistry between us into something more than I'm equipped to offer now. I shake my head. "We're friends. I'm happy with that."

Jake sinks into the chair beside me and stares out at the trees lining the back of the property. "I walked by the office while you two were"—he clears his throat—"in there."

I hear the apology in his voice. I know my brother. He didn't mean to spy, and he's not totally comfortable nosing into my business, but he feels weird knowing there was more to last night than we're letting on.

"So, I can pretend I didn't see anything. That's not a problem, and I won't tell anyone." He winces. "I mean, Ava already knows, but . . . if you want advice or to talk or something, I'm here."

I cough. "Advice?"

"I do know something about having feelings for a friend."

He and Ava might be the very best example of two people who were afraid to risk their friendship for something more but eventually made it work. Keyword being *eventually.*

"Teagan and I aren't you and Ava." I laugh softly. "God, you are a lucky sonofabitch, though. All those years of pining, and look at you now."

"Don't I know it." His voice is thick with emotion. Fatherhood has softened him, leaving all those gooey emotional insides showing. "If you ever want to talk, I'm here. And I don't mean about your love life. I mean . . . I know you miss Max."

Shit. Not off the hook like I hoped. "I'm coping," I say.

"It was awful."

"It's part of the job."

"Have you talked to anyone?"

"Bethany has been a good friend through this. She gets it, you know?"

He studies me for a beat, but I can't tell if he's about to call me on my "talks" with Bethany or if he's trying to decide if he should insist I see a professional. "Good." He nods—once, twice, three times. Like he's trying to convince himself. He pokes my bicep. "You're getting soft."

"Just because I'm not working out with you doesn't mean I'm not working out."

He arches a brow. "Is the same true of eating? You've lost weight."

"I'm fine." I used to meet my brothers at the gym every morning I wasn't on duty, but I haven't returned to that old routine since the warehouse fire. There's nothing appealing about the idea of hanging out with my brothers and trying to banter with them and pretend everything's okay.

It's something I should get back to. Maybe I will. Soon, I'll make myself join them again. Just . . . not yet.

My phone buzzes, and I pull it out of my pocket.

> *Myla: If I'd known you needed a fake girlfriend last night, I'd have gone to the fundraiser. Did Teagan keep you safe from the crazy ladies?*

Well, at least Myla knows it was an act. Before I can reply, another text buzzes through.

Myla: Want me to come over tonight? I can bring beer and pizza . . . and my mouth, of course ;)

Jake snorts. "Shitty closer, my ass."

I scowl at him and turn off my phone screen. "Don't read over my shoulder, fuckface."

"I didn't *mean* to, but . . ." He shrugs.

"But what?"

"Like I said, I'm worried about you."

I stiffen and shove my phone back into the pocket of my jeans. "Why? Because I have a healthy sex life but no girlfriend?"

Jake's brows disappear under his shaggy hair. "One might argue that's not possible."

"What?" I laugh, but the sound wouldn't fool anyone. I don't find this conversation amusing. "Now that you're married, you're going to lecture single guys about sex without emotional commitment?"

"Since when is this what you *want*?" he asks. "I've seen women throw themselves at you for years, but you've never been promiscuous before. You wanted more than that, but now . . ."

"Now I'm *what*?"

Jake groans and braces his hands on his knees. "You've been different since Max died. You try to hide it, but that shit? Your phone blowing up with offers for blowjobs or booty calls or whatever the fuck she was offering, and you drinking too much, then disappearing with random women—"

I fly out of my chair and spin on him. "Like you didn't have a little fun before you and Ava settled down. Hell, you almost slept with your sister-in-law. I really don't think you're in a position to lecture me right now."

Jake's nostrils flare. He doesn't like talking about that night with Molly. It was fucking *years* ago, and long before he and Ava, or Brayden and Molly got together. I'm a jackass for throwing it in his face like this, but I'm not about to be lectured just because he's finally settled down.

Jake stares me down. "I don't give a shit if you want to sleep with every single woman in this town, but Teagan is practically part of this family. If you're planning to make her one of your new fuck buddies, do us all a favor and make sure she understands it isn't actually about *her*, but some half-assed coping mechanism."

I feel my hands curl into fists at my sides. I haven't punched one of my brothers in more than a decade, but I'm itching to knock this one out right now.

Jake's gaze flicks to my fists before meeting mine again. Slowly, he stands. "I see what the rest of them don't, and I haven't said shit because I know you're grieving. I know this is hard for you."

"You don't know shit about how this is for me." I shove him, and he stumbles into the chair but doesn't fall. I wait for him to shove me back or take a swing—I fucking *want* him to—but he doesn't. He looks . . . devastated.

He shakes his head one last time, then turns around and heads inside, stopping only when he has one foot in the door. "You're my brother. There's nothing I wouldn't do for you. For a while, that meant giving you space to deal with what happened, but right now, it includes calling you on your bullshit."

Chapter SIX

TEAGAN

I scored big when I found a house in my budget within walking distance to downtown Jackson Harbor. I love that I can get almost everywhere I want to go on foot, and when the weather is nice, I usually do. But after talking to my mom this morning, I hesitate outside my front door, fidgeting with my keys. It's a beautiful October evening. The sun sinks low on the horizon, painting the sky in red and orange and casting a magical glow around the rainbow of autumn colors in the trees. The light breeze is cool and bites at my cheeks, but I know it'll feel amazing when I start walking. *If* I can convince myself to walk.

Rich Nasser isn't in Jackson Harbor. He won't be here for another few days. But knowing he's coming has made me skittish in my own town.

"Screw you, Rich." I shove my keys into my purse and head

to the sidewalk. I won't let the anticipation of his presence scare me into hiding.

It's a ten-minute walk to the bar, but I get there in eight, my steps quicker than usual. Usually, I enjoy the solitude of the short walk, but tonight, I'm anxious for company. I get my wish the moment I step into Jackson Brews.

The bar is bustling with activity. The Chicago Bears are playing on the big screens, and the booths are filled with familiar faces enjoying a meal as they watch the game. I'm struck by a tug of tenderness. For this place. For this town.

Saanvi planned to do a destination wedding from the start—her genius way of avoiding the massive guest list of virtual strangers Mom and Dad wanted to put together for a wedding at home. When she picked Jackson Harbor, I was thrilled and not even a little surprised. She fell in love with this town at first sight, just like I did. She would've moved here after college if her fiancé, Liam, didn't already have a job back in Alexandria. She might not be able to move here with me, but if she can have her special day in the town that stole both of our hearts, I'm happy.

Or I was until I found out about Rich.

Now I wish Saanvi had allowed our parents to throw her the wedding of *their* dreams back in Virginia. I hate the idea of Rich being in this town—*my town*—even for a few days.

I could tell Saanvi I don't want Rich to come, and she would want to accommodate me. If I could find the courage to tell her the truth about him, she probably wouldn't have let my parents invite him in the first place. But when it comes to that secret, I've always been a coward.

I shake my head, trying to scatter the thoughts of my ex and his talents for getting whatever he wants. I take a seat at the bar and put my purse on the vacant stool beside me to save the space for Carter.

"What can I get you tonight?" Cindy asks, already pulling out a pint glass.

"I'll have the pumpkin ale."

Nodding, she pours my beer and slides it in front of me.

I scan the crowd, looking for Carter. It's odd. I don't know that I've ever had plans with *only* Carter. With many combinations of Jacksons and their girlfriends/fiancées/wives, sure, but Carter and I haven't had a reason to hang out, just the two of us. And if I'm honest, I would've found a way around it even if we did have one. Carter is far too tempting, and I wouldn't trust myself to resist him if we spent more time together.

My cheeks heat with the memory of how poorly I resisted temptation last night, and I bow my head and close my eyes, indulging in a moment and letting the memory wash over me.

"What I'd give to know what's going through that mind of yours right now."

I snap my head up to see Carter smiling at me. "Hey! You made it." He's in the same long-sleeve T-shirt and jeans he was wearing at my house this morning, but he looks a little disheveled, his thick, dark hair a mess, like maybe he just got up from a nap.

Or rolled out of someone's bed.

Jealousy stabs my gut at the thought, but I ignore it. I move my purse from the stool I was saving for him and hang it from one of the hooks by my knees. "I saved you a seat."

He nods but doesn't take it. He leans against the bar and studies me. "Are you going to tell me, or aren't you?"

My eyes go wide. "Tell you what I'm thinking? *Hell* no."

"I'll consider that a good sign." He chuckles, and the sound skitters across my nerve endings like a sensual caress. That's what I imagine it would be like for me to be Carter's lover. Because it's always been laughter and silliness for us. The flirting isn't new. Only the touching. Only the very real possibility of crossing that line again.

Maybe that's why it's so easy to imagine more. Maybe that's why, even with my rules, I want to look him in the eye and tell him I couldn't get through the day without imagining what would have happened if I had gone home with him.

He studies my lips, hovering there for a beat before shifting downward. He scrapes that hot gaze over my breasts and hips with so much intensity that I can practically feel his hands on me.

"Carter, if you keep looking at me like that, I'm going to make decisions we'll both regret tomorrow."

His lips quirk, then his amusement fades in a blink and he sighs. "I'll try to behave."

Please don't. I shake my head, as if I can make my sex-starved inner troublemaker go away that easily. "I asked you here because I need a favor." I take a deep breath, telling myself that my plan is a good one, that I'm not making a terrible mistake.

"Hey, Carter!" Myla Quincy calls from across the bar. She hangs her jacket on the coatrack by the door before sauntering over to him. Myla's a teacher at the local high school. She's also the cheer coach and has the peppy air you'd expect from someone in that position. Never mind that she's gorgeous. Her long, silky hair falls past her breasts in smooth layers, and her jeans and cropped sweater show off her perfect body.

She's doing nothing more than smiling at him, and I already feel resentful, petty, and jealous. I was never the cheerleader type. Is that what Carter likes?

She sidles up beside him and wraps an arm around his waist. I feel a little vindicated when he stiffens. Does it not occur to her that maybe he's standing this close to me because we're on a date?

I frown. It's pretty sad that even with that article in the paper, she still believes I'm nothing more than a friend. An honorary Jackson. I could have been sitting in his lap, and Myla probably wouldn't have thought anything of it.

She whispers something in his ear, and he smiles, but it seems forced, and his eyes dart to me.

"I'll text you," he tells her gently.

"You'd *better*," she says. She winks at him before walking away, smacking her hand against his ass as she goes.

I snort out an awkward bubble of laughter. "Did she just *spank* you?"

Carter has the good sense to look mildly embarrassed—pink cheeks and all. He clears his throat. "Sorry. She's . . . um, a friend."

"Clearly more than that." I hate the bite I hear in my tone. Am I *jealous*? Why? Because he has something with her that he's also offered to me? It's ridiculous. This is Carter. He's not *mine*. He shrugs, as if it doesn't matter that he's involved with Myla and was propositioning me for sex this morning. Maybe that's the only sign I need that I can't go there with him.

"What's the favor?" he asks.

I swallow, taking a beat to get my mind back on track, to push aside my other thoughts and focus on why I asked him here. "My sister's getting married on Saturday. The wedding is here, in

Jackson Harbor. A long weekend of parties and brewery tours and family stuff." I feel ridiculous. "Any chance I could convince you to be my plus one?"

"Can't talk any of your girls into keeping you company?" he asks, laughing.

"I mean . . ." I toy with a cardboard coaster, tapping it on the bar before looking at him again. "I'd like you to be there as my boyfriend."

He blinks at me, and though his body doesn't move, I can feel him pulling away. "Teagan—"

"Like last night," I blurt. Then, softer: "*Pretend*, Carter. I'm not asking you to go steady. Just to continue last night's ruse until the wedding is over."

He swallows, his shoulders dropping a bit. "Good."

I try not to wince and fail. Maybe it makes me a hypocrite, but his relief stings. Sixty seconds ago, he was trying to seduce me all over again, then I said the word *boyfriend* and he looked like a deer caught in the headlights of a big rig. "I'm trying not to be insulted."

He shakes his head. "Sorry. Shit. I . . ."

I roll my eyes. "It's fine." Even though that's a bit of a lie, my conflicted feelings about Carter don't really matter right now. What matters is making it through this week.

"You want a date for the wedding. A fake boyfriend." He nods. "Sure. I'll have to switch shifts with someone, but I should be able to get Saturday off."

"It's a little more involved than that." I bite my bottom lip. "My mom rented out the Hayhurst mansion for the event."

Carter frowns. "I thought the reception was at the Jackson

Brews Banquet Center?"

"The *reception* is, but Mom wants everyone to stay in the mansion together for the event—Wednesday through Sunday, I mean. And since she thinks you're my boyfriend, she wants you to stay too."

Across the bar, Myla is sitting with two other equally peppy girls. She ignores them as she messes with her phone. When Carter's phone buzzes, she lifts her gaze to watch him, but he doesn't even pull it from his pocket. He keeps his attention on me, and his lips curve into a smile. "You're asking me to stay in some swanky mansion-turned-bed-and-breakfast for four nights while pretending to be your boyfriend?"

"Yes."

He arches a brow and gives me such a lascivious grin that my insides do the cha-cha. "Where do I sign up?"

My attention returns to Myla. She scowls and types something else on her phone. Carter's phone buzzes again. Have they been dating and I missed it? I didn't even realize they were more than acquaintances, but Carter has gotten a bit of a reputation lately, and sleeping with the hot cheer coach falls right in line with the things I've heard.

He continues to ignore his phone.

I shake my head. "We won't be sharing a room or anything. My parents are way too conservative for that. But they want to get to know you, so if you're supposed to be my boyfriend, they expect you to join us at the mansion. They'll probably put you in a room with Saanvi's fiancé or my cousin Trevor or something."

"Oh." He rubs a hand over his scruffy beard. "That's definitely less appealing than four nights with you. Do you know if Trevor

LEXI RYAN

likes to cuddle?"

I smack him in the stomach with the back of my hand—and feel the rock-hard evidence of his workouts beneath his shirt. *Damn.* "We'll have to make it believable."

He grins. "I think last night proved we're pretty good at that. I'm not a great liar, but I didn't find it that hard to pretend you're my girl." He tucks a lock of hair behind my ear. The simple touch sizzles through me, leaving need in its wake and making me pull away before I can lean into him. "Do you think *you* can handle it?"

I swallow. "I can. But I think we should set some clear boundaries between us if we're going to do this. No sex. We only need to be affectionate in front of other people, and we can behave normally in private."

"Normal as in . . ."

"Platonic. You might be good at the friends-with-benefits thing, but I'm not sure I have it in me."

"So you did make a decision."

Only just now. "I guess so." I wait a beat, trying to decide how much to say, how much to explain. "Do you remember when that guy from your station wanted you to give me his number?"

He nods. "Hank. Yeah, he still asks about you."

"And you remember what I told you then?"

"That you don't date firefighters?" When I nod, his forehead wrinkles with his frown. "I thought that was an excuse to spare Hank's feelings. That was for real?"

"It was for real." I take a deep breath. I don't like talking about my past, but after last night, Carter deserves more than my typical evasions. "I moved home after college and fell in love.

Heath was a police officer. We weren't engaged yet, but at one point I thought we'd get married. Spend our lives together. He died in the line of duty and . . . it sucked, Carter."

"Shit. I didn't know. I'm sorry."

"It's not your fault. I don't really talk about it," I say. He searches my face, as if he can tell there's more to the story and he's trying to read it on my skin. I hope he can't. "Those months after were like nothing I can explain. It hurt, and I was reckless and made bad decisions. When I moved here to start over, I promised myself I'd never be with a guy whose job puts him in danger every single day. So, yes, I'm attracted to you. Last night was fun, and I *am* thinking about how good it would feel to keep going down that road." I lick my lips. "But you're my friend, and I like that. If we started sleeping together . . ." *It would be too easy to fall for you. You would be so damn easy to love.*

But Carter isn't offering me love. He's offering me sex, so I choose my words carefully. "I would worry and make you crazy."

"So you're saying I can only kiss you when other people are watching?"

"Exactly." My gaze drifts away from him—from the temptation of his mouth and those dark eyes that seem to devour me. Myla's friends are talking to each other and don't seem to notice that her expression has slowly morphed from mischievous to sad. As she tucks her phone back into her purse, I realize what I'm asking might be much more complicated than I anticipated. This isn't the same as taking a guy to a wedding at home and pretending he's my boyfriend. It's not even the same as pretending to be together for a night in front of a crowd of strangers. My family is coming *here*. To Jackson Harbor—the place we go about our individual lives that are very much *not* romantically entwined.

"Maybe this is a bad idea," I say. But the alternative? Being under the same roof as Rich Nasser and letting him know I'm single? Giving him any hope that he might be able to win me back? The hair on the back of my neck stands on end. I wish it didn't scare me as much as it does. "You wouldn't be able to date anyone or even tell anyone who you can't trust one hundred percent." I nod toward Myla. "Before you agree, you need to consider who might get hurt."

"I'm not dating anyone, so it's not a problem," Carter says. He shrugs, as if I'm asking to borrow a cup of flour and not for him to test his acting skills. "We carry on with what we started last night. I certainly owe you after that. But can I ask why?"

"Because my parents think we're together, and that's the way they are. If their daughter is dating someone, they want to meet him and . . ."

"They're protective of their daughter and want to know if I'm worthy. I get that, but why do you need a boyfriend? Why not tell them the truth about last night and go to the wedding without a date? It doesn't seem like you to deceive your family."

"It's not, and I hate it. But . . ." *But you don't understand Rich. You don't know how well he manipulates people into doing what he wants. You don't understand how disappointed my parents are that he and I didn't end up together.* "Do you remember the last time I asked you to pretend to be my boyfriend? About a year ago?"

"The ex who was in town." He chuffs out a laugh. "That's the favor I was calling on last night. Of course I remember."

"His name is Rich, and he's going to be at the wedding. And staying at the mansion. *He's* the reason I need a fake boyfriend."

CARTER

I grip the back of my neck, squeezing on the knots forming there. I only briefly met Rich that one time, but it was enough to know I didn't like him—enough to know that whatever past they had together wasn't good. If it was that obvious to me, surely her family knows how she feels too. "Why was he invited?"

She grimaces. "Rich and I were high school sweethearts. My parents adore him, and I know if they're bringing him along, it's because they want to reunite us."

"And you . . ."

"Would rather chew on poisoned rat carcasses than be with him again."

"That's oddly specific and pretty intense."

She shrugs. "It's honest."

"What did he do to you?" I ask softly. I've wanted to know since the day I met him, but she refused to tell me then, and I can tell by the determined set of her jaw that she's just as unlikely to tell me now.

"It doesn't matter."

A shock of protectiveness surges through me. I'll be damned if I'm going to leave her vulnerable when she's scared of this guy. "I'll do it. Be your devoted boyfriend, stay at the mansion, whatever you need. I'll do it."

"Are you sure?" Her gaze darts to Myla again. I can't decide if she's jealous of Myla or worried she might blow our cover.

"I owe you."

"Do you? Doesn't last night make us even?"

"Last night was . . ." *So good. I can't stop thinking about it. Can't stop the memory from playing on a loop in my mind.*

She's put together tonight in her red sweater and fitted jeans, her dark hair pulled back in a clip, and she has colorful hoops dangling from her ears—the antithesis of what she was this morning in her robe and the little she had on beneath it.

I like her both ways. I *want* her both ways. But I'm going to have to let that go. Despite what Jake seems to think—despite how I acted last night—I know she isn't a convenient lay I can use to numb myself without worrying about emotional entanglements. She's a friend, an honorary Jackson, and we're already entangled.

"Last night was what?" she asks, and I realize her gaze has drifted to my mouth again. *Fuck me,* but I like that she keeps doing that. *Love it.*

"Last night was a bigger favor than you realize."

"Oh, no. I felt all those eyes on me when you called me up onstage. I realize how big it was. Huge. You owe me *so big.*" She laughs, not serious at all.

"I should have warned you. And I would have if it had occurred to me before that moment on the stage. So, yes, I owe you. But I can't lie to my family."

"I wouldn't expect you to." She mutters a curse. "It all seemed so simple before, but maybe it's not. Your family will see mine. We're doing a beer-tasting tour that includes a stop here, and the reception is at the banquet center." She clenches a fist in her lap, and I don't say anything because I can tell she's thinking out loud.

"The lie is already out there. Can it really hurt to keep it up? Do you think your family would play along?"

I nod slowly, imagining the conversation, my mom's reaction and subsequent hope, Jake's judgment, and Shay's knowing grin. "If they think it's important, they will. They care about you."

"I wouldn't ask if I didn't think it was important," she says.

I straighten and close the distance between us. Sitting on the barstool, she's nearly eye level with me, and she stays perfectly still as I wrap a hand behind her neck. "I'll have to touch you like this." I graze the tender spot behind her ear with my thumb, then follow the path I kissed last night to the light purple bruise at the base of her neck. Some base, possessive part of me likes seeing my mark on her. Wants to mark her in other spots too—over her hipbones, on her inner thigh, her ass . . .

"I'll have to endure it, I suppose." Her lips twitch. "To make it believable."

"But no sex," I say, my gaze glued to her wicked smile.

Her smile falls away, and she lifts a hand and threads it through my hair. When she speaks, her lips nearly brush mine. "No sex." For a beat so brief I almost miss it, her gaze flicks to Myla.

"Are you jealous of Myla Quincy?"

"Why would I be jealous? You and I are just friends. This is all for show, but I don't want anyone thinking that you're cheating on me with her." She swallows. "Or vice versa."

"Understood."

"Is it too much to ask you not to see anyone else until after the wedding?"

"Consider it done." I'm surprised how little I hesitate, but I'd agree to anything to protect her from a man who terrifies her the way Rich so clearly did the day he was in town. "Any other rules?"

"Only one."

I arch a brow, waiting. "Name it."

"Don't ask me about Rich. Don't make me explain."

Chapter
SEVEN

CARTER
ONE YEAR AGO . . .

O ne minute I'm standing at the bar at Jackson Brews, talking to Jake about his newest IPA, and the next someone grabs me by the shirt and molds her body to mine.

Not just someone. *Teagan Chopra.* She balls a fist in my shirt and tugs me close as she backs against the wall. It's instinct to follow. Instinct to lean in and feel every curve of the body that's starred in a good number of my fantasies. In fact, I might be dreaming, because I've had more than a few start like this—so many that blood is racing to my dick. *Just. Like. That.*

I'm not going to look the fool, though, so I arch a brow and play it cool. "Can I help you with something?"

She guides my head down until my lips are only a breath from hers. "Could you play along? *Please?*"

Play along as in . . . kiss her? Or play along as in stand here, painfully close to the mouth I dream about on a regular basis?

Her lips are bare tonight. No red lipstick or shiny gloss. Just naked pink lips so close to mine that my stomach knots with the desire to *taste*.

I flatten a palm against the wall behind her to steady myself. "You're going to have to be more specific."

"Pretend to be my boyfriend or . . . something?" Her gaze slices to someone across the room then back to me.

I smile slowly. "What's in it for me?"

I'm not an ass, but what she's asking is going to cost me. Every time she inhales, her breasts brush my chest, and her citrus and lavender smell is filling my head and making me think about the last time we were this close. At my family's cabin last summer, swimming in the lake. We were laughing. *Flirting.* I thought it'd be a good idea to pull her into my arms and kiss her. Arrogant fuck that I am, it never occurred to me that she'd react so badly when I lowered my mouth to hers—her panic more appropriate for a woman who was about to be shoved underwater than one who was about to be kissed. That memory makes me want to back up and forget how good she smells, how soft she is under the palm that's slid toward her ass of its own volition.

I yank away my rogue hand as if I've been burned. *Shit.*

"I'll owe you, okay? Any favor you want at the time of your choosing."

I arch a brow. "*Anything?*"

"Please?" That's when I see the fear in her eyes.

I swallow. "Yeah, okay. Sure." So I step closer, lean in, and tilt my head, as if we're in the middle of an intimate conversation and not two friends who have agreed to stay that way. I drag my knuckles up her side and feel her shiver under my touch. "Who is he?" I want to turn around and see him for myself—*him*, because I have no doubt this is about a guy—but I won't look. I'll stand here and play along. For her.

"An ex." She wraps her arms behind my neck and buries her face in my chest. I hold her close, even when Jake flashes me a questioning glance behind the counter, even when I feel the eyes of the stranger behind us.

"Teagan?"

Her beautiful olive skin pales at the deep male voice. I keep my body angled toward hers but slowly turn my head.

Here's a fun fact about guys who lift: we notice when other fit dudes are around. Measure ourselves against them. And the guy staring at Teagan right now makes me feel small. He's not just built, he's musclebound in a way that reminds me of the little brother from *A Christmas Story*. *"I can't put my arms down!"*

I don't recognize the guy as a local, but she clearly knows who he is—knows enough to want me to act as an emotional shield between them. Maybe a physical one, too.

Dismissing him with little more than a sneer, I turn back to Teagan and lower my mouth to her ear—a lover whispering a secret. "Need me to get rid of him?" I ask softly.

She shakes her head and shivers again. She's not trembling from my touch or in anticipation of my kiss. She's *terrified*, and that alone is enough to make me hate this man. I press my body closer to hers, the need to protect as instinctive as my pull toward her.

I hold her close, whispering, "I've got you. I'm here, okay? You're safe."

"Teagan, is that you?" the guy asks.

She swallows, and I can feel the faint tremor of her shaking hands as she grips my arms. In the next moment, she pastes on a smile and turns her attention to the ex. As if noticing him there for the first time, she steps out from between me and the wall. "Oh my goodness! Rich? Is that really you?"

The bastard's gaze is all over her. I understand the instinct—she's gorgeous, and tonight she's wearing black shorts that show off her legs and a Jackson Brews T-shirt that stretches tight across her chest. Any hetero, red-blooded male would struggle not to look twice. But there's an ownership in the way this guy looks at her that makes my blood boil.

Teagan takes my hand and squeezes hard. "Carter, this is my old friend, Rich. Rich, this is my"—she stumbles for a beat—"Carter."

I extend my hand to Rich, who takes it in his meaty fist and tries to crush my bones. I smile and give him my typical firm handshake. Unlike Meathead here, some of us don't need to crush bones to convince people we have functioning dicks.

Rich drops my hand and smiles at Teagan. "Much more than *friends* during the good times," he murmurs.

She stiffens beside me, but her only response is a noncommittal hum.

"Can we talk?" he asks, nodding toward the booths at the back of the bar.

"I . . ." Her eyes dart to mine, panicked. "I would, but . . ."

"We're celebrating our anniversary tonight," I say. "We'd love to catch up another time, man, but tonight is about us."

"Anniversary?"

Teagan nods and steps into me. I wrap my arm around her, flattening my palm against her stomach.

Rich's expression wavers between disappointment and disbelief. "Your mom didn't tell me you were seeing anyone."

"It's . . . new," Teagan says.

"New?" He folds his arms. "You just said you were celebrating your *anniversary*."

"Two months," I say before dropping my mouth to her ear and stage-whispering, "The best two months of my life."

"I'm here for a conference," Rich says, eyes searching Teagan's face. "Maybe we can meet for breakfast before I head home tomorrow?"

"Tomorrow? I . . . well . . ."

"We'd love to," I say, unreasonably satisfied by his scowl when I invite myself, "but Teagan has to work."

"I do."

"Coffee on your break, then?" he asks.

Dude can't take no for an answer.

"I don't think that's a good idea," she says softly.

"I miss you." He steps forward. "We all miss you. Your parents want you to come home."

"She is home." Everything else about this conversation might be an act, but those words couldn't be truer. Jackson Harbor is where Teagan belongs, and it wouldn't be the same without her. I smile down at her. "We should plan a trip to see your folks soon. I can't wait to meet them."

She swallows. "Yeah, they'd love that."

Rich gives her a final hard look. "I don't need to leave until lunch tomorrow. You know how to reach me if you change your mind." He holds my gaze as he backs away. "Happy anniversary."

I pretend I can't hear the derision in his voice. "Thanks, man." I pull Teagan fully into my arms, like holding her is the most natural thing in the world. It kind of is.

I hold my friend until her panic subsides. Until fear I've never before seen in her eyes fades away and she steps back. "He's gone. He left. Thank you."

"Who is he?" I'm cold everywhere her body touched mine.

"A mistake," she says, shaking her head. "And the man my parents desperately wanted me to marry."

Damn. "Do you want to talk about it?"

"There's nothing to talk about." It's not her words as much as her body language—the stiff posture and the space she puts between us—that informs me I've been firmly shoved back to my side of the friendship line she's drawn between us.

"Hey." I want to chase after her, to drag her into the light somewhere so I can see her face and have a clue what she might be thinking. "Are you okay?"

"I'm fine. We should probably find Jake and explain before he tells Ava and the rumors start flying."

Chapter
EIGHT

TEAGAN
PRESENT DAY...

"Okay, mister, how's the pain level this morning?" I ask as I head into my latest admit's room.

Isaiah Goldright turns his sleepy eyes on me and gives me a wide grin. "Better now that I'm looking at you."

Shaking my head, I check his vitals and IV fluids. "I'm sure."

This kid has been charming the pants off the pediatric nurses since he came in through the ER. I know what brought him here—the blood-alcohol level of point-one-two that made him steer his car right down the side of the hill and into a tree at sixty miles per hour. Still, the social worker and ER both gave him lectures already. It's not my place to pile on, even if that means biting my tongue every time I walk in the room.

"Your vitals look good." I step over to my laptop to add details to his chart, but when I turn, I see he has a visitor I didn't notice before. "Oh. Hi."

"Good morning," Carter says. I haven't seen him since I left Jackson Brews last night, after he agreed to be my fake boyfriend for my sister's wedding. It was harder to leave than I want to admit. I was worried that the second I left, Myla would be all over him, but if we're going to do this, I have to trust him.

"What are you doing here?" I ask softly, looking back and forth between him and my patient.

"Just checking in on Isaiah and making sure he's not giving you all too much trouble up here."

This must be the friend he visited yesterday morning. How do they know each other? "He's pretty damn lucky."

"If you can call a guy who had to be cut out of his car 'lucky,'" Isaiah grumbles.

"You are," Carter says.

"My football season is *over*."

Carter shrugs. "Now maybe you'll know what I mean when I warn you that actions have consequences."

"I only had a couple of beers."

Carter grunts. "Five is not a couple."

"I thought . . ." Isaiah scowls at the ceiling. "I thought I could drive fine."

"You're fucking lucky your car and the tree took the worst of the damage."

"My car is totaled," the teen says.

Carter folds his arms. "Would you rather you'd killed off some innocent family? You want a few deaths on your conscience for the rest of your life?"

I shoot Carter a look. I understand the need to shake some

sense into the kid, but Isaiah's parents are probably going to give him all the come-to-Jesus lectures he could ever want and more.

"I know I fucked up," Isaiah says.

"Language," I say, even though I don't really mean it, not when he spoke softly enough that his voice won't carry outside this room. I feel awkward standing here while they're having this conversation.

Carter grunts. "This boy's poor vocabulary is the least of my worries right now."

"Does that mean you're going to quit threatening to wash my mouth out with soap?" Isaiah asks. His words are edged with a sulk even as he fights back the ghost of a smile—as if he wants to be annoyed but, deep down, he likes that Carter gives him a hard time.

"Don't count on it." Carter pushes out of his chair. "Promise me you'll be nice to the nurses. Teagan here is a good friend of mine."

Isaiah's lips curve into a broad smile. "Oh, yeah? Why haven't you introduced her to me before?" His grin turns cocky, and he slowly looks me over from head to toe with those sleepy brown eyes. "Are you single? Because my girlfriend broke up with me, and you look like the *best* cure for my loneliness. I could use a little exotic flavor in my life."

I fold my arms and fix him with a glare. "First of all, *that's* offensive. I'm a woman, not some wild animal. Second of all, *child*, you wouldn't know what to do with me."

He hums. "But how can I learn if you don't let me try?"

"Dream on, kid," Carter growls. "She's mine."

An irrational thrill races through me at those words. I busy myself updating his chart in the laptop, hoping the screen hides my pink cheeks. I guess I need to get used to this if we're going to pretend to be together.

Isaiah scoffs. "How on earth did your ugly mug manage to land someone like her? Are you a secret millionaire or something?"

I laugh at that. "That's also offensive, my friend. Who made you think women are after money?"

"Girls don't wanna have to pay for their own shit." Isaiah shrugs. "A man should be able to spoil his woman."

"You little punk. You think you can get away with anything just because your dad died!"

Carter and I whip around to the door at the exact same moment and see a blonde walking into Isaiah's room.

"Excuse me, can I help you?" I ask, but I'm thinking about what she said. His dad is dead, and his mother shows up in his hospital room practically foaming at the mouth. *Poor kid.*

Carter clears his throat. "This is Shasta Murphy, Isaiah's mother."

Shasta looks about thirty pounds underweight. Her pale face is covered with acne, and her hair is greasy and stringy. I met enough addicts back when I worked ER to know one when I see one. I would pin Shasta's drug of choice as meth.

"Nice to meet you, Shasta." I step forward and offer my hand. "I'm Teagan, and I'm Isaiah's nurse today."

"I don't give a flying fuck who you are, lady. I'm here to talk to my son. This little shit has no common sense."

"This is a pediatric unit," I say, infusing my voice with calm. "There are young children here. I'd like you to lower your voice and watch your language, please."

"Yeah, *Shasta*," Isaiah says, emphasizing her first name in a way that makes me think she hates when he uses it. "Nobody wants you here."

"You know who came to my door yesterday?" She points a dirty finger at him, her nail bitten to the quick. "The police. That's who. You and your stupid decisions made them come 'round asking me questions."

"*My* stupid decisions?" He grunts. "I guess I learned from the best."

"You'd better show your mom some respect," she says through clenched teeth.

"Shasta, this isn't the place," Carter says.

She spins on him, a bundle of nervous energy—twitching shoulder, fingers drumming her thigh, foot tapping the floor to an irregular beat. "This isn't your concern. You both get out of here."

Carter takes one step forward and folds his arms. It's not much, but it's enough to put himself between the woman and her son, and his posture speaks volumes. If she wants to talk to Isaiah, she's going to have to go through him.

"The police came to my *door*," she repeats, jabbing a finger in the air toward Isaiah.

"I'm sure that must have been very stressful for you," I say. I try to hide the sarcasm in my voice, but she spins and glares at me. "You must have been very worried about your son." *So worried that it took her another twenty-four hours to make it to the hospital.*

"I want to talk to your boss. I won't have some bitch talking shit to me."

I smile sweetly. "I'd be happy to get the charge nurse for you." I press the call button beside Isaiah's bed and give the charge nurse the code for security. Better to have them on the way if this woman is going to keep up her attitude. "Why don't you come with me, and we'll find her together?"

"I'm not done talking to my son yet."

"Yes, you are," Carter says.

"You can't tell me what to do."

"Shasta doesn't have custody of her son," he tells me softly. "She has no legal rights here."

"And you think you have rights? Did *you* carry him for nine months? Did *you* destroy your body to give life to this ungrateful little shit?"

"Mom, *leave*," Isaiah growls.

Shaun, one of our security officers, steps into the room in record time. As discreetly as possible, I nod toward Shasta.

"Can I help you, ma'am?" he asks, stepping forward.

The woman stiffens at the sight of a man in uniform, but she lifts her chin. "Yeah. I want to file a complaint against this nurse. She's disrespecting me."

"Let's go to my office so you can give me the details." Shaun shoots me a look, solidarity in that stern expression. I haven't had to deal with security often, thankfully, but of all the guys on the team, Shaun's the best at defusing volatile situations.

"Don't you ever come around asking me favors again," Shasta shouts to Isaiah as she follows Shaun out of the room. "Don't you dare bring trouble to my door."

I count to twenty after Shaun leaves and then excuse myself, so Isaiah and Carter can speak in private.

CARTER

"I hate my mom," Isaiah says. "I hate her so much."

My gut twists. Isaiah has never bothered to hide how he feels about his mother, but I don't think I've ever heard him say it so directly. Maybe I should scold him for saying something so awful, but I won't. Not when he's already lost so much this year. Not when I have to live with the role I played in that loss. "I don't blame you."

He sighs and shifts in bed, grimacing. "Is that hot nurse really your girl?"

Get used to the lie now. "Haven't you read the papers? Our picture was on the front page of the *Jackson Harbor Gazette* yesterday."

He grunts. "No one under the age of sixty reads the newspaper, C. Sorry."

I laugh. "I guess you're right."

"Did she grow up here like you? The nurse?"

"She moved here a few years ago. Her family's from Virginia, and she went to college with Ethan's wife, Nic, in Alabama." I take the cup from his bedside table, refilling the ice as an excuse to stand closer. "You said Jess broke up with you?"

"I'm not talking about it."

"I didn't ask you to."

91

He scowls at me then sighs. "She said she cares about me, but it felt like it was getting serious too fast. Then she was all over Hayden Traelle at the party on Saturday, so obviously she doesn't care that much."

Suddenly, Isaiah's very uncharacteristic decision to drink and drive makes more sense. Nothing excuses it, but I understand a little better now that I know. "That blows. I'm sorry."

He lifts his chin. "Why? It's not your fault."

"I'm still sorry. Broken hearts suck."

"Preach." He snags his phone off the bed next to him and starts scrolling.

"I work tonight and tomorrow. You need anything before I go in?" I work twenty-four-hour shifts every three days; he knows how it works.

He shakes his head. "I'm good."

"Text if you change your mind. Otherwise, I'll see you Wednesday."

"Got it," he says, but his attention is already off me and on his phone.

I head out to the nurse's station to find Teagan.

When I find her sitting right next to Bethany, I freeze. I planned on talking to Beth this morning, but damn if I don't feel awkward about it seeing her next to Teagan.

After Teagan left Jackson Brews last night, I went to break it off with Myla. Unfortunately, she'd already left. When I texted her this morning, I found out she's out of town for a conference for the next few days. Even if we were casual, I hated ending things over a text, but I couldn't risk Myla blowing our cover in front of Teagan's family when she comes back to town. I told her I was seeing Teagan and we were going to be exclusive. Her response left little doubt in my mind as to how Myla feels about the sudden change to our relationship.

Three words: *Wow. Fine then.*

After getting that curt response, I was glad I could have the conversation with Beth in person, but now, I'm suddenly dreading it.

"Hey, Carter," Beth says, flipping her red hair over one shoulder.

Teagan blinks up at me. "Do you know *everyone*?"

"Beth's a good friend of mine," I say. "She used to work at the department with me."

Beth folds her arms and fights a smile. I know her well enough to know she's thinking, *Yeah, and we fuck on a semi-regular basis.*

Teagan shakes her head. "I'm sorry, Beth. I knew that. I swear, I forget what a small world Jackson Harbor is."

"No worries," Beth says, her eyes darting back and forth between Teagan and me, as if she can judge the status of our relationship by nothing more than the air between us. "I forget too, believe it or not."

Her words are heavy with meaning, and I can tell she's not going to talk about *us* in front of Teagan, but there is a conversation to be had. I shake my head—*later*. "Teagan, can we talk for a minute?"

"Sure." She puts down her pen and swings around the nurse's station. I fall into step beside her, and she leads the way to an empty room labeled "family comfort area." Inside, there's a television, a couch, a couple of chairs, and a shelf stacked with paperbacks and magazines.

"Are you going to get in trouble because of Shasta?"

"Isaiah's mom?" Teagan grins. "Oh, hell no. Shaun wanted to get her out of the room. I'll talk to Isaiah's guardian, and if she agrees, Shasta won't be allowed on the unit next time she tries to visit."

"Marta will agree. She's had enough of Shasta to last her many lifetimes." I exhale. "He doesn't need her around while he's trying to recover."

"How do you know him?"

"Isaiah is Max Goldright's son."

"And Max is . . ." I see the moment the name snaps into place for her. Sympathy casts shadows over her face. "He was on your team at the fire department. He was the one who died at that warehouse."

The one who died. The one who should still be here raising his son. "Max was raising Isaiah on his own, so Isaiah had to move in with his grandma after . . ." An unwelcome surge of emotion presses down on my chest. I focus on my breath. *In and out.*

"After Max died," she finishes for me.

"Marta's a good woman. She looks after him as best she can, but . . ." I shrug. Teagan's studying me so intently that I'm afraid she can see right through that shrug and to the shredded heart in my chest. "Seventeen-year-old boys need their dads, and he doesn't have that." *He'll never have that.*

"I didn't realize . . ." She bites her bottom lip and studies me again with that burning intensity. "I'm so sorry."

I roll my shoulders back, but it does nothing to lessen that feeling that she's seen too much. "It sucks. For all of us, but especially Isaiah."

The little radio clipped to her scrubs beeps. "Teagan, the mother of the patient in 2B wants to talk to you."

She presses a button. "Thanks, I'll be right there." She drops the radio and cocks her head. "Have you given any more thought to the wedding?"

"Are you afraid I'm going to back out?"

"Not exactly. I just . . ." She studies the sign on the wall that lists the visiting hours and rules. "Did you talk to Myla? Is she okay with it?"

"Myla isn't my keeper. I don't need her permission." I sigh when I realize that doesn't make Teagan feel better. "I told her that you and I were seeing each other. I promise she won't get in the way."

"I'm sorry you had to do that."

I'm not. I'm a little surprised to realize it's true. Myla knows I'm not looking for a relationship, but lately, I've felt like she's been hoping for more. I don't want to lead her on, even unintentionally. Maybe it was time for us to end things. "It's not a big deal."

I don't tell Teagan that I'd do anything to protect her from Rich. I don't tell her that my few minutes talking to the guy last year was enough to make me grateful she asked for my help. "I work tonight and tomorrow, but I was able to get the rest of the week off."

"Thanks." She gives me a shy smile as she pulls the door open. "Then I guess I'll see you Thursday."

"I can't wait," I say, and I mean it. I'm looking forward to this weekend far more than I should.

Chapter NINE

CARTER

When Teagan is gone, I sink into one of the waiting room couches, lay my head back, and close my eyes. Between my anxiety about the hero worship at the auction, Isaiah's accident, and everything that's been going on with Teagan, the past few days have been a rollercoaster. And now I need to talk to Bethany.

My phone buzzes, and I grab it from my pocket.

Unknown Number: You didn't respond to my text. Does that mean you don't want to see me?

Shit. I completely forgot about the text from this number yesterday. When I decided it was a wrong number, I put it from my mind. But here she is again.

Me: Who is this?

Unknown Number: Sabrina. Did you never put my number in your phone? I would have done it for you if I hadn't had to run out to catch my flight.

I blink at the screen until the name snaps into place with *flight*. Right. Sabrina was the reporter who came to do a story on the stupid viral picture. It was almost a month ago, right after I'd stopped accepting interviews, but she was ballsy enough to come to town and smart enough to catch me at Jackson Brews and pretend she *wasn't* a reporter. We had a few drinks together, and I took her home. I didn't even know she was there for a story until the next morning, when she scrambled to ask me some questions so she wouldn't get in trouble with her boss. I wasn't thrilled.

I add the name to my contacts in case she decides to text me again.

Me: Hey, how are you? I must have lost the number.

A lie. Once I found out what she'd come to town for, I wanted nothing to do with her. But a harmless lie. No need to tell someone I'll rarely see that her lie by omission totally turned me off.

Sabrina: Well, good thing you have it now. So . . . this weekend. I get in Friday morning and will be there until Sunday. I'll be kind of busy with family stuff, but I'm sure I could sneak away for you. I've been dying to see you again.

I feel like an ass if that's true. She's been thinking about me, and I barely remembered her? Jake's right. It's time for me to make some changes. Maybe this thing with Teagan is exactly what I need to kick my ass out of this rut I've been in.

> *Me: I'm flattered, but I'm seeing someone now. I'm sorry.*
>
> *Sabrina: Is this because I didn't tell you I was a journalist?*

"Is there a reason you're scowling at your phone?" Bethany asks, sticking her head in the door. "Do you need another minute, or can you talk?"

Shutting off my screen, I sit up and rub my eyes. "I'm fine. Come on in."

She shuts the door behind her and takes a seat on the couch across from me. "Isaiah's probably going to get discharged this afternoon." She shakes her head. "I'm not really supposed to tell you that, but I know you're worried about him."

"Is that . . . good? Do you think they're sending him home too soon?"

She shrugs. "It's normal. Insurance doesn't like to pay for any more time in the hospital than necessary, and he'll be able to rest at home better than he can here anyway."

I pinch the bridge of my nose between two fingers. Bethany worked with Max when she was still with the JHFD, and she understands why I'm so protective of Isaiah. "His girlfriend broke up with him."

She arches a manicured brow. "Seriously? While he was in

the hospital?"

I shake my head. "No. Before. I think that's why he drank too much." I sigh. "Maybe why he got behind the wheel when he knew he shouldn't. He's been different since Max died—more reckless."

"Must be going around," she says, so softly that I almost think I misheard her.

I study her for the first time all day. Bethany is a gorgeous redhead with the energy to match, but today she looks tired. "What do you mean? Are you okay?"

She cocks her head to the side and gives a small smile. I know that smile. It's the one she gives guys who are trying to pick her up at the bar. The one that says, *Oh, you're so cute, but you're too oblivious for your own good.* "I'm fine. It's you I'm worried about."

I laugh. "Seriously? Why?"

"Isn't Teagan one of your best friends?"

"Sure. I mean, she's a family friend." I shrug.

"And now you're sleeping with her too?"

"Bethany—"

She holds up a hand. "I knew the deal, Carter. And, honestly, I never expected this to last as long as it has. I thought . . ." She sighs. "I thought you'd be better by now."

"Better how?"

"Come on. I know how hard Max's death hit you. That's why you reached out to me the first time, remember?"

"I remember you dragging me to your bed." I'm trying to make her laugh, but she looks sad.

"Well, I was trying to help." Her smile falls away. "But instead, I became this crutch that you've used to keep yourself from moving on—me, Myla, God knows who else."

Her lecture sounds too much like Jake's, and irritation rankles so hard that I almost miss what she's saying. "You're . . . ending this?"

I'm not even sure how I'm supposed to feel. I should feel like I'm losing something. Bethany is smart, funny, and beautiful. I've truly enjoyed the role she's played in my life this last six months. She was a bright spot when I had so few. But mostly, I'm relieved that she's doing it so I don't have to.

"If only there were something here to end," she says. She takes my hand in hers and squeezes. "I don't want to be an excuse. Max's death was awful, but you weren't to blame. It's past time that you forgive yourself and go back to the Carter Jackson you were before—the one who was hunting for a woman to spend his life with and not one to warm his bed." She stands, then leans down to press a kiss to the top of my head.

The maternal gesture is at odds with the relationship we've had lately, and it catches me off guard.

I cradle my head in my hands, close my eyes, and try to collect and steady myself. Because suddenly my world feels like its shifting beneath my feet.

TEAGAN

Shay Jackson opens the door to her apartment after my first knock. Her eyes light up when she sees me. "Speak of the devil," she says. "I just got off the phone with Ava, who talked to Jake, who said you and Carter were looking *mighty* friendly at the bar last night. You two are making a habit of that."

Of course she already knows. Secrets are a rare commodity in the Jackson family. There's no way he and I are going to pull this off without being the subject of their ongoing game of telephone—even if they do know the truth. "That's why I'm here. I wanted to talk to you."

Shay beams and pulls the door wider. "Good. Because I want to know all the details." Cringing, she shakes her head. "Scratch that. No sex details. You're my friend, but he's my brother, and . . . yuck."

I toss my purse on the counter and go straight to her fridge for a beer. One of the best perks of being friends with the Jackson family is that they always have good beer in the fridge, and after the last few days, I feel like I deserve the empty calories. I grab a second and wave it at Shay.

She shrugs. "Sure. Are you going to explain why my brother was feeling you up last night?"

"My mom saw the picture of us online, and I didn't tell her it was fake."

Shay's eyebrows shoot up. "Oh."

"My sister's wedding is this weekend, and I asked Carter to go with me—to pretend to be my boyfriend until it's all over."

"But your sister's wedding is *here.* In Jackson Harbor. This isn't like taking a guy home and pretending you're a thing when you're not."

"I know. I do. But Shay . . ." I put down my beer then take her hand and squeeze it in both of mine. "The guy my parents want me to marry is coming, and if I'm single, they'll be relentless in their efforts to set me up."

"Why not pretend you have a boyfriend who lives in California or something?"

I squeeze her fingers again. "Because my mom has already seen the news about me and *Carter*. If I'm going to lie, doesn't it make sense to go with what's already established?"

She frowns. "I guess. But I wish you didn't have to lie at all."

"You and me both," I mutter. Truth be told, I can't think about it too much. Every time I do, there's an ache in my chest, like I'm a child who's gotten away with breaking a rule. "I feel like a total shit for doing this to my family."

"Then why do it? Why not tell them the truth and explain that you don't want this guy there? Surely they value you enough to listen."

I shake my head. It's hard to explain Rich and how well he's entrenched himself in my family's life. Hard to explain the fear and shame that keeps me from telling anyone the whole truth— whether it's my family or Shay. Or maybe I don't want to explain that I'm too much of a coward to ask my sister or mother not to let Rich come—too afraid they'll ask questions I don't want to answer. Or worse, that it will piss off Rich and he'll tell them my secrets. "It's not that simple."

"But this is?"

"Pretending to be with Carter beats any alternative I can come up with." Even if it makes me a liar and a coward. God, I wish I weren't so damn afraid.

She folds her arms and arches a brow. "And that's it? Just pretend? No ulterior motives in choosing Carter?"

"He was convenient."

Shay grunts. "I'm sure that's all there was to it."

I shrug. We won't discuss how good it felt to have him pressed against me or the flurry of butterflies that swarmed in my belly when he touched me at the bar. It would've been so easy to stay in his arms all night, to thank him for this favor by taking him home with me. But after running through the details of our weekend together, I left. I didn't trust myself to stay. Not with the peppy cheerleader lady looking at Carter like he'd broken her heart.

"Do you know anything about Carter and Myla?" I ask. "She was blowing up Carter's phone last night." Never mind the fact that she whispered something to him and smacked his ass.

Shay snorts. "Her and *most* single, age-appropriate women in Jackson Harbor. He's become such a flirt."

"It seemed like more than flirtation. Have they been dating?"

"Myla Quincy, right?" She frowns and grabs her phone. "I don't think so."

"Who are you calling?"

She grins. "Ava. She used to work with Myla. She might know something."

I snatch the phone from her hand before she can connect the call. "Don't. Please?"

"If you and Carter are involved, don't you want to know?"

I wave a hand. "I have no claim on him. I was just curious." *And jealous. More jealous than I want to admit.* I find the bottle opener, open my beer, and drain half of it in one go.

Shay laughs. "I guess you don't want a glass?"

That easily, the subject of Carter and me is pushed aside. This weekend might be difficult, and maybe I'm making the biggest mistake of my life—lying to my family because I'm too scared to tell them the truth and risking my friendship with Carter when he deserves better—but for now, Shay and I are back to being a couple of single girls. *Just the way I like it.*

Chapter TEN

TEAGAN

There are books you read when you're lonely and need to smile, but sometimes, those are the same books you definitely shouldn't read when you're actively lusting after your fake boyfriend. I've been waiting for this novel to come out for months—a sexy friends-to-lovers romance about a woman who sets out to seduce her best friend and falls in love in the process. It isn't doing my libido any favors. I either need to find something else or tell Carter I'm changing the rules of our arrangement, because the way this heroine thinks about her friend feels all too familiar.

One more page, then I'll put it down and find something else to do.

My phone buzzes before I have to confront how badly I just lied to myself.

Carter: You home?
Me: In my pajamas and curled up with a book. I'm trying to enjoy the calm before the chaos tomorrow
Carter: Want to come to the door?

Frowning, I push the blanket off my lap and peek out the window. Sure enough, Carter's Jeep is parked in front of my house. I run to the door and pull it open to find him standing on my front step, a bouquet of bright sunflowers in one hand and a bottle of wine in the other. My stomach flip-flops, practically reaching out and dancing happy circles with my libido. I try to ignore both. *Friends.*

"What's this?" I ask, pulling the door wider to let him in.

"Can't a man bring his girlfriend flowers and wine?"

"Sure he can. But that doesn't answer my question."

Chuckling, he heads to my kitchen, sets the wine on the counter, and opens cabinets.

I follow him and grab a vase from under the island. "The wine glasses are by the fridge." As I reach for the flowers, the brush of our fingers sends a buzz of warmth through me—the twin to the buzz I felt when I opened the door and saw him. It's been a long day running errands and preparing for the wedding. I should've been too busy to think Carter's name . . . and yet I found myself alternating between giddy anticipation at spending my weekend with him and worries about spending it near Rich.

Every time I caught myself thinking about Jackson Harbor's most eligible bachelor, I'd feel a little pathetic, but seeing that he's clearly been thinking about me too? Yeah, *hello, warm buzz.* "Is this some sort of bribe?"

"I missed you, honey." He makes a face. "Sweetie? Baby? Love bunny?"

I yank the flowers away and laugh. "*Teagan* works fine."

"Oh, no. No one's going to buy it if I don't call you by some sort of endearment from time to time. What about *legs*? I really, really like your legs, so it would be from the heart, at least."

I roll my eyes and pull the kitchen scissors from the drawer. "You're not serious."

"Well, if I called you *tits*, I'd make myself look like an ass."

I snort then laugh fully when I can't hold it back anymore. "If you called me *tits*, *I* would think you were an ass. And then I'd kick you *out* on your ass."

"Then you'd *call* me an ass. Or a dick. See? Calling people by body parts is totally normal."

"And widely considered offensive. Please, resist."

"But *earlobe* has a nice ring to it. It's unique. Everyone would assume there was some heartfelt story behind it."

"Not legs, not tits, and definitely not earlobe."

"Are you sure?" He grins. "If I recall, you rather enjoy it when I give attention to that body part."

"I'm sure."

He opens the drawer by the sink and pulls out a corkscrew. "What did Heath call you?"

My hands still over the flower stems I'm cutting, and I have to swallow hard and take a deep breath before I can answer. "He . . . Why does it matter?"

Carter studies me for a beat, and I think he's going to ask me a question about it, but then he shrugs. "Only because I want to be original. It wouldn't do for me to call you the same nickname he did. Or Rich, for that matter." Is it me, or is there jealousy in his voice when he says Rich's name?

"No one will think it's strange if you call me Teagan."

"Whatever you say, pinkie finger."

Another snort of laughter bubbles out of me. Not because it's that funny but because it's *not* that funny and he's amusing the shit out of himself with it. "Oh my God. What has gotten into you today?"

He shrugs as he pours our wine. "I'm in a good mood. I have the next five days off, and I'm spending them with a beautiful woman. Can you blame me for being upbeat?" He hands me a glass and takes a long sip from his own before making a face. "Oh, hell."

I frown. "What?"

He wipes the back of his mouth with his hand. "Jake's trying to make wine. This is his first batch, and . . ." He shudders and takes my glass away. He dumps them both in the sink. "Let's just say that either sleep deprivation from the baby is starting to affect his judgment, or he should stick with beer."

He reaches for the bottle, but I snatch it off the counter before he can dump it too. "I want to try."

He folds his arms, watching me as I bring the bottle to my lips.

I take a sip, then cough. "Dear Lord. It tastes like vinegar."

"I was trying to be gallant and save you."

Pursing my lips, I shove the bottle at him. "And not even good vinegar."

"Agreed." He dumps the bottle down the sink. "I thought we should make bourbon, but Brayden did a market analysis and insisted the market for wine is better for our clientele."

"I have beer in the fridge." I return to the flowers while Carter rummages through my fridge to find us some drinks. By the time I'm done arranging them in the vase, he's opened a bomber of the Jackson Brews Blueberry Sour and poured us each a glass.

"Much better," he says, sighing.

I take a sip and nod. "Don't you all have enough to do without adding wine to your offerings? What's next? Buying a vineyard?"

"That would be awesome, but no. We're all big thinkers. We can't help but imagine new opportunities for the company." He shrugs. "But I'm not here to talk about the family business, ligament."

I cough on my beer. That might be the worst one yet. "Why are you here? Other than to call me seriously disturbing pet names?"

"Your family arrives tomorrow."

I nod. "We'll head over together after lunch if that's still okay with you."

"It's great." He pulls a stool out from under the island and sits on it, settling his glass in front of him. "But if we're going to be convincing, I figured we should make sure we have our bases covered in terms of information. I need to know everything I'd know about you if we were truly involved."

I lean back against the opposite counter and study him. "Don't we already know each other pretty well?"

"As friends, sure, but I don't know you *intimately*."

"After Saturday, you certainly know me more intimately than most of my friends," I mutter. When he shoots me a mischievous grin, I roll my eyes. "Fine. What do you want to know?"

"Well, first we're going to need to explain why we told Rich we'd been together two months a year ago and then I told everyone on Saturday that we'd been dating for two months."

Crap. He's absolutely right. It's obvious, and yet I'd been so relieved to know Carter would be by my side that I hadn't given that explanation any thought. "Okay, we were dating last year for a couple of months, but things were getting serious and you didn't want that."

He gapes, pressing a hand to his chest. "*I* didn't want it? Do you want to make me look like a commitment-phobic asshole?"

"What if I broke up with you because you called me really obnoxious pet names?"

"How about saying it was mutual? Things were getting serious, and neither of us was ready for that."

I consider, running it over from a couple of angles in my head before nodding. I don't want either of us to sound like a jerk in whatever story we concoct. "That works."

"Though I secretly was ready," he says. "I just didn't want to rush you because I understand that my job was part of the reason you were afraid to get too close."

I flinch. They say the best lies are based in truth, but that one feels like it's too close to home. So close it's knocking on my damn door. "My sister would certainly buy that."

"But then we started dating again a couple of months ago," he says. "This time I'm determined to make you fall as hard for me as I've fallen for you."

It's weird to have this conversation and weirder to stand here wishing this weren't pretend, that we were describing our history instead of manufacturing it. I take a long pull from my beer and sigh. It's so good that I want to drain my glass, but I've made that mistake with this one before. "I haven't eaten much today," I tell Carter. "I should probably find some food if I don't want this to go straight to my head. Are you hungry?"

"I could eat."

I open the pantry and frown at my pitiful selection. I eat out too much and hate cooking for one, and that's completely obvious by the lack of food in my house.

Carter comes to stand behind me. "You're worse than Shay. At least she has whole-wheat bread and stuff for sandwiches most of the time." He pulls open my freezer and fridge, then nods to the stool. "Sit. I'll cook, and you can fill me in on the lesser-known details of Teagan Chopra."

I open my mouth to protest then decide not to. I don't know if Carter is any good in the kitchen, and that does seem like something I should know. "Okay, you know I have one sister, younger. Her name is Saanvi."

"And her fiancé?" he asks. "Leroy?"

"Liam." I'm honestly impressed that he's even that close. I don't remember talking about Liam, but I'm sure I have. He came to Jackson Harbor last spring to help Saanvi finalize some wedding details, but I've never had the chance to introduce either of them to my friends.

Carter nods as he pulls a package of chicken breasts from the fridge. "And you like Liam?"

I have to smile at the question in his voice. Given how protective I am of Saanvi, maybe it's odd for me to love her guy so much. "Once I would've thought no one was good enough for my baby sister," I admit. "But when she started dating Liam, I realized it isn't about whether he's good enough—it's about how happy he makes her. How much better her life is when he's in it."

"I like that." He puts a pan on the stove and drizzles it with oil, letting it warm while he pulls out a cutting board and knife. "I guess I feel the same about my brothers. I want them to be happy, and if the women they marry bring them joy, then I approve."

"The KonMari method, but for spouses."

He laughs, and I watch as he butterflies the chicken with the smooth, steady movements of someone who's done it a hundred times. "I guess so. And your parents? They're still together, right?"

"LouAnn and Kamal. Yes. They're both doctors—Mom's an OBGYN, and Dad's a general surgeon."

"Wow. I didn't know that. Did you feel pressured to go to med school?"

"Not at all. They love what they do, but since they live it, they know the downsides of the career. They wish I'd become an NP and will probably bring it up at least three times while they're in town, but I've become adept at ignoring them."

The chicken sizzles as Carter places it into the bubbling oil. "NP?"

"Nurse practitioner. I'd have to go back to school, but it would mean more pay. It's a hard pass for me. I don't want to get stuck working in an urgent-care clinic. I love the hospital, and there's not a lot of opportunities for NPs working there." I cock my head as he grabs an apple out of the basket, washes it, and starts slicing on a clean cutting board. "What are you making?"

He looks up from his work and grins. "You had some Havarti in there. I thought I'd make apple-and-cheese-stuffed chicken."

"That is . . . impressive."

"You're impressed that I can cook?"

"I'm impressed that you know how to make more than frozen pizza," I say.

"We cook at the station all the time. Nothing fancy, but we can't eat crap constantly if we want to stay in shape."

"Still. I've never been close to a guy who could hold his own in the kitchen."

He checks the chicken then pulls the cheese out of the fridge. "Jake would be totally offended if he heard that."

I wave a hand. "Jake doesn't count. It's his job." And that wasn't what I meant. I meant I'd never *dated* a guy who could cook, but since Carter and I are only fake-dating, I don't want to make this awkward by explaining.

"I can cook," he says, "though nothing like Jake and Nic."

"You're beyond competent, based on what I'm seeing here, and it's kind of hot." *There's that beer. Going straight to my head and loosening my tongue.*

"Oh, yeah?" He waggles his brows. "I also do my own laundry and put the seat down after I use the restroom."

A giggle bursts out of me, and it's so unexpected that I snort. "God, Carter. *Do me right now.*"

"I thought that might get you." He grins. "Tell me more about your parents."

"Okay . . . Mom can be bossy and is very conservative, but she loves her girls. I've never doubted that. She hates that I moved away, but I know she's proud of me. And Dad dotes on her. When I was a teenager, I thought it was annoying. He'd do whatever she wanted. Vacations, home renovations—everything was up to her. But I understand now that it wasn't because he was a pushover. He truly didn't care about the details. If Mom's happy, Dad's happy." I hesitate, but I know I need to ask. "What about your dad? I know you lost him a few years ago, and I know the brewery was his business, but I don't know much else about him." When his grin falls away, I wish I hadn't asked. "I'm sorry. We don't have to—"

"No. It's fine." He takes a deep breath. "We lost him six years ago this month. Some days, it feels like it's been longer than that, and other times it feels like it was yesterday."

"You really miss him a lot."

He nods but doesn't meet my eyes. "Especially lately."

Since he lost his friend in the fire. "I'm sorry, Carter."

He pokes at the chicken, and I'm not sure if he even heard me, but after a long pause he finally says, "Dad was my mom's joy. He'd usually come home when she was working on dinner. The house was always chaotic—five kids, half of us with a friend or two over, and throw in a dog most years—but it was a managed chaos, thanks to Mom. She was always doing five things at once after school—helping us with homework, talking to someone on the phone, making dinner—but no matter what she was doing, she stopped everything when Dad came in the door. I didn't always appreciate the magnitude of that gesture, but when I spent time at my friends' houses, I realized a lot of parents start sniping at each other when they're both home. Mom and Dad certainly had their disagreements, but they saved those for another time."

"That's sweet." I never considered how different our childhoods were. My parents are attentive and loving, but when I was a kid they both worked a lot, and my after-school memories are mostly with one nanny or another. I loved those women like grandmothers or favorite aunts, so I didn't resent my parents for leaving us in their care.

Carter rubs his chest, and I wonder if he even realizes it. "Most of the time I feel okay with not having him here for me. I mean, I miss him, but I'm fine. Mostly. But I really, really miss Mom having him."

"I love your mom. She's definitely one of the kindest people I've ever met. But I think she's doing okay."

He nods, seeming lost in his thoughts, and busies himself with the chicken, turning it and browning the other side before adding the cheese and apples and covering the pan.

"Tell me something I don't know about your mom," I say, more because the silence is breaking my heart than because I think I really need to know more. When it comes to knowing about each other's families, I definitely have the advantage here.

"She didn't want me to be a firefighter."

"Oh." I'm not sure what I expected, but that wasn't it.

"She didn't try to talk me out of it. Mom is nothing if not supportive of our goals and dreams, but she told me that it terrified her and that if she could choose, I'd join the family business or do something—*anything*—less dangerous."

"Was that hard? To pursue a spot with the department when you knew she wished you wouldn't?"

He takes a long pull from his beer before shaking his head. "No. I knew she'd support me no matter what, and I always wanted to do something good too much to let her worries stop me." His chest shakes with silent laughter and he rolls his eyes. "Ridiculous childhood fantasies."

"You do, Carter. You're quite literally a hero every day."

"Don't call me that, okay?"

His voice is so low that I can barely hear the request, but something about the intensity behind his words sends a chill through me. I want to push—to ask him why that label bothers him so much. But I also want to wash away the pain I see on his face. It'll wait. Another time I'll get him to let me in and understand that wound. Or maybe I won't. Maybe we both carry old hurts we will never share with anyone. "Okay. I promise."

Chapter ELEVEN

CARTER

I love watching Teagan enjoy a meal.

It's nothing new. I've done it a thousand times at the bar, at Sunday brunch, at Ethan's . . . but something about the way she closes her eyes and moans around a bite of something *I* cooked makes this even better. I find myself wishing I could feed her again and again, wishing we had more time to prepare for this wedding. I'm not worried about our ability to pull it off, but I want an excuse to come over here and cook for her, flirt with her. I want to watch those cheeks flush while I tease her and impress her with my rudimentary culinary skills. As it stands, tonight is the only one like this we'll get. Tomorrow, everyone comes to town, and I'll have to share her with her family. And then Monday, we're back to friends.

I push all thoughts of Monday from my mind and focus on

her now.

We've opened our second bomber, and her cheeks are flushed, her posture relaxed. I'm glad I didn't warn her I was coming over. She answered the door in cotton shorts that don't cover much more than her panties did Sunday morning. Her wide-neck sweatshirt falls off one shoulder, and I can't keep my eyes off her exposed cherry-red bra strap. One little strap has my imagination running wild, landing over and over again on her in bed in nothing but a red bra and panties.

"Why are you looking at me like that?" she asks, pushing her plate away. She leans back in her chair and puts a hand on her stomach in a time-honored gesture of satisfaction.

"Like what?"

She sighs. "I'm not sure. You seem . . . maybe regretful? What's going on in that pretty little head of yours, Carter? Are you worried I'm going to become one of your stalker fangirls and chain you in my basement now that I know you can cook?"

"Well, I wasn't, but *now* I am," I say, and she laughs. "I was thinking that tomorrow's the big day. Are you worried about this?"

"Not . . . really."

"That wasn't very convincing."

"It'll be fine. It's just that I've been looking forward to Saanvi's wedding, and this changes things. I won't be able to let my guard down because I'll be worried about slipping up."

I want to ask why she's so determined this is necessary, but that would mean asking about Rich, and I promised I wouldn't. "I think we'll be fine."

She rolls her shoulders back, and determination steels her

jaw. "Okay, what else do you need to know?"

"I'm not sure." In some ways I already know her so well, but in other ways I feel like I know nothing. Mostly, I want an excuse to stay—to listen to her laugh and look into her eyes instead of getting in bed and resigning myself to the nightmares that await me. "What's your favorite color?"

She laughs. "I haven't been asked that question since I was eight. I don't think I have one. What's yours?"

My gaze lands on her bra strap. "Red." As of sixty minutes ago, but it still counts.

"I guess I like red too. Definitely not pink." She shudders.

"Why not?"

"It's the color of my childhood bedroom. Mom had pink *everything* in there. The furniture, the bedding, the rug, the walls. It reminded me of the medicine she'd give us when we had a stomach bug." She shrugs. "A little pink is okay, but it's definitely not my favorite. Saanvi still loves it, though. And it suits her. She's even girlier than I am. What else?"

"Steak or chicken?"

"Steak. But don't tell my parents. They don't know I eat beef."

"Oh, are they Hindu?"

She puts her arms over her head and stretches, yawning. "No, it's for health reasons, really."

I wince. "Sorry. Was that an asshole white-guy assumption?"

"No, it's fine. Dad's parents were secular Hindus. Religion wasn't really that important to them, but then he met my mom, who is a devout Catholic. He knew it was important to her, and he was happy to convert. Some of his childhood habits stuck, though, like the red-meat thing. I had my first hamburger in college and thought I'd died and gone to heaven. What about you? Steak or chicken?"

I stand up and start clearing plates. "Steak every time."

She grabs my wrist, stopping me before I can pick up her plate. "You cooked. I'll clean."

"But I like taking care of you." I don't just mean the meal or the cleanup, and when she lifts her eyes to meet mine, I see the heat there. Is she thinking about Saturday night too?

"Only *you* could turn a discussion about who loads the dishwasher into a come-on line, Carter." She's trying to be flippant, but I don't miss the way her gaze dips to my mouth or the flutter of her pulse at the base of her neck.

"I don't know what you mean." I wink and take the plates away before she can protest again.

"Thank you," she says, even as she grabs the leftover salad from the table and follows me into the kitchen. "I know you prefer coffee to tea and beer to wine. What about hobbies? Any I should know about before I do one hundred introductions?"

"Other than collecting little bits of your hair?"

She throws her head back and laughs. It's the best fucking sound, rich and full. "I'm so proud of myself for that," she says.

"You should be. It was golden. And now all those damn 'Carter the puppy hero' Facebook fan pages are probably filled with tales of my creepy hair-collecting ways."

"You really hate everyone making a big deal of that, don't you?"

I scoff as I load the plates into the dishwasher. "Trust me, you'd hate it too. I'm not shy, but I like my privacy, and when this all blew up, suddenly I had to fight for it. I'm ready for it to be over."

She's quiet, and when I look up, she's frowning at me. "Is that it? Really?"

I know what she means, but I can only shrug. "There are men and women fighting every day in the military, firefighters risking their lives, police officers facing dangerous criminals. Hell, even Molly coming back to Jackson Harbor and facing her jerk of a stepfather showed more bravery than what I did that day. I'd rather we acknowledge actual heroics instead of mislabeling something because we want an excuse to look at a shirtless guy carrying a puppy."

She's quiet again. I'm afraid she can see right through me, so I turn to fill the sink with soapy water. I'm not much of a housekeeper, but I've always enjoyed the ritual of cleaning up after a meal, and I find my pulse slows and my breathing settles as I scrub the pans.

"So . . . hobbies?" She puts the leftover salad and the bottle of dressing in the fridge and leans against the counter beside the sink. Close enough to touch.

"Working out, remodeling my house, helping Levi restore a random car here and there. Nothing exciting."

"I didn't know you were remodeling your house."

"I like working with my hands and figured when I bought it I'd be able to add some value with minimal investment and lots of elbow grease. I've ripped up the old carpet and refinished the hardwood beneath. Right now, I'm working on replacing the trim. I thought I'd be able to strip off the paint, but it's a mess, so I pulled it all off and started over. When the trim's done, I'm going to finish off the attic to add another bedroom."

"I'd love to see it sometime."

LEXI RYAN

"Sure. I'd love to show you." I finish rinsing the dishes and place them into the dish drainer. "What about you? Any hobbies other than trying to keep my sister from being a shut-in?"

"I like to run. Sometimes. And I knit."

I can't help it. I gape. "You? Knit?"

"What? Why is that so surprising?"

I try to picture it and can't. "Isn't that, like, an old-lady hobby?"

"Carter, you just offended hipsters everywhere by your unironic mocking of one of their favorite pastimes."

I hold out my palms. "I'd never intentionally offend a hipster, but you . . ." I rake my gaze over her. "You're no hipster."

"I'm not, but I do love to knit. Knitting and reading are the only ways I can really relax."

Right, she was reading when I got here. I come from a family of big readers, so I always take that for granted. I don't understand people who don't read. It feels like willful ignorance to never try to experience anything from a different point of view. "What do you like to read?" I ask, drying my hands.

"Anything. Mostly fiction, with a hard preference for books with kissing." She shrugs. "Actually, my unironic enjoyment of Taylor Swift and romance novels may be my best proof that I'm *not* a hipster."

That makes me laugh, but then I think about how much my mom loves romance novels and my smile falls away. "I told Mom about what we're doing."

Teagan cringes. "And?"

I scrub a hand over my face as I remember my mom's folded arms. Her arched brow and tight jaw that made me feel like I was sixteen again and being lectured for staying out past curfew. "She's not a fan of the lie, and she'd rather we get married and make her some grandbabies than pretend to be together." With a sigh, I shrug. "So it pretty much went as expected."

"I'm sorry," she says softly.

"I'm not. I'd rather her be irked at me and know the truth than lie to her."

She ducks her head, and her shoulders curl in slightly. "Right."

"Hey." I take a step to close the distance between us and lift her chin. When her dark eyes meet mine, they're full of worry. "I know you don't like having to do this. I might not totally understand it, but I know you well enough to know you wouldn't lie to your family if you didn't think it was necessary. You're handling this in the best way you know how."

"Thank you, Carter. You're a good friend." She scans my face before her gaze settles on my mouth.

"I think I should kiss you right now." The words are out before I think about it. I want her, and fuck, if I won't do just about anything to see the hunger in her eyes from Saturday night.

"Yeah?"

I wonder if she knows she leans into me, that her lips part and her pupils dilate. The sight is enough to make me dumb with lust. "Yeah."

"But we're alone. And we have rules."

"But we need to look natural this weekend, right? I think we should practice."

"Oh." She swallows. "Okay."

I barely have to move to touch my mouth to hers, but when

I do, she parts her lips and moans. I suck on her bottom lip, and the hand she has tangled in my hair tugs lightly. Lust surges down my spine.

"How's that?" I'm breathless from a simple kiss. *Damn.*

"Not bad," she answers, equally breathless.

I pull back and tuck a loose strand of hair behind her ear. "I'll see you tomorrow, eyebrow."

She draws in a shaky breath. "Tomorrow." She walks me to the door and opens it, smiling softly.

I stop on her porch and turn back to her. "One more question."

"Shoot."

"Top or bottom?"

She blinks. "What?" When I flash her my most lascivious grin, she rolls her eyes. "Goodnight, Carter." Then she shuts the door.

Chapter TWELVE

TEAGAN

"Welcome, welcome!" Mom says, grinning widely as she greets Carter and me at the doors to the Hayhurst mansion. Tall, lithe, and exuding class, my mom is as beautiful today as she was when I was a little girl. She has honey-brown hair that she wears in an asymmetrical bob and blue eyes that brighten when she takes in Carter. "I'm LouAnn, Teagan's mom. I'm so happy to meet the local hero!"

Beside me, Carter stiffens, but he takes her offered hand and shakes it. "It's a pleasure to meet you, ma'am. Teagan's told me a lot about you."

"I wish I could say the same," Mom says, flashing me a glare. "But my daughter's been keeping your relationship a secret."

"We didn't know if it would go anywhere," I say. I'm sure I'm going to have to repeat the words a hundred times this weekend.

I love my mom, but she takes the whole Catholic mom guilt-trip cliché to the next level.

"*She* wasn't sure," Carter says, grinning at my mother in a way I'm sure will melt the ice-queen thing she's got going on, "I've been biding my time until she was willing to give me a chance."

"Well," Mom says, softening as I knew she would, "I can certainly see why she couldn't resist."

Dad steps up beside her and smiles. I feel ten again at the sight of him in his typical dress pants and suit jacket, his dark hair parted to the side. I favor my father—the olive skin, and full lips, the build that leans more brickhouse than ballerina. Dad offers Carter his hand. "I'm Kamal. You must be Carter," he says, his words still curled with shades of the accent that hasn't quite disappeared in his thirty-some years in the U.S.

"I am. It's a pleasure to meet you, sir."

"Don't mind my wife. She likes to worry." He turns to me and opens his arms. "How's my beautiful girl?"

I step into his warm embrace, letting him hug me and wrap me in the scent of the cologne he's worn since I was a little girl. "I'm fine, Daddy. How was your flight?"

"Oh, fine, but I'm glad to finally be here. I don't get to spend enough time with both of my girls under one roof anymore." He kisses the top of my head before pulling away.

"Kamal, we need to meet with the wedding planner," Mom says. "She has a few items to run by us."

Dad huffs good-naturedly and tells Carter, "She means checks she needs me to write."

Carter laughs. "I won't keep you. It was nice to meet you both."

"Likewise, Carter. We'll all talk more at dinner, I'm sure." Mom looks me over and frowns at the décolletage exposed by my V-neck sweater. "Try to dress appropriately, darling. It's not at some wild dance club."

Carter doesn't bother disguising his snort of amusement, but I sigh. "Yes, Mother." And we both watch them go before Carter turns to me and examines my jeans and sweater.

"Am I supposed to believe your mother thinks that sweater is scandalous?"

I shake my head. "Like I said, *conservative.*"

"Wow." His gaze dips to the same V my mom disapproved of. "I hope you won't be taking her fashion advice anytime soon."

I open my mouth to respond but am cut off by a shrieked "Tea-Tea!" and I turn to see my sister rushing toward me, her arms wide.

I can't help but smile when I see her. In my mind, Saanvi will always be the baby sister I got for Christmas. Many people told little-girl me that she wasn't *mine*, but I didn't believe them. When you ask Santa for a baby for Christmas and he delivers, she's *yours*. So Saanvi was and always has been. Since I moved to Jackson Harbor, I haven't gotten to visit her nearly as often as I'd like, but that hasn't changed the surge of love that fills me every time I see her.

She wraps her arms around me, and I hug her right back. "You're glowing," she says as she pulls away. Her gaze shifts to Carter as she gives a coy smile. "I think I know why."

I hate lying to her. My parents, I can deal. But Saanvi? Yeah, getting through this week is going to be hard. "This is Carter Jackson, my boyfriend." The words are like glue on my tongue and don't want to come off. But he takes my hand in his and gives me an extra squeeze of reassurance. I'm so epically grateful for his friendship. "Carter, this is my sister, Saanvi."

Carter flashes her his charming, panty-melting smile though, to be fair, I'm not sure he has another one. "It's a pleasure to meet Teagan's favorite sister."

"I'm her *only* sister," Saanvi says, smiling. "I'm glad to meet you too. I've heard so much about you—your whole family, actually." Saanvi ignores his offered hand and pulls Carter into a hug. He rolls with it. The Jacksons are all comfortable with physical affection. Maybe it's one of the reasons I adore Carter's family so much. Right up there with *everything about them*. My sister squeezes his biceps as she pulls back. "Dang, I can see why Tea likes you! Well done, muscles."

"Don't you have your own man to grope somewhere around here?" I ask my sister.

"He's upstairs getting us settled into our room."

I arch a brow. "Your room? Mom's letting you share a room with Liam *before* you say your vows?" I can't imagine the parents *I* was raised by allowing their daughter to share a room with her husband *before* the wedding.

"I insisted," she says with a shrug. She lowers her voice. "I've discovered that if I play the *but it's my wedding* card, Mom will bend to almost anything I ask."

Carter shifts to stand behind me. It's not a struggle to act normal when he wraps his arms around my waist and pulls my back to his front. In fact, the struggle is in reminding myself that this is all pretend. This is going to be our "normal" this weekend, and I need to remind myself that it doesn't mean anything. Even if it feels . . . *easy.*

A moment later, I catch sight of Rich out of the corner of my eye and understand what Carter's doing. Rich is in the common living area off the foyer talking to my uncle, but I can feel his attention on me. On *us.* I lean into Carter's touch. His heat. *Damn, he smells good.*

"Saanvi?" A tall brunette in a pencil skirt appears from the hall, hands folded as she walks over to us. "The chef wants to run a couple of ideas by you for breakfast. Would you follow me?"

"Valarie, this is my big sister. Teagan, this is Valarie, my wedding planner," my sister says. She whispers, "Val is the best money Mom ever spent. She's a genius."

Val gives me a broad smile and nods. "I've heard so much about you, Teagan."

"It's nice to meet you," I say. "Please let me know if there's anything I can help with."

"Oh, no," Valarie says. "My job is to take care of the details. Yours is to enjoy yourself."

"I'll see you tonight," Saanvi says to me. Her smile's so wide she's glowing. God, I hope I'm that happy if I ever get married. "It's nice to meet you, Carter."

"You too," Carter says.

"Oh, and I have a surprise for you." She digs into her pocket and pulls out an envelope, tossing it to Carter. "That's the key to the other honeymoon suite."

My eyes go wide. Why is she putting Carter in a suite?

"I talked Mom into letting you two share a room." Saanvi winks at me. "You can thank me later."

I can only blink as she walks away. *This was not the plan.*

I spin in Carter's arms, cringing. "I'm sorry. She means well. It's just—"

He puts his thumb on my bottom lip and lowers his forehead to touch mine, and I stop talking. Even if he hadn't put his thumb on my lip, I'm not sure I'd be capable of forming coherent sentences with the full intensity of Carter's gaze on me.

He lowers his mouth to my ear and whispers, "Your old boyfriend is watching, so if you want him to believe we're together, maybe you should tone down the disappointment over sharing a room with me."

At least, I think that's what he says. I only pick up every other word or so, because his lips brush my ear as he speaks and the sensation sends licks of pleasure up my spine, reminding me of his touch, his mouth, his magical fingers . . .

I'm still frozen with lust when he pulls back. "What do you say we go check out our room and unpack our clothes?"

I nod stupidly. Right. We should definitely go to our room and take off our clothes—or put them away.

He chuckles, as if he can see right into my pathetic, lust-addled brain. "Come on, Teagan. I won't bite. Not again. Not unless you want me to." He presses his thumb to the faded mark on my neck. And after that bonus jolt to my libido, he takes my hand and leads me toward the stairs.

CARTER

Having lived in Jackson Harbor my whole life, I'm familiar with the Hayhurst mansion bed and breakfast, but I've never had a reason to stay here. I knew it was a nice place, but I didn't realize how big or opulent until today.

Our suite is incredible. There's a kitchenette, a large bathroom with a tile shower that has half a dozen showerheads, and a Jacuzzi tub by windows that overlook the lake. On the other side of the kitchenette is a sofa facing a massive four-poster bed.

One bed.

"Your sister must really like you," I say.

Teagan threads a hand through her dark hair as she surveys the room. "Go, Saanvi. Thanks for making sure I can sleep with my fake boyfriend." She wanders toward the bed, where a little red box is wrapped with a black ribbon. She pulls the card off the top and reads, "'For my big sister. Congratulations on finding an epic love. I'm so excited for you.'" She squeezes her eyes shut.

"Are you going to open it?"

"I should have told her. She could have kept the secret."

"You still can," I suggest softly.

"It feels dirty lying to my sister at her wedding, but if I tell her now, I'm going to create drama where there should be none. I want her to focus on having the best weekend of her life, not on me and Rich."

I understand her angst, but her sister is going to ask about the gift later, so I step forward and take the box. "May I?"

"Knock yourself out." She sinks onto the bed then lies back, her hair splayed out all around her. She's a beautiful sight, and it

131

would be easy to stare at the way her body sinks into the fluffy duvet, but I don't let myself.

I pull the lid off the box and drop it to the bed, pulling a lacy black fabric from inside. Grinning, I hold it up for her. There's not a lot to it, and if Teagan put this on, I'd be able to see every curve, every private inch beneath the fine black threads. "I *really* like your sister."

She grabs a pillow and hurls it at my chest. "Shut up!"

I sigh heavily. "You know you have to model it for me."

She springs upright. "No, I don't!"

"What if she asks about it? I don't want to mess this up." I press a hand to my chest. "I take my job here very seriously."

"You're a pig," she mutters, but her lips curl into a smile and some of her tension falls away.

I take her hand and pull her up to stand in front of me. "Relax, Teagan. I'll sleep on the couch. This is not a crisis."

"I'm not a good liar."

And yet you've spent years in Jackson Harbor without telling any of us what you're so afraid of at home. In all that time, you didn't breathe a word to me about losing the man you planned to marry or hiding from another guy who terrifies you.

I'm not supposed to ask about Rich, but maybe there's a way around that. "You know what we didn't cover last night?"

"What?"

"Our romantic histories—you know, serious relationships. I know you don't want me to ask about Rich, but what should I know that you feel okay talking about? And what about other guys?"

She nods slowly. "Rich was high school—my sophomore to

senior year, his senior year, and then his first two years of college."

I know the shock is clear on my face. "That's a long time, considering how young you were."

She toys with a loose lock of hair at the base of her neck and twirls it around her fingers. "I guess so, but I didn't think of it that way at the time."

"What happened between you? To end it, I mean."

"I got a track scholarship to go to school in Georgia, and he gave me an ultimatum. If I wanted him, I had to stay."

"That's a little intense. You were only eighteen."

She rolls her eyes. "No shit. It was an easy choice for me, though it wasn't a clean break. The summer before I left, we kept . . ." She shakes her head. "Anyway, it was good to get away, and once I started college and realized I suddenly had more freedom than I'd had in three years, I knew I'd never get back together with him or be with anyone that controlling."

I wonder if that's the extent of her fear. He was controlling, and she doesn't want that in her life again. But I know there's more. If there weren't, she wouldn't have stipulated that I not ask about him. "Then in college?"

She chews on her thumbnail. "Nothing significant. Lots of dating. A few boyfriends. Nobody who gave me butterflies or made me see a future together with them."

"And then Heath was after you moved back home? He gave you butterflies?" I'm not sure what to think about the jealousy that tears through me at those words. I'm jealous of a dead man for his relationship with my fake girlfriend. That might be a new low.

"Yeah. Butterflies and . . . thrills." She sighs, tugging on that same lock of hair. "My parents didn't care for him, and given how much they approved of Rich, I think that made Heath all the more appealing."

There's a knock on the door. "Bellman."

"Hold that thought," I tell Teagan, going to the door.

"Good afternoon, sir," the man says. "I have your luggage."

"Thanks. You can leave it by the couch."

He nods and hauls our suitcases into the room, thanking me when I pass him a tip. Then he's gone and we're alone again, but judging by how diligently she's avoiding my gaze, I wonder if she's planning to change the subject.

I pick up my suitcase, put it on the bed, and unzip it so I can hang up my clothes as she does the same with hers. "What was Heath like?"

She stills, hand tightening around some vibrant red material. When she releases a puff of air, I realize she's quietly laughing. "Like you, I guess."

"Because of his job?"

Her lips twitch into a reluctant smile, but she still doesn't meet my eyes. "More because of his . . . love of women?"

I cough. I was not expecting *that*. "What?"

"It's not a secret that you like to keep your bed warm, Carter. Or that you've come to prefer . . . variety to commitment."

"Jesus." I remove a stack of clothes and put them into a dresser drawer. I guess it's not just Jake. I've somehow managed to get a reputation as a player. "Is that what you think of me?"

"I'm not judging. A lot of guys are like that."

But I want to be better than a lot of guys. I release a breath and drag a hand through my hair. This isn't about me. Not right now. "How'd you end up with a guy like that? Heath, I mean."

"He was charming, and I wasn't looking for forever." She slides a dress onto a hanger. "I moved home right after graduation and met him my first weekend back."

"How'd you meet?"

She stills again, and she's quiet so long that I'm about to repeat my question when she says, "Rich introduced us."

"Oh."

"Sounds crazy, doesn't it? But then, I believed Rich had moved on as completely as I had. No hard feelings, no weirdness. And he was best friends with Heath—they'd gone to the police academy together and worked out of the same precinct. I actually think Rich meant to set us up, as crazy as that sounds. If I knew then what I know now, I'd have run far away from anyone Rich wanted me to meet."

And what do you know now? I don't want to push her, so I continue unpacking and wait for more.

"Heath had a revolving door of women in his life when I met him, but we hit it off. I liked him. But after a couple of weeks, I knew I couldn't be one of many, and I told him if we were going to keep seeing each other, he had to stop seeing everyone else. Rich encouraged me to have that talk with him. He said Heath was the kind of guy who'd need it spelled out, but I'm not sure he was giving Heath enough credit. He was young and single, not an ass. It didn't take much convincing. And after that . . . we fell in love fast and hard. He was romantic and sweet, and so damn good in bed."

I grunt. I *don't* want to think about another man physically pleasing her.

"Not that bedroom skills are required for a relationship, of course," she says quickly.

"Of course."

"My family accepted him, but Rich was always around, and he always found ways to look better than Heath. At first, I didn't think he was doing it on purpose. Rich knew my family from the years we'd been together in high school, and he stayed close to them after I left. He'd know Mom needed help getting the salt to the basement for the water softener, and of course he'd remember how much she loved to get lilies at Easter." She releases a small huff of air. "I guess I can't really talk about Heath without talking about Rich, and that was always the problem. The harder I fell for Heath, the more my family wanted to see me get back together with Rich."

"Why?"

She hangs another dress, taking her time before responding. "Rich has a way of twisting things—making people look bad for nothing without straight-out lying. I know this sounds crazy, but I need you to promise me now that you won't let Rich get to you. He might try to be your buddy or he might just be an ass, but whatever he does, he'll be trying to manipulate you."

"Is that what he did to you?"

She shrugs. "He'd call my mom after Heath and I had a silly spat and ask if I was around because he was worried about me. She'd have to pry it out of him, but he'd admit that Heath and I had been fighting or that I'd been upset or that Heath hadn't done something I asked. He had a way of turning nothing into something awful, and a way of making my mom hold on to the idea that he and I might get back together."

"But was it bad? You and Heath? Do you think you could

have been happy with him if . . ." *If he hadn't died.* I swallow, wishing I could take it back and feeling like a jackass for asking at all.

"No," she says tightly. "We couldn't have. And that was my fault."

The guilt in her voice sets off warning bells in my head. "How so?"

She shakes her head. "I don't want to talk about it. I'm sorry."

"No, it's fine." I force myself to give her a reassuring smile. "I didn't mean to push."

She lifts her gaze to meet mine. "What about you? Serious relationships, I mean."

I groan. I guess I'm the one who brought it up. "I had a girlfriend for a couple of years in high school. Her name was Marjorie and we were pretty happy, but we kind of grew apart." I haven't thought about her in a long time, but the memories are mostly good ones. Marjorie was my first love . . . my first all-around. "Then lots of dating, lots of searching for that elusive *the one.*"

"Did you ever think you found her?"

My gut knots when I think of Renee. We weren't together long in the scheme of things, but I'd thought she was *it* for me. "I dated a woman named Renee when I first started at the fire department. My dad was sick, and she was the one who was there for me. We dated for six months."

Teagan cocks her head, frowning. "Renee French? The one who runs the yoga studio by the bar?"

I grimace. For better and worse, Jackson Harbor is a small world. "That's her."

"What happened? Why'd you break up?"

"She didn't want what I did, and she found lying about it easier than honesty." I shrug. As if it's nothing. As if losing her wasn't like having the earth yanked from beneath my feet while my world was falling apart around me. I hate being lied to. "But really, I've never had a long-term, serious relationship. Ethan says I'm too damn picky and I should stop looking for Miss Perfect."

"You want Miss Perfect, and yet you tried to start something with *me*?" Her cheeks flush, and she averts her gaze. She opens a dresser drawer, and I try not to stare as she fills it with her undergarments. "Or maybe I misread that day at the lake."

"When we were in the water?" I drop my toiletry bag back into my suitcase and step toward Teagan, threading a hand into her hair. "And I did this?"

Her throat bobs. "Yeah. That day."

"You didn't misread anything." I scan her face, her dark eyes, that perfect mouth, remembering how easy it felt to pull her into my arms and how natural it was to lower my mouth to hers. I told myself I didn't care that she pushed me away, that it was better we stay friends, but in truth, I always wished she'd let me have that kiss. "I wish you would have told me about Heath then. About my job being a problem for you. I would have understood."

Her flinch is there and gone so fast that I'd have missed it if I hadn't been trying to memorize every inch of her face. "You're a good friend, Carter."

Friend. There's that word again. "I try."

"You don't have to sleep on the couch. It's a big bed. I think we can manage."

Right. "We'll see." I might be a good friend, but if she's serious about the rules she laid out for us, the couch is the right place for me tonight.

Chapter
THIRTEEN

CARTER

Rich Nasser is an ass. Granted, my introduction to the man skewed my opinion, but after thirty minutes in the same room as him, I can't imagine what Teagan ever saw in him, and I'm at a complete loss for as to why her mom and dad still adore him.

Teagan needed to meet with her mom and sister for a while, so I came down to the game room to kill time and shoot pool. Rich, Liam, and Travis, one of Liam's groomsmen, were already in here. I thought about turning around and going back to our room, but I decided to use the time to feel out the ex who's managed to keep a foothold in Teagan's life.

Had I not felt the way Teagan shook when she first saw him, and were he not obviously struggling to hide his irritation with my presence this weekend, I might have even fallen for his "everyone's best friend" act.

It's not just that he's hung up on Teagan. He tries too hard to be what everyone wants. And sure, during a celebratory weekend, everyone should play nice, but it's more than that. An agreeableness that almost ventures into *creepy*. I've learned very little except that the guy puts off a bad vibe and likes to talk about all the favors he's done for Teagan's parents and brag about how much they love him.

My phone buzzes with a text alert. Once. Twice. Three times. I pull it from my pocket to see messages from Myla.

> *Myla: Sorry if I was a bitch about everything.*
> *Myla: You don't owe me any explanations. You said this was casual from the start.*
> *Myla: I guess I caught feelings somewhere along the way.*

"You and Teagan seem happy," Rich says, and I quickly darken the screen so he can't read over my shoulder.

"We are."

He smirks, as if he knows our secret. I don't care if he has me and Teagan figured out. Even if everyone involved in this wedding weekend knew the truth, I'd still want to spend it with Teagan. I won't leave her to fend for herself with this guy.

"Interesting," he murmurs, studying the pool table before leaning over to line up a shot. "Three ball, corner pocket." He points to the opposite side of the table then pulls his stick back to take the shot. The cue ball smacks into the red three, sending it spinning into the hole.

I scan the table. I'm decent at pool, though it's never been my favorite pastime. But Rich? He's running the table and threatening to sink the eight ball before I have a chance to make my move. Normally, I wouldn't care. I can be competitive, but I'm also completely comfortable with turning off that instinct in situations where it doesn't matter. But this guy? With his swagger and a *BOSS* tattoo on his bicep? I can't help but want to crush him at everything.

"You two need to get your story straight." He lines up his next shot. "When I was here last year, you said you'd been together two months. Funny to hear you say the same thing now, a year later."

"Can't both be true?" Liam asks. He hands me a beer.

"Thanks," I say, taking the bottle. I like Liam. Mostly because he seems like a genuine guy who's truly in love with his bride, but in my short time in here with them, his disdain for Rich has become apparent. If I'm honest, that makes me like him even more.

Rich shrugs. "I wonder how happy you can really be together if you keep breaking up." He hits his next shot, and the yellow solid rolls into the side pocket. "Maybe it's a sign."

Liam and I exchange a glance. Rich is trying so hard to bait me, but I'm not biting.

"Quit making trouble, Rich," Liam says. "They're obviously happy, and Teagan doesn't need you playing guard dog." Rich scowls at him, but Liam only laughs. "Dude, let it go. Sometimes your obsession with her is creepy as hell."

At least someone else sees it. Hell, I was starting to think everyone connected to Teagan's life back home was blind.

"Fuck you. I'm not obsessed. I'm concerned. I watched her grieve for my best fucking friend, okay?"

Liam ducks his head at that, shamed. "I'm sorry about that. But this isn't the same."

Rich hands his stick to Travis. "I'm tired of this game. I'm heading out."

Liam watches him go without a word and only turns to me when the game room doors swing closed behind Rich. "I'm sorry about him." He shakes his head. "I don't like him, but he's done a lot for Saanvi's parents. They think of him as family. He means a lot to them, but if it had been up to me, he'd never have gotten an invitation."

"Don't worry," I say. "I can handle a little pouting."

Liam grins. "I like you, Carter. I'm glad Teagan has you by her side. She deserves a good guy."

The continued buzzing in my pocket suggests that Myla has more to say. Maybe sometime in the last six months, I stopped being the good guy I always thought I was.

Teagan warned me that her parents don't do *anything* halfway. If the welcome dinner is any indication, I can see what she means. It's extravagant. The party bus picked us up at the mansion and brought us to the Luckette Winery, where we were served a six-course meal with accompanying wines and surrounded by the happy chatter of a family reunited.

We finished the meal twenty minutes ago, but everyone's lingering to talk and finish off the remaining wine.

"Thank you for changing your schedule at the last minute so

you could come." Saanvi sighs. "Even my own cousin wouldn't take today and tomorrow off work to be here, and she's a *bridesmaid.*"

I grimace, uninterested in stepping in that kind of drama. "I'm sorry to hear that."

She waves a hand. "Whatever. She's a journalist chasing the next hot story. I should have assumed something would come up, but regardless, it means a lot to my family to have *you* here for the whole thing—Teagan included, whether she admits it or not."

"I'm glad she invited me." And, hell, I mean it. Across the room, Teagan is grinning at one of Liam's groomsmen as he tells her a story. I can't hear the whole thing, but I think he must be a medical professional too, because I keep hearing hospital jargon. She looks beautiful tonight in a red dress that straps behind her neck and clings to her curves all the way down to her knees. And then there are the shoes . . . I'm not sure I've ever met a woman who looks as good in heels as Teagan. I've certainly never cared before her—maybe because they're as much a part of her personality as the way she takes no shit from my brothers and loves my nieces and nephews as if they were her own. Tonight's heels are red and wrap around her ankles with ribbons. If shoes could talk, these would scream *SEX.*

"Has anyone ever told you that you look at her like a teenage boy with a crush?" Saanvi asks.

Reluctantly, I tear my gaze off Teagan to look at her sister. "No, but I'm not surprised. That's pretty much how she makes me feel."

Saanvi beams. "I love that! And to think she was planning to hide you from us." She lowers her voice. "Not that I can blame her. My parents *are* all over the 'What are your intentions?' talks. Dad asked Liam that when we'd been on three dates. I'm lucky Liam didn't run screaming."

I laugh. "I bet he already knew."

Saanvi bites her bottom lip. "I like to think so." She waves a hand. "Enough about us. Tell me how you two got together."

I swallow hard and let my gaze drift back to the woman in question. "She's been part of my life for most of her time in Jackson Harbor. She knows my brother Ethan from the hospital and is friends with my sister and my sisters-in-law, so she's always around, but she was reluctant to get involved with me."

"Because of your job?"

I nod. "I didn't know that was the reason at first." Four years, and she never breathed a word about my profession being an issue for her. Has she told Shay or Nic about Heath, or is he a secret she's kept from everyone?

"It was hard when she lost Heath. She was . . ." Saanvi shakes her head. "She wasn't herself afterward. And Heath might not have been my favorite person, but I hate that she had to lose him like that. His death made her lose a piece of herself that she's never managed to reclaim."

I have so many questions I want to ask, but I don't—not just because I should probably already know all of the answers, but because I owe it to Teagan to get information about Heath from her and no one else. "Do you think he knew how lucky he was?"

Saanvi seems to consider this for a beat. "I think most people don't know the value of what they have, but Heath seemed to at first. Then things changed, and . . ." She shrugs. "Maybe that's normal. But we were talking about *you*. About what you love about my sister."

I drag a hand through my hair and grin. "Everything, Saanvi. There's honestly nothing about her I don't value." My stomach knots, because I know it's true. "She makes me laugh when I don't think I can anymore. And she cares about everyone around her. That's why she's such a good nurse and friend, and why she fits so well with my family."

"She loves your family. She talks about them all the time. Especially the little girl—what's her name?"

"Lilly."

"Yes, Lilly! Teagan loves her, and I think she's ready to trade our mom in for yours."

I smile, thinking of the way my mom feels about Teagan and her none-too-subtle request that I turn pretend into something real this weekend. "Mom loves Teagan, which is the true test of character. I mean, my mom likes everyone, but she's selective about who she'd want for her boys, and she's been wishing Teagan and I would end up together for a long time."

"It looks like her wish came true." Saanvi's so damn sincere, and I understand why Teagan hates lying to her. I wish she'd let Saanvi in on the ruse. "I'm glad she has that here—even if it means she might never come back home."

"She misses you," I say, and Saanvi nods, the feeling clearly mutual. "Did you two always get along?"

"Oh, heavens no! I made her crazy when she was a teenager. I'd steal her clothes and tell Mom if she snuck out of the house. I was awful, honestly, but we had each other's backs when it mattered."

"Well, if you and Liam ever decide to relocate, I know she'd love to have you in Jackson Harbor."

Saanvi pats my shoulder. "Thanks, Carter. That's good to hear." She takes a few steps away then hesitates for a beat before turning back to me. "I'm sorry Rich is here this weekend."

I shrug, as if it never even crossed my mind. As if Rich's presence isn't the very reason I'm standing here, pretending to be a loving boyfriend when I've dodged commitment for the last six months. Rich isn't at this dinner, for whatever reason. The moment the bus started pulling away tonight, Teagan's posture shifted as the weight lifted from her shoulders. It took me a minute to realize why—Rich wasn't with us. My mind keeps spinning with theories about their relationship. Was he abusive? Controlling beyond what she described? Possessive?

"He's still in love with her," Saanvi says softly. "And if he thinks he has a chance, he'll fight for her."

"Don't worry," I say. "I'll fight harder."

"I'm rooting for you." She winks and wanders across the room to talk to another guest.

"Me too," I murmur to myself. Then I draw in a deep breath, because I realize I mean it.

Teagan crosses the room to me. "Was Saanvi telling you all my secrets?"

"Surely you don't keep any secrets from me, amygdala."

She laughs. "Whipping out the big words doesn't make your awful nicknames any funnier, Carter."

"But I made you laugh, didn't I?" My phone rings. When I pull it from my pocket to silence it, I see the call is from Marta. "I'm sorry. I'm going to take this."

Teagan nods. "Of course. No worries."

Stepping away, I swipe to accept the call and put the phone to my ear. "Hello?"

"Oh, Carter, I'm so sorry to bother you. I was wondering if you could come over tonight. It's Isaiah."

Terror grips my lungs in a vise. "What happened?"

"No, no, nothing bad. I'm so sorry. He's not eating and won't take his pills. He doesn't want to talk to me, and I wondered . . ."

"Sure. Of course." I look at my watch, then at Teagan. I know she'll understand, but I still feel bad for leaving. "I can be there in twenty minutes."

Chapter
FOURTEEN

CARTER

"**Y**ou didn't have to come," I tell Teagan as we climb out of the cab. I didn't want to wait for the party bus to take me back to my car at the bed and breakfast, but when I told Teagan what I was ordering a cab for, she insisted on coming.

"I wanted to." Her heels click on the sidewalk beside me, and she slides her hand into mine. "I have a soft spot for this kid, and if he won't listen to his grandmother about the meds, maybe he'll listen to his nurse."

I want to kiss her for that, but instead I squeeze her hand before knocking on Marta's front door.

Marta must have been waiting for me, because she opens the door quickly. "Thank you for coming." She nods at Teagan. "And you brought the pretty nurse. Well done."

I laugh. "She wanted to come. Our little charmer won her heart."

Marta grunts softly and pulls the door wide. "Of course he did."

As we step into Marta's house, I'm instantly hit by the familiar scent of chicken soup and pine-scented cleaner. I've visited regularly since Max died, so Marta's home is as comforting to me as my own. *I wish Isaiah felt the same.*

"It's my fault he's in this mood," she says, leading the way into her kitchen, where there is indeed a pot of soup bubbling on the stove. "He overheard me on the phone with my brother talking about medical bills, and it upset him. He doesn't need to worry about money. That's my concern."

"I can help. With the bills, I mean." My throat goes tight. If only Max were still here . . .

She waves me off. "You coming over here is help enough. He's in his bedroom. Go see if you can talk him into eating something. He's stubborn as a mule."

"I'll wait out here with Marta," Teagan says. "Let you two talk for a minute first."

I nod and squeeze her hand one last time before heading to Isaiah's bedroom at the back of the house. As I pad toward his door across the green shag carpet, I can hear the muffled beat of his house music.

I knock, and when he doesn't answer, I push inside.

Isaiah's propped up on a pile of pillows, his casted leg straight before him, his other bent at the knee and his eyes directed at the ceiling. "What do you want?"

"I thought you'd like to go on a run with me. Come on. Five miles. Let's go."

He tears his gaze off the ceiling long enough to scowl at me.

"You're not funny."

I sigh and close the door behind me. In some ways, the room is a stereotypical teenager's hovel with piles of clothes—some folded, some crumpled—littering the floor, but in other ways it's the room of a boy who's tried to fit his old life into a space where it can't. After his dad died, they had to sell his house. Marta couldn't handle the mortgage or the upkeep on her own. When Isaiah moved in here, he brought a couch, chair, Xbox, and TV from his old basement and crammed it all into the bedroom, leaving barely enough room to walk between one piece of furniture and the next.

I take a seat on the couch and rest my elbows on my knees. "How's the pain?"

"It's pain. Can it be *good*?"

"It can be better if you take your meds." When he ignores that, I sigh. "You haven't been replying to my texts."

"I haven't felt like talking."

"Marta said you're not eating."

"Not hungry."

I stand, too irritated to sit still. "Listen, I get that this situation sucks, but you're not going to make anything better for anyone if you mope and ignore the doctor's orders."

He levels me with an angry gaze. "Do you have any idea what it's like to be nothing but a burden? Grandma can't afford to take care of me, and she's been cashing out her retirement to get by, and now she has my medical bills on top of it. Because *I* fucked up."

I wince at his language—Marta doesn't allow cursing in her house—but let it go and focus on the rest. "She doesn't think you're a burden."

"Do you know why Jess broke up with me? For real? She was sick of dealing with my grief over Dad. She said I'm too young to be so sad all the time, and she didn't want me dragging her down."

Fuck. "I'm sorry, Isaiah. She's being immature, and that's not fair to you. You're entitled to all the time you need to grieve, and—"

"Stop. I don't want your inspirational speech."

The soft rap on the door saves me from trying to come up with a response. "Hello?" Teagan calls, stepping into the room.

Isaiah gapes. "You brought *her*?" He looks around his room, as if he's going to jump up and start cleaning. "Jesus, Carter, a little warning?"

Teagan chuckles softly and leans against the doorframe, a glass of some dark liquid in one hand. "No appetite?"

By whatever magic, her words seem to take the sulk out of Isaiah, and he shakes his head. "I don't want to eat."

"How about a milkshake?" Teagan says, lifting the glass. "Just a little something to coat your stomach so you can take your pain meds."

"I don't need 'em. I can handle it."

"I'm sure you can, but the human body isn't made to sleep through pain, and the less you sleep, the longer it's going to take to heal." She steps into the room and offers him the glass and a straw.

He holds her gaze as he accepts it and takes a few sips.

"Nice," she says, and her voice is sincere, as if she's complimenting him for solving some complex math problem and not for drinking a chocolate shake. She hands him pills and the water bottle from his bedside table. "Now these."

He takes them without complaint, a slight flush to his cheeks. He's just a kid, but he's too proud to let a pretty woman see him sulk.

She surprises me when she sits on the edge of his bed and puts a hand to his head. She tilts his face side to side, looking into one eye then the other. Seemingly satisfied with what she sees, she lifts his hand and looks at her watch as she takes his pulse.

"Do you do house calls for all of your patients?" Isaiah asks.

"Only the ones I like." She releases his wrist. "Even if you get to the point where you can sleep without the pain meds, I need you to keep taking that antibiotic—all of it until it's gone, okay?"

"I know," he says softly. "The doctor told me."

"Then why—" I shut up when Teagan shoots me a look.

"What can I get you, Isaiah?" Teagan asks.

I wonder if it's the question or the tenderness in her voice that makes his eyes fill with tears.

He looks away and shakes his head. "I'm good," he says gruffly.

"I'm glad to hear it," she says.

"I think I want to sleep now," Isaiah whispers.

"Sure," Teagan says, standing. I follow suit, and we edge around the bed back to the door.

I let Teagan leave before I turn back to Isaiah. "Text if you need me. I'll be back in a couple of days."

"You don't have to visit me."

"But I want to." I grin. "And you're stuck in that bed, so you can't avoid me."

He rolls his eyes and *almost* smiles. "Thanks, Carter."

TEAGAN

I wake up to the sound of thrashing and sit up in bed. It takes me a few panicked beats of my heart to remember where I am—the hotel suite, with Carter.

It's still dark, but I can just make out his silhouette on the couch, blankets thrown off and scattered on the floor. He waves his arms over his face as if he's trying to throw someone or something off him. "Get the fuck out of there," he shouts.

I climb out of bed and cross the room. "Carter?"

He thrashes again and grumbles something unintelligible. But his face—*my God*—his expression is that of someone in excruciating pain, and my chest aches at the sight of this big, powerful man decimated by his own nightmares.

"Carter," I say, louder this time. And when I brush his shoulder with my fingers, he grabs my hand and holds it tight.

"We have to get out of here."

"Carter, wake up."

"Get the fuck out!" he growls. He squeezes my arm hard enough that it brings tears to my eyes.

"Okay," I say, swallowing hard. "Let's go."

His whole body relaxes and his shoulders go loose, but he keeps my hand in his and brings it to his chest, pressing it there under both of his. "I almost lost you."

"I'm fine," I say gently. "We're safe." But even now his expression is so tortured that my heart breaks a little.

The couch is too small and he's too big. There's not really room for me to sleep beside him, so I grab a blanket and crawl on top of him, resting my cheek against his bare chest.

When I wake up a few hours later, Carter's awake and staring at me. I see the confusion on his face.

Light pours in through the open curtains, casting the room in the soft yellow glow of morning sun. After curling up on his chest, I slept like a rock. I'm normally a terrible sleeper.

"Teagan?" he asks. The sound of his voice this early in the morning—all grumbly and low—makes me want to snuggle into him. Instead, I scramble off the couch and stand, picking up the remaining blankets on the floor to avoid his gaze. He looks around blearily. "Was there something wrong with the bed?"

My cheeks heat. Did I really think he'd want me to sleep on top of him? "You were having a nightmare."

"Shit." He tugs on his messy hair. "How bad was it?"

I shrug. "Bad enough I knew you were upset. You have them a lot, then?"

"I guess. I'm sorry I woke you. Why didn't you go back to bed?"

I feel like such an idiot, but I try to act like it doesn't matter. "You seemed calmer when I touched you. You were saying we needed to get out, and I played along. I agreed and told you we would. That seemed to make you relax, but then . . ." My cheeks blaze hotter. I really should have gone back to bed. Maybe after seeing him like that, *I* needed the comfort of being close to *him*. "You didn't seem to want to let me go, and I was afraid you'd have another if I left. I thought maybe you'd sleep better if I was there."

"You played along?"

"Yeah." Sighing, I smile at him. "I worked nights for a while. I never really adjusted to the schedule, so I was constantly overtired, and when I actually managed to make myself sleep during the day, I'd have these crazy dreams that I was at work and no one was helping me. I'd sleepwalk and talk to my roommate— eyes open, like I was totally awake. I'd demand that she help me with patients and apparently get really pissed if she told me I was dreaming or tried to get me to go back to bed. She eventually learned it was easier to play along. She'd smile, nod, agree to help me. Yes, she'd help me with the IV on the patient in 301C. Yes, she'd call the doctor to follow up on Mr. Frasier's reaction to the new pain meds. It was the only way I would relax enough to go back to sleep."

He arches a brow. "That's crazy."

I laugh. "She loved to regale our friends with stories of my sleepwalking when we were at parties." I shrug. "It seemed to work for you too."

"It's clever."

I hesitate a beat, not sure if I'm crossing a line by asking. "Is it the warehouse fire? Is that what the nightmares are about?"

His expression is cautious as he meets my eyes and nods.

"You tried to get Max to leave before the building collapsed, but he wouldn't."

"We got a report that there were kids on the second floor. We were working off a line, trying to get to them so we could get them out, when we were told to leave the building." The words are spoken in a monotone—he's more a robot reporting an event than a man divulging a traumatic experience to a friend. "I couldn't see him very well, but he turned around at the same time I did. I thought he was behind me, and when I realized he wasn't, I had to follow that line back in through the smoke. I should have known he'd be stubborn. He could be reckless, and it wasn't the first time he'd gone against orders trying to make an impossible rescue. I was shouting for him on our portable, but then the building started coming down and I had to make a choice." He shakes his head. "In together, out together," he whispers, "but he never came out."

"You tried."

"I should have tried harder."

"Carter." I reach out to touch his arm, but he stands and shakes his head. I wonder if he has the nightmares a lot or if seeing Isaiah last night triggered something. "It's not your fault—the fire, what happened to Max. You know that, right?"

"Of course I do." He squeezes the back of his neck, then stretches. "Do you want the first shower?"

Just like that, the conversation is over. It doesn't have to be. Maybe he needs someone to make him talk about it. Maybe that someone should be me.

I take a deep breath. "I blamed myself when Heath died." The words aren't as hard to say as I would have thought. Maybe because I've carried them for so long. Or maybe because I know Carter needs to hear this from me.

He blinks at me, and I can see the struggle playing out on his face—the internal war between exposing a broken part of his soul to help me with a broken part of mine, and keeping everything locked down so he doesn't have to admit he isn't whole.

"We were fighting when he left for work that night." My stomach knots with the memory. Heath was so jealous, so angry, and there was nothing I could do to make it right. "He was killed during a routine traffic stop. The guy was high and had a bunch of heroin in the car. Heath should have called for backup, but he was in a mood." I turn away, not wanting to see the sympathy in Carter's eyes. "He was pissed at me, so distracted by our argument that he was reckless. And it got him killed."

"You can't blame yourself," Carter says softly. "You weren't even there."

"Maybe I wasn't there physically." I tap my temple. "But I was there."

"Don't do that to yourself, Teagan. You have no idea what was going through his mind."

"And neither do you—with Max, I mean." I hold up my hands before Carter can shut me down. "I'm not saying it's the same. I know it's not. If I'd been there that night and survived him . . ." I shake my head slowly. "I can't imagine what that was like for you, but I do know what it's like to carry that blame. I know how it eats away at you. How it makes you . . ." I close my eyes, remembering those months after Heath died and before I moved away. "It makes you act differently. Recklessly."

"You think I'm being reckless?"

"I think the Carter I knew before the warehouse fire didn't have a revolving door of women in his bed."

It's not pain that crosses his face with those words but . . . *nothing*. Like he flipped some switch inside him that turns off his emotions and turns his face to stone.

"I'm not saying it's the same," I repeat, trying again, "but I am saying I might understand what you're going through better than you realize."

"Teagan," he says, "let it go. I'm fine."

But I understand *fine*, too. *Fine* is where hopes and dreams go to die.

Chapter
FIFTEEN

TEAGAN

I have to give Carter credit. I'm sure he knows all there is to know about all of the local breweries—and he certainly knows everything there is to know about Jackson Brews beer— but as our tour bus took us from one brewery to the next, he acted like this was his ideal way to spend a day off. I know the Jacksons are picky about beer and think their stuff is the best, but he tasted the samples at each stop like it was all new to him.

We're sitting thigh to thigh at the far end of the bar at Jackson Brews, the last stop of the day. After the tense and abrupt end to our conversation in the hotel room this morning, it was a relief to let loose and do something fun together. Now I'm slightly buzzed from the beer samples. My skin is warm and my eyes are heavy, and going back to our room for a nap is starting to sound mighty tempting.

The best part of the day has been spending it next to Carter. I kept catching my gaze drifting to him as we toured the breweries. My sister is completely smitten by him. Or maybe she loves the idea of me being with someone she believes makes me happy. He plays the role of my boyfriend effortlessly—walking hand in hand with me and whispering comments into my ear. He's so natural that I'd almost believe he *did* adore me. I almost want him to.

The worst part of the day has been Rich watching our every move. He wasn't at dinner last night, but I should've known the reprieve would be short-lived. I haven't talked to him since he showed up in Jackson Harbor last year. I don't know if he's tried to call or text. I blocked his number a long time ago, and Rich is perceptive enough that I'm guessing he's figured that out. My friendly Apple Store tech informed me that I can listen to the voicemails he leaves if I go to the Blocked Messages folder. Thanks, but no.

I don't realize that my thoughts have made me frown until Carter leans over and brushes my hair behind my ear. "Are you okay?"

I swallow and push away thoughts of Rich—as much as I can when I know he's in the same room, sitting three chairs down from us. "I'm fine. What about you? Are you having an okay time?"

"If this is your family's idea of bonding, I can see why you fit in so well with the Jacksons," he says.

"I think this was more Saanvi and Liam's idea of fun than Mom's." I lean my head on his shoulder. We're supposed to be a couple, after all, so wouldn't I touch him like this? "But maybe my parents have loosened up a little in recent years."

"They did put us in the same room."

I huff out a laugh. "Mom cornered me at dinner last night and told me she'd given us the other suite to 'appease the bride,' then warned me of the risks of pregnancy and the struggles of her patients who have babies out of wedlock."

His eyes are wide—perhaps the slightly horrified look of a man who's wondering if there's a shotgun wedding in his future. "And what did you tell her?"

"I told her that I'm a virgin and I've never so much as kissed a boy, and how exactly *are* babies made again?"

He laughs, his eyes crinkling at the corners. "You didn't."

"Oh, yes, I did. She didn't think it was funny, sadly."

He shakes his head and grins. I love when he smiles at me like this—as if I'm the most beautiful thing he's ever seen. As if he wants nothing more to get me alone and kiss me in a way that has nothing to do with pretending we're together. Is that wishful thinking? Do I *want* him to want that?

"Regardless, I'm having a good time. And I'll get bonus points with Brayden when I can tell him about Howell's new sour," Carter says.

I grin. "It's like you're a secret agent."

"Oh. My. God. It's him!" Someone screeches behind us. "I told you it was him."

"He's even hotter in person!"

We turn on our stools to see two women standing right behind us, cameras at the ready.

"Can we get a picture?" the shorter of the two asks, flipping her curly, golden hair over her shoulder.

Carter smiles, and I notice no one but me seems to see the way he pales. "Sure."

"I'll take yours and you take mine," the second woman tells the first.

They squeal and squeak, fawning all over Carter as they get pictures of themselves hanging on him. He doesn't pull away from their touch, but he stiffens every time they stroke down his arms or press against his chest, and he grows even paler when they croon about what a *hero* he is.

"If you'll excuse me, ladies," he says after a few minutes, "I'm on a date with my girlfriend." He nods to me, and the girls look stricken—kids caught with their hands in the cookie jar.

"Oh, wow. We're so sorry. Your boyfriend is the reason we came to Jackson Harbor," the shorter woman says.

"We live in St. Louis. I actually have a golden retriever puppy just like the one you saved," the other says. "We're *huge* fans."

"Jackson Harbor is beautiful this time of year," Carter says. "Enjoy your visit."

The women giggle their whole way out of the bar, and when they're gone, I scoot my stool right next to Carter's, close enough that I can lean on him and loop my arm through his. All I want is to ease the haunted ache I see in his eyes.

I close my eyes and feel him lightly comb his fingers through my hair.

"I'm sorry you're so tired." He presses a kiss to the top of my head, and the gesture surprises me so much that I pull back to look at his face. His brow is creased with worry. "I should have warned you about the nightmares."

I shake my head. "I'm not tired because of that. I'm tired

because I've had enough beer and bar food that it's made me sleepy."

"You should go back to the hotel and take a *nap* when we get back."

Carter and I both turn to see Saanvi standing behind our stools.

"Liam and I are definitely 'napping.'" She makes air quotes around the word then winks before continuing on to the booth where she and Liam have been sitting.

"I think my sister is trying to get you laid," I whisper.

Carter chuckles, and the sound is such a relief after seeing him lock up with those women. I was right. He needs to talk about the warehouse fire, and the shit with the viral photo only made his guilt worse. "I knew I liked her," he says.

"I told you she's good people."

"Obviously."

"But if I know Saanvi, she's more worried about *my* pleasure than yours."

He cocks a brow. "Are those things supposed to be mutually exclusive?"

Heat whips through me, and I swallow hard. "Behave."

His gaze drops to my mouth, and the tension simmers between us. "Do I have to? It's hard when all the beer has gone to my head."

"Is that why you're looking at my mouth like you're starving?" I'm shocked that I let the thought form into words, but once it's out, I'm glad for it. This flirtation is a distraction from real worries—from Rich, from the lies, from the way the compliments of two strangers can make Carter look like he wants to disappear.

His tongue skims his teeth. "Nah. I can't blame that on the beer. Your lips always make me hungry."

"For what, exactly?"

Chuckling, he takes my hand in his and sweeps his lips across my knuckles. "If you ever really want to know, Teagan, I'll happily show you."

"Of course I want to know." I slide off my stool and step in front of him, standing between his legs as I lean closer and whisper so only he can hear, "There's a bar full of nosy people watching us. Make sure you act like my loving boyfriend would."

He cups my chin in his big hand. "And what would your boyfriend do right now?" he says, so low I almost can't make out the words.

"I'm pretty sure he'd kiss me."

"Yeah?" He dips his head and brushes his lips across mine. He retreats a fraction of an inch before saying, "Like that?" I can feel his hot breath on my mouth.

"No." Reaching up, I slide a hand into his hair, guiding his mouth back to mine. "Like this."

The kiss starts slow. It's part show for nosy onlookers, part reassurance for me that he's okay. It starts as no more than a sweep of my lips over his, but the contact sends a rush of need through my blood, and I tug his bottom lip between my teeth.

Carter angles his head and brushes his tongue against my mouth. When he pulls away, his eyes are dark. He draws in a breath, but before he can say anything else, Rich is sidling up to us, his charming smile in place.

"Can I buy you two a drink?" he asks.

CARTER

I'd pay good money for the pleasure of slugging that sonofabitch.

I pull away from Teagan—just enough to glare at Rich. "Rain check, man. I'm kind of busy seducing my girl."

Rich claps me on the back, as if we're best buds and he's all about me taking Teagan to bed. "I don't mean to intrude. I feel like we got off on a bad foot last year, and I wanted to start over. What do you say?"

I already fucking said it. I'm sure he can see the annoyance in my smile. I don't try to hide it. "Another time."

Irritation flickers in his eyes, and he clenches those beefy fists before he walks away. When he's gone, Teagan leans her head against my shoulder and exhales. Her eyes were hazy when I pulled back from our kiss, but her body wound tight the second he walked up to us.

I toy with the hair at her temple. "Sorry about that. I forgot for a minute."

She lifts her chin, looking up at me through her lashes. "Forgot what?"

"Why you had me kiss you. Why we're even here." I shake my head, studying her face, trying to decide if maybe for a minute she forgot too. "When I'm kissing you, I forget everything." I wrap my arms around her, and she leans into me, some of that tension melting away.

Across the bar, Rich is pretending he's not staring, but I know he's watching every move we make. I lean my head down and brush my lips against her ear. "He's still watching." At that, she stiffens. When she starts to turn her head, I take her chin in my hand. "Don't look. It'll ruin my plans."

She arches a brow. "What plans?"

I brush her hair to the side and lower my mouth to her neck, kissing her in the way longtime lovers might. The way a couple planning to spend their lives together might show affection in mixed company.

"Is that it?" she asks when I pull my mouth away.

I tighten my arms around her middle, and I swear the heat in her eyes is real. I chuckle. "Well, your mom and sister are watching too, so I thought it would be best to keep it G-rated. But if you'd like, we could disappear into the kitchen for a while and make them wonder." I'm totally joking, but she giggles and steps out of my arms, grabbing my hand and dragging me back behind the bar and into the kitchen. And because I can't resist when it comes to Teagan, and because I've felt more alive with her these last few days than I've felt in months, I follow.

The second the kitchen door swings shut behind us, I pull her into my arms, immediately lowering my mouth to hers.

Behind me, someone clears his throat.

I ignore my brother.

He coughs, and I pull my mouth off Teagan's long enough to give Jake my best glare.

With a mischievous grin, Teagan points to the stairs at the back—the stairs that lead to Jake's old apartment. Currently empty save for the couch and the bed.

The bed.

I swallow hard, and before I can decide if going up there is a terrible idea or an excellent one, Teagan grabs my hand and rushes for the stairs, flashing me a grin over her shoulder that is both challenge and invitation.

I practically chase her to the second-floor apartment, pushing the door closed behind us right before she presses me against it. "Are you drunk?" I kiss her mouth, her neck, trying to slow myself down when I want to peel this dress off her and fuck her against the door.

"No," she says, breathless. She tilts her head, giving me better access to the tender spot beneath her ear. "Why?"

"I thought we agreed we were just playing pretend," I murmur, my hands already all over her—skimming up her sides, gripping the curve of her ass through her jeans, pulling her as close as I can get her.

"We did," she says. "I like playing with you."

Groaning, I tug her earlobe between my teeth. "We agreed no sex."

"Who said we have to have sex?" she murmurs, unbuttoning my pants. She rubs her hand over the length of me, stroking me through my boxer briefs. "Maybe I just want to make you come."

"Jesus." If I weren't already hard as hell, those words would get me there.

"Have you thought about my mouth on you? Because I haven't stopped thinking about it since Saturday night." Her words threaten to finish me off before we even start. She tugs down my briefs and wraps her hand around me, and my mind goes blank.

"Teagan. I . . ." I can't manage another word. Can't manage a coherent thought. Because she drops to her knees and takes me into her mouth. She flattens her tongue to the underside of my shaft, and her fingers graze my balls, making my hips buck. I press my palms flat to the door, trying to be still, trying not to shove myself deeper in her mouth.

She pulls back, releasing me and licking her lips. "Are you okay?" she asks. She grips the base of my cock and squeezes, dragging her tongue across the tip. "Is this okay?"

"Christ, Teagan." I swallow hard. "I'm trying not to come in the first sixty seconds of your mouth on me like some teenage boy, but you're not making it easy."

She grins and strokes me again. Harder. "I like you undone, Carter. It's better than I even imagined." She keeps her eyes on me as she drags her tongue along the underside of my cock.

I bark out a curse, and she smiles again. This time when she takes me into her mouth, she sucks and pulls me deep. My hips jerk instinctively, and she moans in approval. I lose my tenuous grip on my control. I let pleasure take over as she licks, sucks, and strokes. Every time I rock into her, fucking her hot mouth, pressing into those perfect lips, she moans, sucks hard, draws me deeper.

The sight of her—Teagan on her knees, her mouth around me, her eyes dark with lust—is the sexiest fucking thing I've ever seen. Looking at her fills me with a tenderness and longing I've never quite experienced before. Maybe we shouldn't be doing this. Maybe Jake's right, and Teagan is another diversion in my months of dodging the broken pieces inside me.

No. He's not. Maybe it was like that at first—the night at the auction—but the other women never made me feel like this. I never felt the weight of the day slip off my shoulders just because I heard their laugh. I never wanted to open up to any of them.

I want that and more with her. I want to strip off her clothes and lay her out on the bare floor, fuck her so deep that she's making those sounds right into my ear as we find release together.

Pleasure coils tighter and hotter down my spine, and I thread my fingers in her hair. "Teagan, baby. *Fuck.* I'm about to come."

She draws me deeper and sucks harder. Pleasure jackknifes down my spine as I spill into her mouth.

When she stands, she's a mess of wild hair, swollen lips, and flushed cheeks. I slide both hands behind her back and draw her body tight against mine as I kiss her hard—right as there's a knock on the door.

"Hey, sorry . . ." Jake clears his throat. I can picture him shifting awkwardly from one foot to the other. "The bus is ready and they're asking for you two."

Chapter SIXTEEN

TEAGAN

Mom stands at the foot of the stairs in the Hayhurst mansion. "Thank you, everyone, for an amazing day. Dinner will be served in an hour, and after that, I understand the bridal party has some plans for the evening."

"Hmm, what could we possibly do with an hour?" Carter asks, eyes dancing and all over me.

"It'll have to be a *quick* nap," Saanvi whispers to us. She grabs Liam's hand and races up the stairs.

Carter grins. "What do you say?" he asks, his voice low and husky. "Quick nap?"

My heart races and my stomach flips. I'm not sure what would've happened if Jake hadn't knocked on the door, but judging by the way Carter was kissing me, I know we weren't done. I'm realizing that when it comes to him, I'm not done with anything but lying to myself. I'm sick of pretending I don't want more.

"We should at least go . . . freshen up," I say, my voice a little high-pitched. Because *hell.*

He winks at me, and we're halfway up the stairs when my phone buzzes. I almost ignore it except . . . except this is my sister's weekend, and if she needs me or if my mom needs me to do something for her, she has to come first.

I pull it from my purse to look at the text. The picture there makes me freeze, one hand gripping the railing as the other grips my phone. Without thinking, I scan the faces in the lobby until I find Rich. He's grinning at me, and the anticipation that was flip-flopping my stomach moments ago turns to dread. He must have gotten a new number if this was from him.

Carter grazes his knuckles over my shoulder. "Are you okay?"

No. I'm not okay. Why does Rich even have these pictures? "Excuse me," I murmur.

I race up the stairs to our room, fumbling with the key at the door before closing myself in the bathroom. I slide down the wall, put my head in my hands, and try to remember how to breathe.

The soft rap of knuckles and then: "Teagan?" Carter's voice. Soft. Soothing. *Worried.*

I flinch. "I'm okay. I think maybe I . . . maybe I had too much bar food today." I bite my lip, hating the lie.

"Anything I can do?"

"No. I just need a minute. I'm sorry."

"You don't need to apologize." He sighs heavily, and I imagine him closing his eyes. He knows me well enough that I'm sure he's not buying my lie. Hell, a few minutes ago, I was ready to come up here and jump him, and now I'm hiding in the bathroom.

I was an idiot to think Rich wouldn't find a way to get to me this weekend. I was an idiot who convinced myself I wanted Carter to save me from Rich, when the real thing I need to be saved from is my own mistakes.

CARTER

With the exception of those held in honor of my brothers, bachelor parties aren't exactly my thing. A bachelor party full of strangers is high on my list of activities I'd rather avoid.

I was hoping I'd get a pass, but Liam found me after dinner and insisted I join them. With a broad smile and a smack on the back, he said he'd be disappointed if I didn't go. I like the guy, so honestly, that would have been enough, but I also figured that if I were really Teagan's boyfriend, I wouldn't hesitate.

So here I am, at the back of Jackson Brews with a handful of strangers. Teagan's dad joined us for a drink then excused himself—no doubt wanting to spare himself any inappropriate conversation that might include his daughter and future son-in-law. Liam's dad is here, but he's content to sit at the bar and grill Jake on the science behind the perfect IPA.

The good news is that the party seems to be nothing more than hanging at my family's bar playing poker. The bad news is I managed to find myself seated right next to Rich.

"Teagan seemed upset at dinner," Rich says, eyes on his cards. "Is everything okay?"

I bite back my scowl. "She's great. Why would you say that?" Or she *was* great until someone sent her a text that upset her—a text she wouldn't even talk to me about. She was distant the rest of the evening, claiming she wanted a shower before dinner and then avoiding my gaze all through the meal.

Did he send the text? Is that why he has that knowing smirk on his face?

"Oh, I know Teagan, and she definitely was *not* fine. In fact, she seemed pretty distressed. I would've thought you'd . . ." Rich's jaw drops, and I turn in the direction of his stare as Myla slides into my lap.

"Hey, you!" She wraps her arms behind my neck and nuzzles my ear. "How *are* you? God, I've missed you this last week. Maybe I wouldn't have but that conference was a drag, and I miss our dirty texts, and I've been dying to talk to you and here you are. What do you say we get out of here?"

"Myla." I push her away gently. "You're drunk."

"Does it matter?" She giggles. Rich is watching everything. She wiggles in my lap, and I scoot my chair back to stand, forcing her to her feet too.

"We aren't doing this anymore, remember?" I say softly.

Myla's lips curve into a pout, and I can see the moment the memory registers in her drunken brain. Her eyes fill with tears. "You didn't really explain. I know this wasn't supposed to be serious, but it always felt like more than just fun to me."

Now the whole damn table is watching us. Rich looks cocky as hell, and Liam's brow crinkles as his gaze bounces between me and Myla.

"Can we go outside and talk?" I ask softly.

Myla nods, her chin wobbling, and I lead her outside.

The night is cool but still warm enough that downtown is bustling with people enjoying the last weeks of balmy weather before winter comes. "Come back here," I say, nodding down the alley. We'll talk in the back where there are fewer eyes.

"I'm such an idiot," she says, sniffing beside me. "God, it's no wonder you don't want to really be with me if I get drunk and forget important things, like *Hey, that asshole dumped you.*"

I tilt my face to the sky and make myself process her words.

Asshole.

Dumped.

Myla knew the score. She knew I was seeing other people. Knew I didn't want anything serious. But it doesn't matter, and I should've known this would happen.

"I'm sorry, Carter." She sniffs and wipes away her tears. "Shit. I'm so sorry."

"Myla . . ." I squeeze her shoulder, and she leans into me, placing her head on my chest. "I'm the one who owes you an apology. I should've waited until you got back into town to tell you about Teagan and me. I handled it badly, and I'm sorry."

"I don't understand why she gets more and I'm only good for . . ." She sniffs then straightens, wiping her cheeks. "Damn it, I'm so pathetic."

"You're not. And I *am* sorry."

"I really didn't mean to fall for you." She lifts her chin as if she's grappling to find her pride. "We're friends, and we were never supposed to be more. You never led me to believe otherwise. But

I . . . wanted to."

"I'm really sorry." I could repeat myself a hundred times, but the words aren't enough. I never meant to hurt her, but saying so now makes me sound like a massive cliché. Like I'm just an ass who's delivering lines to get himself out of trouble.

"So . . . *Teagan*?"

I nod, and my stomach knots. "Yeah." For now. And maybe not even that. This afternoon felt like it was about more than pleasure, more than getting off, but when she got that text, she shut me out. For months I've been dodging anything that resembled commitment, but suddenly I'm getting this ache in my gut when I imagine letting Teagan go. It doesn't matter if this weekend is pretend. I already know it'll hurt to see it end. Months messing around with Myla and Bethany and I was never tempted, but a couple of days *pretending* with Teagan and I already wish I knew how to make it real.

Myla drops her gaze to her shoes. "I know it sounds pathetic to ask, but what about her made you change your mind about relationships?"

"She's . . ." *Fucking amazing. Fun. Sexy as hell. And sweet in the most surprising ways.* And this morning when she asked about my nightmare, I thought maybe she really might understand what I've been going through. "I've been carrying a torch for Teagan for a long time, and once she gave me a chance, I knew I didn't want to let her go."

Myla nods. "I'm so *lonely*, Carter. Maybe you and I aren't a love match, but sometimes I think I'm not going to be a love match with anyone, and that is a really crappy feeling."

Her words are a blow to the chest. I know what that feels like.

I was searching for someone special for years before I changed my ways. Being alone and wondering if I'd ever find someone to spend my life with sucked, and I hate that I'm making Myla feel that. She's my friend and I care about her, but right now it's pretty clear that I should have been more careful with her feelings. "You're incredible, Myla." I blow out a breath and drag a hand through my hair. "In fact, I work with a couple of guys who have been hounding me for your number. Hank, in particular, really likes you."

She smiles slowly and looks up at me through her lashes. "Seriously?"

"Seriously."

I swear she stands a little taller. "You could give Hank my number. I mean . . . if that wouldn't be too weird for you." She blows out a breath. "But only if he's looking for a relationship. I think this thing with you taught me something about myself."

"I'll make sure. And I'll make sure he knows that you're an important friend to me, so he'd better not hurt you—not that I'd set you up with anyone I thought might intentionally hurt you."

"You're a really good guy, Carter." She squeezes my arm. "I hope Teagan knows how lucky she is."

"Eh, I'm the lucky one in that relationship."

She shakes her head, her hair swaying across her shoulders. The tear tracks drying on her cheeks glisten in the light from the street lamps. "See what I mean? That's something a good guy would say." She lifts onto her toes and presses a kiss to my cheek. "I'll see you around."

I grab her hand before she can walk away. "Myla, wait."

She shakes her head. "Don't make this harder."

"No . . . I wanted to say thank you. For everything."

Her eyes are full of tears, but none fall. "You're the worst kind of heartbreaker, Carter."

I flinch. "I don't mean to be."

"I know. That's exactly what makes you the worst. This would be easier if I could hate you. Even a little." She pulls her hand from my grasp and jogs down the alley to the front of the building.

I lean back against my car and close my eyes.

"Did you mean it?"

I open my eyes to my brother, who's walking toward me with his hands tucked into his pockets. I tense. I'm not ready for another lecture. Even if I fucking deserve it. "Mean what?" I ask warily.

"Everything you just said about Teagan." Jake takes the spot beside me. We're shoulder to shoulder, both looking up at the sky. "I'll be honest—after you two disappeared upstairs earlier, I was worried, but you sounded sincere."

"I am." My voice cracks. "I've felt something for her for a long time, but I don't know what to do about it."

"You could try telling her."

Jake and I turn to see Shay stepping out of the shadows by her car two spots down. *Fucking seriously?*

I sigh, exasperated but resigned. Never was there a better metaphor for my entire life than trying to have a private conversation and discovering two of my siblings witnessed it. "Is my entire family spying on me, or just the two of you?"

Jake holds out his palms. "I was taking out the trash."

I turn to Shay. "What's your excuse?"

"I wasn't trying to eavesdrop, but you were dragging Myla

into the alley when I got here, and I decided not to leave my car until you two were done talking."

I sigh. I don't really care that they both heard. I'm more upset with myself. How did my life become such a mess that I thought I was single and yet this week has felt like a series of bad breakups?

"Why don't you, though?" Jake asks softly. "Tell Teagan, I mean."

"Trust me, I've dropped a couple of significant hints today."

Shay snorts. "Idiot. Women don't like *hints*. We like kindness and consideration, but you still have to be direct. Believe it or not, we don't *like* sitting around and dissecting what men have said to us."

I swallow hard. I was the one to tell her only four days ago that I don't do relationships, that I had nothing to offer beyond a friends-with-benefits arrangement. And she was with me on that. "She has no desire to be with someone like me."

"A player?" Jake says at the same time as Shay says, "A man-whore?"

"A firefighter," I growl. I roll my shoulders back. "She was in love with a police officer who died on a bad traffic call. She's got a thing against guys with dangerous jobs." I turn to Shay. "Did she ever tell you about Heath?"

"Heath?" My sister frowns and shakes her head. "That name doesn't ring any bells."

I hope Teagan won't mind me asking, but it's weird that she wouldn't tell Shay, one of her best friends, about a man she thought she'd marry. "What about Rich?"

"He's the ex she wanted you around because of, right?" Shay asks.

I nod. "Yeah, but do you *know* anything about him?"

"No, not really." She takes the spot opposite Jake, and we all lean against my car, in no hurry to get inside. "It's weird, now that I think about it. An ex bad enough to merit a fake boyfriend at her sister's wedding, and yet she's never talked about him."

"I met him inside," Jake says, shrugging. "He seemed okay."

I grunt. "Her whole family loves him, and he *seems* nice enough, but . . ."

"But what?"

I cut my eyes to my sister. "I swear this isn't a typical case of ex avoidance. I have a bad feeling about him. It's like he's too nice. Too much of everything her parents want him to be. And I think . . ." I shake my head, trying to piece it together—Teagan's terror when Rich was in town, the way he seems to still know her so well even though they haven't dated since high school, and the text she got today. The way she immediately looked at him afterward and then shut me out. "She's scared of him."

"Think he was abusive?" Jake asks.

"That's the only thing I can come up with," I say. "She's admitted he was very controlling, so it's logical he may have been physical about that need to control her. But even that doesn't completely make sense. Why wouldn't she tell her parents? Or at least her sister?"

"Why don't you *ask* her?" Shay asks.

"Because when I agreed to do this for her this weekend, she made me promise I wouldn't ask about Rich."

Jake lets out a long breath and squeezes my shoulder. "I need to get back in there before Cindy threatens to cut my dick off again, but let me know if I can do anything to help."

"I'm going in too," Shay says.

I arch a brow. "Girls' night tonight?"

"No. I'm avoiding the dissertation."

"Ah, yes, I hear that's the best way to finish it."

She smacks my arm. "Shut up. Writing is hard."

I laugh and wrap an arm around her shoulders, squeezing her. As crappy as I feel about what happened with Myla, I'm glad I got a chance to talk to Jake and Shay tonight. I needed that.

We all head in together through the back door. Shay and I cut through the kitchen and leave Jake to deal with the latest food order while we make our way out to the bar.

"I have to return to the bachelor party," I tell my sister.

"Godspeed," she says, winking.

"Everything okay?" Liam asks when I return to the group.

"Yeah. I think it's all worked out."

"Was she an ex, or . . .?" He looks concerned, and I can't blame him. If a woman had acted that way with him, I'd feel like I had to get that information to Saanvi somehow.

"You don't have to look so tormented. Teagan knows Myla, and I'll tell her about what happened."

"I think Rich might beat you to it."

I follow Liam's gaze to the front of the bar, where Rich is pushing through the doors. When he hits the sidewalk, he turns right, not getting a cab but heading down the street—toward the dance club where the girls are supposed to be spending their night. He'll be able to tell Teagan whatever he wants while I'm stuck here. *Fucking fantastic.*

But maybe it doesn't matter if Rich is going to the girls' party.

I turn to Liam. "You know what I want to do?"

180

"What?"

"I want to find our women and spend the rest of the night with them." I arch a brow. "Can you honestly tell me you want to sit here and play cards when your fiancée is dancing at a club only two blocks away?"

"A man after my own heart." He smacks me between the shoulder blades. "I'll tell the others."

Chapter
SEVENTEEN

TEAGAN

My sister is a happy drunk. Not that she's unhappy sober, because frankly, the girl never stops smiling, but alcohol somehow magnifies that happiness. She lets her guard down after a few drinks, like most of us do, but instead of being sloppy and obnoxious, she exudes joy I want to soak up.

Tonight has been all dancing and booze and laughter. In truth, I wasn't looking forward to the bachelorette party. The only bridesmaid I really know is my cousin Sabrina, and she and I don't exactly have a great relationship. Maybe it's a good thing she's not arriving until tomorrow morning. I can give my attention to Saanvi and enjoy myself without feeling judged by Sabrina.

Saanvi comes up to me on the dance floor and swings one arm around my shoulders. "This is the best weekend ever." She means it, and I couldn't be happier about that. "Do you know *why* it's the best ever?" she asks, swaying.

I grin. "I don't know. Maybe because you're marrying the love of your life?"

She snorts. "I would've done that on the dreariest day in the ugliest courthouse in America. And it does make me happy. But you know what makes that happiness even more awesome?"

Everything, it seems. "What?"

"Seeing you and *Carter*!" She groans. "Oh my gosh. You guys are so cute together! Even Mom is loving him, and she wasn't sure about it, because you know how she feels about Rich."

How everyone *feels about Rich,* I think, because Saanvi likes him nearly as much as my parents do.

"But *Carter.* Damn, girl. No one, and I mean *no one,* is worried about how fast this thing happened between you two now that we've met him."

Guilt is a dull blade twisting in my gut. "You guys were worried about my relationship?"

"Of course we were! Come on, falling for a pseudo-celebrity who has women chasing after him? Yeah, we were worried. Not now, though." She waves a hand, as if what she said shouldn't matter. "I *like* him. I like that you like him, and I like the way he looks at you. I remember the first time Liam looked at me like that. I'm pretty sure that was the moment I fell in love."

I laugh. "And how exactly does Carter look at me?"

"Like you're the first starry night he's seen in a decade." She sighs dreamily, hanging on me a little. "Like you're the moon and he's the sun."

"That's poetic."

She grins. "I figured you'd rather hear that than the truth."

I frown. I kind of liked the idea that Carter looked at me like that. "What's the truth?"

"Like he wants to lick every inch of you and make you come."

I smack her arm. "Saanvi."

"You two haven't done it yet, have you?"

"Saanvi!"

"I can *feel* the tension. I know you haven't. Is it him? Does he have like religious reasons for waiting, or . . ." She narrows her eyes. "Or is it you? Maybe after everything . . ." The joy seems to drain out of her in a rush. "Maybe you're scared to be with someone again."

I roll my eyes. "I've been with men since Heath."

"So why not Carter?"

Why not, indeed? I don't have a good answer. Not one that doesn't involve more lies. "We want it to be special," I finally say, because that feels like the truth.

"Oh my *God.*" She throws back her head and tugs on her hair with both hands. "That is *so hot.* But you do other stuff, right?"

"Seriously, stop." I laugh.

"Come on! Don't treat me like your innocent baby sister. I'm a grown woman, and I want *all* the dirty details."

"No, you don't."

She sighs. "Okay, maybe I just want to live vicariously through you. Liam and I decided to do this stupid thing where we don't do anything more than *kiss* the last month before the wedding, and I'm *dying* over here."

I snort. "I thought you went up to your room to *nap* this afternoon."

"By napping, I meant kissing," she says. "*Only* kissing. And don't get me wrong, the waiting is *hot,* but I might combust before our wedding night."

I laugh. I was so down after getting that text, so down all through dinner, but it's so easy to be happy around her. "I think you can make it a few more days."

"Easy for you to say. You have Carter in your bed." She grins. "Maybe the special moment will happen while you're in the suite!"

A thrill races through me at the thought, and I realize I want to make it a plan. I shouldn't, but . . . "Maybe."

"Would you be okay with that?"

I want to tell her the truth about our relationship. Honestly, I assumed I would at some point, but . . . what a tangled web we weave. "I could see it happening," I admit.

"Then let's get you another drink!"

After a trip to the bar, my little sister and I dance until I'm breathless and my feet are aching. These shoes are hot but not very forgiving. When a favorite eighties song ends, I put a hand on her arm. "I'm going to the table. I need a drink."

She grins and waggles her fingers in a little wave, already moving her hips to the beat of the next tune.

I swing by the bar to get a bottle of water before heading to our booth on the back side of the dance floor. I'm so focused on rehydrating that I don't even notice I'm not alone until I settle into the booth and Rich swoops in to take the spot next to me.

"Hey, beautiful," he murmurs. He slides in so close his thigh presses against mine.

I scoot in farther, and he follows. "Back off." The words

are low, breathless, and probably impossible to hear over the thumping house music.

He holds up both hands. "I'm here as a friend. I just needed to tell you something."

"What?" I snap. I hate the way I feel when he's close. Powerless. Trapped. *Dirty.*

He tilts his head from side to side, stretching his neck. "Why do you look at me like that? I came here because I care about you, but you're looking at me like I'm a monster."

"Where did you get that picture?"

"You already know the answer to that."

"Did he give it to you, or did you take it off his phone after he died?"

"*It*? You think that's the only one I have?"

The knots in my stomach are folding in on themselves. Again and again. Tighter and tighter. Pictures. *Plural.* "If you ever cared about me at all, you'll delete them."

His eyes flash. "No."

"Then you are a monster. And there's nothing you have to say that I want to hear."

"Really? Not even if I know something about your *boyfriend*?"

I still. Shit. He knows. And if he knows, he'll tell my parents. And if my parents know, they'll flip out, and it'll ruin Saanvi's whole wedding weekend. I won't let that happen.

"You deserve someone good, Teagan. You might not want that someone to be me, but it's definitely not him."

He doesn't know. He's just spewing his regular bullshit. I drain the rest of the water and avert my gaze to the dance floor, trying desperately to keep the relief off my face.

"I saw him with another woman tonight."

"So?"

"Oh." He arches a brow. "So you two have an open relationship, then? Interesting. Maybe Heath knew you better than you knew yourself."

"Shut up," I growl. My nails bite into my palms, and I force myself to relax my hands. I take a deep breath. "I'm sure whatever you saw wasn't what you thought. Carter has a lot of friends. He's lived here his whole life."

"They weren't talking to each other in the way *friends* talk. She practically jumped into his lap when she saw him, like she'd done it a hundred times." He smiles slowly, like this is a poker game and he knows he's laying out a winning hand. "And then they left. *Together.*"

I flinch as jealousy slams into me. I know Carter. This is what he's like—the women, the flirting. At least it's what he's been like for a while now. I shouldn't be surprised that a random woman threw herself at him. And he's not really mine, so I have no right to feel this jealous at all.

I want to ask what exactly he saw, what she looks like, and where Carter is now. I want to go over to Jackson Brews and get between him and any woman who dares to get too close. But I can't reveal those insecurities to Rich, and in truth, I have no right to feel this possessiveness rocking through me.

"Do you want to see them?" Rich asks, pulling his phone from his pocket.

At first I think he means Carter and the girl, but then I realize he's talking about the pictures. "No." The one he sent me this afternoon was enough. "All I want is for you to delete them."

"Why are you acting like you didn't like it?" He grins at his phone. "Thanks to these, I don't have to rely on my memory to know you enjoyed yourself."

"I hate you."

"No, you don't. You tell yourself you hate me because you don't want to accept responsibility for how you felt that night. For what Heath could see even when you denied it."

I turn to the wall inside the booth. I don't want to have this conversation, but I refuse to make a scene. I refuse to let him bait me.

"Maybe while Carter's busy with his girl, you could teach him a lesson." He tucks a lock of my hair behind my ear, and I flinch.

"Am I interrupting?"

I yank away and look up to see Carter standing at the foot of our table, his angry gaze leveled on Rich. "Not at all," I say. I want to stand up—to put distance between me and Rich and prove this isn't what it looks like—but Rich has me trapped inside the booth.

"I was telling Teagan that you left Liam's bachelor party with some woman who was all over you," Rich says. "But I guess you finished with her already."

Carter's jaw is hard, but he keeps his gaze steady on me and extends a hand. "Dance with me," he says, as if Rich isn't even there.

It works. Rich steps out of the booth and out of my way. "You two have fun. Let me know if I can help." He winks at me, and my stomach churns at the kind of *help* I know he's referring to.

I'm so happy to get away from Rich that I fold myself into Carter's arms on the dance floor.

"Are you okay?" he asks, his mouth against my ear.

I nod. "Fine."

"When I found you and saw him so close . . ." He gently grips the base of my neck and guides me back so he can look into my eyes. "I wanted to drag him out of the booth and away from you, but I couldn't tell if you wanted him there or not."

"I'm glad you came." I stiffen, remembering the girl Rich mentioned. The one Carter didn't deny leaving with. I step back, putting distance between our bodies. I've made a mess of this weekend. Of my relationship with Carter. Of *everything.*

"Why do you keep pulling away from me?" Carter asks. He sweeps his knuckles down my jaw, and his throat bobs. "One second I'm touching you and I swear you feel it too, and the next you're pushing me away. One second you're on your knees, my fucking fantasy come to life, and the next you won't look me in the eye."

I open my mouth to lie, to give one of the dozens of excuses I have in my resist-Carter-Jackson-at-all-costs arsenal, but instead I drag in a deep breath and push away my insecurities. Carter wouldn't be bringing this up if he didn't want me to let him closer. "Did we already screw this up?" I ask softly. "Did we open Pandora's proverbial box last weekend and irrevocably change things between us?"

Something I can't place flashes in his eyes. Worry? Sadness? "I don't know." He shakes his head. "I do know that my whole family would be disappointed if our drunken decisions made you disappear from our lives. The girls would be pissed and my brothers irritated that I did something to upset their women. But most of all . . . I'd miss you." His smile is different than before.

Gone is the cocky guy who throws around sexual innuendo, and suddenly I'm face to face with a very vulnerable Carter—perhaps the one side of him I absolutely can't resist. "I didn't tell you, but Jake and I fought at Brayden's on Sunday. He was pissed that I was treating you like an easy lay. For using you as a distraction from my own issues. I don't know if he was right—if I was treating you like that—but I never meant to."

I realize I've stopped dancing and wrap my arms behind his neck, but I keep enough distance between us that I can look up into his face. Carter even admitting that he has issues feels *immense.*

"Would it be so bad?" he asks, settling his hands on my hips.

"Would what be so bad?"

He squeezes my hip. "If things were different between us? If they changed? If maybe this all wasn't one big lie or another way for me to cope, but the beginning of something real?"

"I . . . I don't understand." I bite my lip. "You just left the other bar with another woman. And now you're asking me . . . ?"

"The woman was Myla. She was drunk." He sighs heavily. "I screwed up there. I thought we were friends. I didn't realize she'd started imagining we'd become more."

"But you two *are* more. You have been more. You can feed yourself whatever lies you want, but if you're sleeping together, you're not just friends. And if you're still sleeping with her, I can't . . ." I shake my head. "I can't be one of several. I don't work like that."

"I didn't go home with her. I haven't slept with anyone since before the auction."

I laugh, but it's more hysterical than joyful. "That's less than a week, Carter. Am I supposed to be proud?"

"No, of course not. I just . . ." He scans my face, searching for something, and I realize that maybe I'm as closed off as he is. "I didn't think I wanted *more* with anyone at all, Teagan. The idea of letting someone in when I'm as fucked up as I've been? It scared me to death." He swallows. "With you, it's a different kind of scary. It's not the scary of nightmares. It's the scary of holding on to something precious and feeling responsible for what happens to it."

My breath catches, because I know exactly what he means. The feeling he describes is the exact one I had when he pulled me into his arms in the lake more than a year ago and I pushed him away. It was like having someone place a rare gem in my hands and choosing to put it back in the safe deposit box—protecting it rather than enjoying it.

"*You* are precious," he says, "and a chance with you is something I want enough to be brave. So I'm asking you if it would be so bad if things did change between us."

My heart races, and I struggle to keep my footing as I waver between wanting to run from the edge of this cliff and wanting to leap off it. "The idea scares me," I admit. I let myself step closer and lean my head on his chest.

He strokes his hand up my side. "Because of my job?"

"Not just that. I like you," I say softly.

"But . . . ?"

I flick my eyes up to meet his, but there's no judgment on his face, no hurt or caution. Instead, his eyes are full of open curiosity, caring, and maybe a little sympathy. "But I think that if I let down my guard, it would be a fast fall from lust to love. I already know it would be so easy to fall for you."

He gives me a sad smile. "But you don't know if you can trust me to catch you." It's more reluctant observation than question. He pulls me against his chest, and we dance. "I don't need an answer now. Just to feel you. All I want tonight is to hold you close so that jackass can't get to you."

We dance, letting our bodies rock to the music, letting go of this pretense that neither of us wants more. And it's enough. For now, it's enough. On the other side of the dance floor, Liam and Saanvi are doing the same. My sister is so happy when she looks up at her groom—there are stars in her eyes for everything he is to her. And I realize that for all the dating I've done since coming to Jackson Harbor, for all my searching for someone, I haven't been looking for what they have. I've been scared of it—scared of what it will mean for me if I give up a piece of myself again. If I let myself love someone so entirely that I might break myself just to prove that love.

But maybe what I did for Heath—maybe that's not what love is. Maybe love is the person who reminds you of who you are. Maybe it's the person who helps you see yourself so clearly that you have the courage to say no when you're being asked to give too much.

"We're getting out of here," Saanvi says over the music, pulling me away from my spot nestled in Carter's arms for the first time in many, many songs. Liam's standing behind her, his arms wrapped around her waist. "Want to share a cab with us?"

I look to Carter, who gives me a gentle smile. "Whatever you want," he says softly. I realize he doesn't only mean the cab. He means us. This. Trying for more.

I nod, and he lifts my hand and holds my gaze as he presses a kiss to my knuckles.

Chapter
EIGHTEEN

TEAGAN

We don't talk to anyone as we exit the taxi, and Saanvi gives me a knowing smile as we head straight to the stairs. To our room.

When I shut the door behind us and hear the snick that lets me know we're finally alone, I jump on him, my hands in Carter's hair as I nudge him toward the wall. I yank his shirt from his pants and unbutton it with shaking fingers. My thighs clench at the memory of the sounds he made earlier—the thrust of his hips as he pressed himself deeper into my mouth and the feel of his hands in my hair as he came.

He lowers his mouth to mine, and I open for him, tasting him, needing him. He groans into me, and his hands drop to my waist—gripping as if he's afraid I'm going to disappear. And God, it's good. His kiss, his heat, the way he pulls me closer and closer even as he unzips my dress, as if he can't decide between getting me naked and keeping me as near to him as possible.

"I need to tell you something," he says breathlessly.

"What?"

"I never liked your rules."

I smile against his mouth. "But sometimes rules are fun." I step back, letting my unzipped dress fall off my shoulders and into a puddle on the floor. His shirt's unbuttoned, revealing the undershirt beneath it. I can almost make out the ridges of his abdominal muscles through the thin cotton.

His eyes are all over me, taking in every inch of my skin and black lace underwear. I put them on thinking of him. Thinking of this room we share and hoping he'd catch a glimpse. Maybe I knew we'd end up here tonight. Maybe I hoped.

"I've loved the way you look at me since the day we met." I draw in a ragged breath. "I've wanted you since then, too . . ."

He groans, and then we're on each other again. I'm peeling his clothes off. His hands are on my hips, my stomach, my back, cupping my breasts. Everywhere all at once. Greedy and demanding in a way that makes my blood blaze. And my hands are on him, unbuttoning his pants and pushing his clothes to the floor.

He turns our bodies until I'm against the wall, and he pins my arms above my head as he lowers his mouth to mine. He positions a knee between my thighs and grips both of my wrists in one big hand.

"Not fair," I say. "I can't touch you."

"You had your turn." He drags a hand down my side and back up, his knuckles rubbing over the lace covering my breast, and I rock into his thigh, desperate for more of his touch. More of him. I love him holding me like this, even as I ache to pull him into my mouth again. "You're so fucking beautiful," he says into my ear. "Do you have any idea how hard it was to make myself sleep on that couch last night when I wanted to hold you in my arms?"

"You could have," I say. "I told you there was enough room for us both to sleep there."

"I wasn't interested in *sleeping*. I wanted to feel you against me. Naked in my arms. I wanted to hear the sounds you'd make as I slid inside you." He nips at my neck, then soothes away the sting with his open mouth. I want to tell him that I want him too, that my rules were a pathetic attempt to protect myself—an attempt to protect a heart I know would be so easy to put in his hands. But his mouth on my neck, his teeth scraping across my collarbone, and his hand between our bodies . . . I can't think through the pleasure, and lose all capability of speech.

His mouth dips to my breast, and he sucks my nipple through the lace.

I cry out. "Please."

"Please what?" he asks. "Tell me what you want."

"I want you," I murmur.

He pulls my earlobe between his teeth and slips a hand into my panties. I whimper at the feel of him cupping me and the gentle pressure of his fingers poised between my thighs.

"Please," I repeat. "Carter . . ." I part my legs and lift a knee, hooking a leg around his waist to urge his hand where I need it. But he's too stubborn to give me what I want.

"What about your rules?"

"I don't care about my rules."

When he pulls his hand away, I nearly scream in frustration, but then he releases my wrists and wraps his arms around me, picking me up.

Squealing, I wrap my arms behind his neck and laugh as he carries me to the bed. "I *can* walk."

"What fun would that be?" His voice is husky and his eyes hot on me as he lowers me to the mattress.

Holding his gaze, I remove my bra. He licks his lips and reaches for me. I lift my hips, helping him peel off my panties. He throws them to the floor, and the rest of his clothes follow in a frantic rush of both our hands. Then he's nude in front of me, and my mouth goes dry with need as I take in his muscled form, his impressive erection.

I part my legs and crook my finger, urging him forward, but he doesn't crawl on top of me. He looks me over. Slowly. Thoroughly.

"Nice shoes," he says, his gaze skimming down my legs to where my heels are still strapped to my feet.

I grab his wrist and tug. "Come here."

"Oh, hell no. Not when I have a fantasy right at my fingertips." He drops to his knees, slides his hands under my ass, and tugs me forward, positioning each of my legs over his shoulders before he lowers his mouth between my thighs and licks me in one long, smooth stroke.

I gasp, my hands in his hair and tugging. I don't know what I want. More of this? Him on top of me? More of *everything*. He splays a hand on my stomach and teases me with his tongue and lips, tasting and sucking on my sensitive flesh.

When he lifts his head and meets my eyes from between my legs, he asks, "Have you ever thought about this? About me, here?"

"Yes," I whimper.

He licks me again—a reward and a promise. His greedy hands graze my stomach and thighs as he pushes the limits of my pleasure. Yes, I've imagined this. More times than I'd ever admit. But I never knew how much the chemistry between us would heighten my body's physical reactions. I should've known. How many times, alone with my hand, did I picture him to get me there? How many times did my fantasies of a faceless lover become Carter?

When he thrusts a finger inside me and licks my clit, I arch off the bed and bite down on a cry. He pulls back, those fingers moving in and out of me, his eyes smoky and hot as he flicks his gaze from between my legs to my face and back again. "I want to hear you," he says.

I shake my head. Had we gone to my house or his house—anywhere else—maybe I could let go, but here there are too many ears beyond these walls.

"I know, baby." He chuckles and presses a kiss to the inside of my thigh. "Soon, though. Soon, I need to hear you. I'm going to take you home and make you come so hard you scream." Then his mouth is on me again, that hand pumping in and out of me, making me bow off the bed and press against his lips, and that sweet, torturous flicking of his tongue. He changes the angle of his hand and, at the same moment, sucks on my clit. It's like being filled and emptied all at once. Like being destroyed and given life. And I come with the feel of his hair between my fingers and the sound of his hungry groan filling my ears.

CARTER

I stroke her as she comes down from her orgasm, still kneeling before her, still worshipping her body. I graze the underside of her breasts and her taut nipples, run my fingertips over her stomach, then flatten my palms down her sides and her hips. On the insides of her thighs, I press gentle kisses until her breathing steadies.

Those hands in my hair . . . Christ, I've never experienced anything as hot as Teagan tugging on my hair as she came against my mouth.

"It's my turn," she says as I stand. She reaches between our bodies, gripping me. My cock pulses—harder, thicker—into her stroking hand.

"I want to fuck you," I say, tracing the line of her wrist and rocking into her touch. "Will you let me, Teagan? Let me break your rules?"

She draws up her knees and places those sexy fucking shoes on the edge of the bed. "I'd be very disappointed if you didn't."

I grin and open the condom I placed beside her on the bed when I took off my jeans. Keeping my eyes on her, I roll it on. I love the way she looks at me. Makes me feel like fucking Superman and a god all wrapped into one. Add that to the sounds she makes when I touch her, to how hard I made her come? I'm not sure I'll be able to get my ego back out the door.

I climb over her, propping myself on my elbows as I position my body over hers. My cock is nestled between her legs, and I ache to get inside her.

"What are you waiting for?" she asks, those fingers toying with my hair again.

I scan her face. The flushed cheeks, swollen lips, her dark hair splayed out around her on the bed. "I'm not waiting for anything. Just trying to remember everything in case I wake up."

Her eyes widen then soften. She lifts onto her elbows, pressing her mouth to mine and tilting her head. She kisses me with a depth and patience I'm not sure we've explored yet—a slow rhythm I could revel in for days . . . weeks . . . years. We're still kissing when we shift our hips and I sink into her, slowly inching deeper and letting her body adjust.

She gasps against my mouth, her body coiling tight around my cock. "Carter." I feel her cry before it comes and muffle it with my mouth. She whimpers against my lips, and I slowly move, pulling out and sliding deeper with each pass.

I don't know how long we stay there. Kissing as our bodies rock. But it feels more intimate than anything I've ever shared with anyone else before. And when her body tightens around me and I feel her orgasm coming again, I pull back to watch her face—to memorize the way she looks as the pleasure washes over her. She bites back a moan, her dark lashes on her cheeks as she lets her release roll over her again.

Something unlocks in my chest. For the first time in months—maybe for the first time ever—I understand what it means to make love. I've used sex to hide from the shitstorm inside me, but lovemaking *is* the storm. As I move inside her, the connection between us tears down the walls around my ravaged soul and throws them open for her to see. For her to judge and decide if I'm worthy. And for the first time since the warehouse fire, I *want* to be worthy. I want to be enough for someone's tomorrow. I finally want to plan my own future.

The thought fills me with more elation than fear, but there's an even stronger emotion that grips me as I press my mouth to hers. For once in too long, it's one I want to share and not hide, and it fills me with hope as I find my own release.

"We should probably sleep." I stroke a hand up Teagan's bare stomach to settle between her breasts. I can't stop touching her, holding her, feeling her. Tomorrow is a busy day that starts with us spending hours apart, and I feel like I have to soak up as much of her as I can tonight so she doesn't slip away in the morning.

"Probably," she says on a sigh. She's no better, keeping her fingers threaded through mine or a hand in my hair, on my chest, my thigh. We crossed a line tonight—not just physically, but emotionally—and neither of us is in any rush to fall asleep.

"You have to be up early for the . . . What did you call that ceremony?"

Teagan turns in my arms, rolling to face me with a hand under her cheek. "It's called a Mehndi party, and it's a tradition where the bride and her bridesmaids have henna designs applied to their hands and feet." She smiles softly. "Saanvi's will be the most complex, so we'll keep her company and entertain her while it's done. It's more fun than it sounds, but it gives the bridal party time to give the bride advice before her big day."

"I can't wait to see it."

"I'm glad Saanvi wanted to pair some of the Hindu traditions with the traditional Catholic wedding ceremony, which"—she rolls her eyes—"is *long*."

I've always thought Teagan was beautiful, but right now, flushed from lovemaking and curled up next to me, there's a glow to her that makes me ache for more. More from her. More from us. If I could steal hours from next week to give us tonight, I'd do it. Instead, I settle for kissing her again, running my hand down her back, mapping out each tiny peak and valley of her spine.

She breaks the kiss and traces an imaginary line across my pecs, as if she wants to memorize me in this moment as much as I want to memorize her. "How will you spend your morning?"

"I'm going to check on Isaiah. He's healing, but without his dad around . . ." Some of the night's warmth and joy drains from me. "I don't know. He probably doesn't want me there, but I can't let him push me away."

She scoots closer, nestling her head in the crook of my shoulder. When she sighs, her breath dances across my chest. "You're right. He needs you."

I shift uncomfortably. "I don't know about that."

"He does. He talked about you a lot."

"When?"

"On Monday—after you left and before he was discharged. He admires you, and I'm sure he misses his dad, but he knows— on *some* level—that he's lucky to have you."

"Thank you." Taking the words as more than blown smoke is hard, but I make myself do it—even if that little bit of truth feels heavier than I expected, like a weight I'm not sure I can carry or deserve to.

She returns to tracing across my chest then dips her hand lower to take a similar tour across my abdomen.

"You were right this morning, you know." I focus on my breathing. *In. Out.* It's so hard to talk about this shit, but I want to try with Teagan. I want her to understand. "I'm sorry that I shut you down when you tried to talk to me about Max this morning. It's just . . ." I search her face. "I do blame myself, and maybe if Isaiah's mom weren't a total piece of crap, it wouldn't be so hard, but I feel like I failed to protect the person that kid needed most in the world."

Her fingers trail up my side, then my neck, and into my hair, until she's nudging me to my back and rolling to straddle me. When she looks into my eyes, there's sadness in hers. Or perhaps . . . compassion. Understanding. "It wouldn't be easier if you'd died next to Max. The kid was dealt a shitty hand, but it would only be worse for him if you were gone too." She grazes my stubble with her fingertips. "I know it's hard to be the one who lived, the one who carries that, and maybe it's self-centered to perceive your grief through my own needs, but I want you to know I'm *so* grateful you made it out."

I shake my head, trying to find the words to speak around the thickness in my throat. But there's nothing to say, and this feeling in my chest? I needed to hear that. I never realized I needed someone to say it out loud. "Thank you." I grip her hips. "I spent a lot of months getting through each day by pretending everything was normal. It was the only way I knew how to cope."

"It's fine to pretend that things are okay if that's what it takes to get through. And it's fine to sometimes pretend with some people that *you're* okay, even when you're not. But you need to have people in your life you can talk to. People you can confide in when you're *not* okay. People you trust to see you that vulnerable."

"Are you volunteering to see my ugly insides?"

She puts her hands on either side of my head and leans forward, her dark hair falling like a curtain around us. "Yes, Carter. I'm a nurse," she says, smiling softly. "Ugly insides are my specialty."

Chapter
NINETEEN

CARTER

Teagan and I fell asleep after two. For the first time in too long, I didn't have a single nightmare. I slept hard, but habit has me up at five.

I tuck the blankets around Teagan, pull on my jeans and a T-shirt, and head downstairs. I don't want to wake her up, and I'm dying for a strong cup of coffee.

The dining room is quiet, but the kitchen staff has set out some pastries, fruit, a selection of teas, a carafe of coffee, and . . . I sniff. Oh, sweet baby Jesus, I smell bacon.

"Good morning, sir," a young blonde says, stepping out of the kitchen. "May I get you some hot breakfast? We have bacon, scrambled eggs, and French toast this morning, in addition to the offerings on the buffet, of course."

I blame my upbringing, but when I'm short on sleep, I don't

just crave coffee to get moving. I crave *bacon*. Or at least I used to, before my appetite abandoned me.

I grin at the server. "Bacon and eggs sound great, thank you." I take a seat at one of the white-clothed tables, sip my coffee, and scroll through emails on my phone as she retrieves my meal. Brayden sent out third-quarter Jackson Brews P&L reports—which I'll open and skim only enough to say I did and send back with my approval. Beth sent me an email with a link to a story about a firefighter who lost his father (also a firefighter) with a note about it.

I've been sitting on this for a month, waiting for the right time to give it to you. It's a story of grief, guilt, and forgiveness. Thought of you. Hope you're well.

My chest goes tight. She's only tiptoed around the subject of the warehouse fire before, but this is definitely less of a tiptoe and more of her taking my hand and urging me to take a full step. A month ago, it would've pissed me off and I'd have deleted it, but now I think I might be ready. I flag it for myself to read later.

"Here you go, sir," the server says. She places a plate of steaming bacon and eggs in front of me, and I thank her before digging in. I feel a little odd eating down here without Teagan, but she already told me I'd be doing breakfast on my own this morning. She and the bridesmaids and mothers will be taking breakfast in Saanvi's suite.

I'm scrolling through Instagram when I hear someone clear his throat. I lift my head as Rich pulls out the seat beside me and sinks into it. *Shit. Just the asshole I don't want to see.*

"Good morning, Carter." He has a steaming cup of coffee and holds it between two hands as he studies me. "I wanted to apologize about last night."

I arch a brow. "Yeah?"

He nods. "Liam's right. I get a little . . . unreasonable where Teagan's concerned. You know how it is, right? She was my first love, and then we grieved over my best friend together."

I nod but take another bite of my breakfast instead of responding. I have so many questions, but I'm not sure I should be getting my information about Teagan and Rich's history from Rich—especially considering the warning she gave me about how he manipulates people.

He blows out a breath. "I don't think I'll ever stop feeling protective of her, and I'll probably always love her, but I do know she's a grown woman who gets to make her own decisions. I'm sorry if I came off a little too intense. I'm going to make an effort to be better. I don't want to be in the way of you two enjoying yourselves this weekend."

Well, hell, that sounds downright mature. "Thank you, Rich."

"You're welcome. Let me know if I can help at all, okay?"

Unlikely. "I don't think we'll be needing anything, but thanks anyway."

He nods. "I know it's hard for her to talk about the past, so if you have any questions, I can fill in details. I want her to be happy."

"I think what she needs to be happy is for you to let her go." I pause a beat. "Completely."

Anger flashes in his eyes—there and gone in a beat—and then he smiles at my nearly empty plate. "I remember those days."

I frown at the bite of eggs remaining. "What days?"

"The run-ragged-by-Teagan days." He looks at his watch, then back to me. "I mean, here you are before the sun's up, trying to get some basic sustenance." He holds up his hands, palms out. "Been there, done that. I'm not judging."

Dude, you almost *made it through a conversation acting like a civilized adult and you had to go and ruin it.* "Maybe you should mind your own business."

"I'm just being friendly. And hell, I remember what it's like. If Teagan's anything like she used to be with me . . ." He looks around the room, ostensibly to make sure we're still alone, before dipping his head and adding in a quieter voice, "And Heath? That dude was my best friend, and I mean no offense when I say he couldn't keep up with her, and he *tried*. Not that it mattered to Teagan. She's a modern woman with *needs* . . . And I didn't mind helping her out with those." He winks at me and stands, and I'm fucking speechless.

Maybe guys in his world talk to practical strangers like this, but I'd never even say this shit to my *brothers* about a woman I was seeing or saw in the past. It's bad form and more than a little sleazy. And what's he trying to say, anyway? That Teagan stepped out on Heath? With him?

"I'm saying that you should do what you can to keep up with her if you're not into sharing . . . if you catch my drift."

"I don't think I do, Rich," I say, forcing calm into my voice. "What are you trying to say?"

"Nope." He mimes zipping his lips and locking them, and slowly backs away. "I don't kiss and tell." He points both index fingers at me, wagging them as he heads to the door. "Godspeed, sir."

He leaves the dining room, and I make myself count to ten. On the one hand, I want to run after him and punch him in the face. On the other hand, I'm here to save Teagan from drama, not to cause more, so I make myself stay seated until I finish my coffee.

I'm about to leave when Saanvi comes in. She's a shorter and thinner version of her sister, but they both have a smile that lights up their whole face.

"Good morning," she singsongs.

"Good morning, Saanvi. How are you feeling this morning?"

"I'm great! No hangover, thanks to copious water, Gatorade, and some healthy exercise to clear some of the booze out of my system before sleeping."

Exercise. It's rare that I feel like the biggest prude around, and yet my first two conversations of the day are certainly making me feel that way. I like Saanvi and I like her fiancé, but I really don't want to know about the "exercise" they did last night.

She must spot my cringe because she laughs. "A *walk*, Carter. Liam and I took a midnight stroll along the lake. As in, actual exercise."

"Right. Sorry. And good. I'm glad you're well this morning."

"How's Teagan?" Saanvi asks, filling a plate with Danishes.

"Good. Sleeping." I motion to her plate. "I thought you were having breakfast with the girls this morning."

"Yeah, but that's in, like, two hours." She lowers her voice. "And I am a *little* hungover."

"The truth comes out."

"Worth it." She grins and takes a seat beside me. "Liam likes you, you know."

"He's a good guy. I'm glad he approves."

"He said Rich rubs you the wrong way, though." She says this casually, as if she's just putting the information out there, but I can tell by the way she watches me from under her brows that she's trying to read my reaction.

And how exactly am I supposed to respond to this? I blow out a breath. *Fuck it.* "That's putting it mildly. I can't stand the guy."

She nods slowly, tearing a lemon pastry into bite-size pieces. I'm not sure if she's going to eat it or play with it. "You'd probably feel differently if he'd started off on a better foot with you. I mean, he planned on coming here to sweep Teagan off her feet, and then suddenly, last weekend he found out she has this boyfriend— you. He's trying, but I don't think it's easy for him to put on his best face when you have what he wants most."

"Did it ever occur to him that Teagan doesn't want him to sweep her off her feet? That their relationship has been over since high school, and he needs to let her go?"

Saanvi drops the pastry and pushes her plate away. "Is that what she told you?"

"She doesn't want him."

"Not that. The . . . She said they haven't been together since high school?"

She said I couldn't ask questions. She said he pushed his way back into her life. "I know it was complicated between them," I say, carefully evading what I clearly don't understand. Rich's insinuations rankle me. Am I the only one here who doesn't know what the fuck went down between them? How am I supposed to help her if I don't know the whole story? "She removed him from her life for a reason." I hesitate for a beat, then decide to take a chance. "I guess that's why I don't understand why your parents would insist on inviting him this weekend."

Saanvi sighs. "I guess because as far as my parents are concerned, Rich saved Teagan's life."

I don't try to hide the shock I'm sure is all over my face.

"Not literally, I suppose, but she was a disaster after Heath died. Rich pulled her out of bars when she was too trashed to know her own name, got her away from guys who wanted to take advantage of the fact that she was trying to lose herself." She picks at a cuticle, her eyes far away, as if she's remembering those days. "We were all grateful for him. He was the only thing that kept her grounded when she was spinning out of control, and even when her grief made her treat him like shit, he stuck around. He kept her safe."

I swallow hard. "I'm not sure she sees it that way."

She squeezes my shoulder and sighs. "I love that you want to protect her from her ex, but I want you to understand that he's not a bad guy. To me, to my parents, he's just a guy who'd do anything for Teagan."

"So would I," I say softly. "But with all due respect, I hope that if she ever wants to start over without me, you and your family won't push me back into her life."

Saanvi stares at me with those big, sad eyes. "I wasn't blowing smoke when I told you I'm rooting for you. Regardless of her history with Rich, I like her with you. She blossoms when you're around."

"Thanks, Saanvi. I'm rooting for me too." I wink at her, then head out. All this talk about Teagan's past without her around makes me uncomfortable.

When I enter the room, the bathroom light's on but all the other bedroom lights are still off. Teagan's asleep in the bed. She's curled on her side, her arms tucked into her chest and her dark hair spread out on her pillow.

I strip off my shirt and my jeans, and when I'm in nothing but my boxers, I slip into bed behind her, pulling her tight against me. I press my mouth to her neck. She's so damn warm and smells like springtime. Like a new life and second chances. The thought makes me laugh at myself. I've never been a poet, but she makes me wish I had it in me—the pretty words and the perfect explanations for my mistakes. She makes me wish I were better in so many ways, but I'm not. All I have to offer is this: myself. My battered, broken heart. And my desperate wish to become whole again.

I might not know all the details about her past, and I might not be the one who dragged her out of bars when she was grieving for the love of her life, but I'm here, and I care about her so much that I feel shaky when I imagine letting her go. Maybe it's true. Maybe Rich did save her in some way, but right now—this weekend, for all its scheming, lies, and pretense—she's saving me.

I slip a hand up her shirt, greedily skimming my fingers over the soft skin of her belly. Her sleepy moan sends a whip of pleasure down my spine. She arches into me, and my cock hardens against her ass.

My kisses on her neck grow greedier, and when I cup her breast in my hand and pinch her nipple, she gasps. Then all of the sudden she cries, "Stop!" She yanks out of my arms and jumps out of bed.

"Shit. I'm sorry." I sit on the edge of the bed, facing her, and turn on the bedside lamp.

She squints against the light and blinks at me. She takes in deep, gulping breaths, like she's trying to calm herself down.

I'm an idiot. I should've woken her up before touching her. I fucking know better. "I'm so sorry."

She gulps in air and puts a hand flat against her chest. "It's fine. *I'm* the one who's sorry. I haven't had anyone crawl into bed with me in a long time. It scared me." She gives me a wobbly smile and steps forward. She drags her fingers over my stubble and straddles my lap. "I'm glad it's you." When she presses her mouth to mine, the kiss is gentle. Shaky. "You think I'm crazy, don't you?"

I shake my head. Will she ever trust me enough to show me all of her ugly insides? "I think . . ." I trail my thumb down the side of her neck, and she closes her eyes. *I think you might be as broken beneath the surface as I am.* "I don't ever want to scare you."

"You don't." She presses her lips to mine again, but this time the kiss is firm and sure. She pours herself into it.

I saw the fear in her eyes—I recognize that haunted terror as well as I recognize my own reflection—but I let her drown her fear in me. I kiss her in return. I grip her hips and rub my tongue against hers until the connection between us is all that matters.

She draws back enough to pull her shirt over her head and toss it on the floor. Before she can press her body to mine, I roll her onto the bed and prop myself on one elbow so I can look down at her. I kiss her gently. "I'm sorry I scared you."

"It's okay." She strokes her hands down my back. "I'm fine."

I don't think you are. There's more she's not saying, so much she's not telling me. But I won't push. Not right now. I'll give her whatever she needs. Distraction. Pleasure. Oblivion.

And I'll give myself what I need too. *Her.*

She wraps a hand around my bicep and tries to tug me down. "I want you closer."

I chuckle, scanning over her again. I memorize every inch, catalogue her beauty even as my mind spins wildly with all the ways I want to touch her. "I like the view from here."

She arches, as if the words alone shoot pleasure through her.

"I love looking at you." I bend, flicking my tongue against her peaked nipple. Gasping, she jerks beneath me. "Love tasting you." I press my open mouth to her breast and trail my hand down her body, slipping my fingers beneath the waistband of her panties where she's already slick. "Touching you."

"Carter." My name is a moan on her lips as my fingers dance across her clit. She parts her legs for me, letting me toy and play and touch until her whimpered pleas become louder and more frantic and she's grabbing a condom from the bedside table and begging for me.

Pushing this morning's conversations from my mind, I silence her moans with my mouth and we lose ourselves in each other.

"You're beautiful." I rake my gaze over her after taking care of the condom. She looks like a goddess in the warm light of the bedside lamp—flushed skin against white sheets in nothing but her satisfied smile—and contentment wraps around me as I climb back into bed with her.

Her pulse flutters wildly at her neck, and I dip my head to press a kiss there. "Your heart's still racing."

"You do that to me."

I groan. "I want to do it again and again."

Panic flashes across her face. "Carter . . ."

I roll to my back. "No rush. I meant it when I said so last night. You know what I'm offering. All you have to do is decide if you want it."

She rolls onto me. "The truth is I'm not so sure you're going to want me. Not the way you mean. You deserve that perfect girl Ethan said you're looking for."

I don't want her. I want you. "What? You're telling me you're not perfect?"

She huffs. "Shut it. You know I'm not. And if you think I am, you're going to be disappointed."

"I don't want perfect, Teagan. Perfect is boring."

"Okay, well, how about a little less screwed up, then?"

"You think I can't be with a woman who grieved so deeply she had to be dragged from bars?" I watch as she pales and decide to go all in. "Tell me about your ugly insides, Teagan. Tell me about Rich."

She lowers her body onto mine and curls into my chest, placing her palm flat against my pounding heart. "Sometimes I think Rich wanted me to be with Heath because he knew it was the only way he could get me back. Heath was Rich's best friend and partner, and he was . . . Heath was a good guy. He didn't do anything halfway. He loved me fiercely and made me feel like I was the most beautiful woman in the world. He was passionate about his job, about me, and about his friendships. That included Rich, so I never dared ask him to push Rich away."

Sadness seems to seep from her pores, and I realize I never saw this side of her until she started opening up about Rich and Heath. Teagan is happiness and sunshine. It radiates from every inch of her. She sags against the weight of the story, curling into herself as if she can defend her heart from the pain of the memory. Seeing her like this is like watching her fade away. And it kills me.

I stroke her back in gentle circles, trying my best to comfort her.

"Rich and I were both a mess after Heath died. I told you losing Heath made me reckless, but what I didn't say was . . . I slept with Rich."

I wait for jealousy to ratchet through me, but it doesn't. There's nothing to be jealous of. I want her, but I'd never want to turn into a regret, and that's all Rich is. "It happens. Grief can make us impulsive."

She swallows. "The night I buried my boyfriend, I slept with his best friend. We were drinking, and I started crying. Rich held me, and the next thing I knew, we were kissing." She buries her face in my chest and draws in a long, deep breath. "It wasn't about sex. Not for me, at least. We were lonely and grieving and comforting each other. But Rich . . .

"I knew it was a mistake immediately. Hell, I think I knew it was a mistake even while it was happening, but Rich didn't see it like that. He thought we'd be back together in no time. I was still a new nurse and I'd come home from work, exhausted from the long days and the demands of a new job, and he'd be there, waiting for me."

She's quiet for a long beat, and I can almost feel her sorting through the memories—analyzing them from every angle and trying to find the right details, the right words. "It was fine at first. I mean, I felt so bad for sleeping with him—for leading him on like that when I knew he was grieving too. I put up with his presence in my life for a while. And at first, I didn't mind. I was lonely, but at least with Rich around, I wasn't *alone.* Then things changed—they'd *been* changing, but so slowly I hadn't even realized what was happening, and by the time I realized it, I was already under his control again. Like in high school. He'd show up to my house and grill me about who I'd seen that day. Who I'd been with. His cousin saw me at lunch with another guy—was I fucking him? He'd show up to the hospital and sweet-talk my coworkers and feed them little bits of my life and struggles. He'd tell them I was drinking more, but he was keeping an eye on me. That I wasn't sleeping, but he was working on getting me to take the sleeping pills the doctor prescribed.

"He made my parents believe we'd fallen in love again while comforting each other. He made all our friends believe we had this secret love. He made them believe I was too ashamed to tell anyone I'd moved on. We weren't even together as far as I was concerned, and he convinced everyone—*everyone*—that he was the only steady thing in my life, the only thing keeping me from falling apart completely. He worked them so well that if I dared object and say we weren't involved, they'd give me a lecture about how I was lucky to have him, how it was okay to move on, how they understood how guilty I must feel but I deserved happiness."

She shakes her head, and some of that sadness I saw in her eyes before burns away into anger. "I let it go on too long. Because I felt bad for *him*. Because I knew *he* was struggling with his own guilt and grief, I kept my mouth shut too long. He copied the keys to my house and always seemed to know where to find me. It wasn't until later that I realized he put one of those trackers on my phone."

"Jesus." I thread my fingers through her hair and hold her tightly, as if I can somehow protect her from what he did all those years ago. I'd guessed it was bad, and if no one around her could see him for what he was, she must have felt trapped.

"He took control of my life inch by inch, and by the time I tried to take it back, it was too late. My friends turned on me. My family begged me to be reasonable. I got my locks changed and started going out again—bringing men home to spite him. I told Rich I didn't care if everyone thought I was the biggest bitch in the world. We weren't together and never would be."

I kiss the top of her head. "That must have been awful."

"I thought since I'd finally put my foot down, that would be it. I was an idiot. I should have done it weeks sooner. One night I came home from work—my house with its new locks that were totally going to keep me safe—and he was there. 'You think you can lock me out?' he asked, and when I threatened to call the police, he laughed in my face. He *was* the police. Everyone he worked with saw how crazy I'd become after losing Heath, and who were they going to believe?" She pauses for a long time, as if she needs to catch her breath. "Then he told me to pack my things. He couldn't *trust* me living on my own anymore, and he'd talked to my parents about how I'd been sleeping around, and they agreed that I needed help. That I was self-destructing."

"Your parents listened to him?"

She shrugs. "That's just it. Rich's manipulations were so good because he didn't need to outright lie. I *was* sleeping around. I *was* drinking a lot. I was dealing with my own grief through all of this, but my parents are old-fashioned. They didn't see Rich as a controlling narcissist. They saw him as the good guy who was trying to save me from myself. He'd manipulated them so completely that I couldn't go to them for help. My friends didn't trust me because of the poison he'd whispered into their ears. And he was a police officer, so I didn't feel like I could call the cops either."

"So you moved."

She nods and slowly sits up again, returning to straddling my waist and tracing the muscles of my torso. "I didn't just move. I ran. And until I saw him at Jackson Brews last year, I thought he'd finally let me go." She trails her gaze up my chest and finally meets my eyes. "But you were there, and you understood I needed you. You have no idea how much that meant to me."

I want to be there *every* time she needs me, but I'm not sure if she's ready for that yet. I sit up, pulling her body flush with mine. She wraps her legs around my waist, and I cup her face in my hand and kiss her slowly.

"Don't let him get to you," she says against my mouth. "I don't know what I'd do if he got in your head the way he's gotten in everyone else's."

"I don't like the guy, and I don't trust him. You don't have to worry about me."

"But I do." She studies my face, and I know we're not talking about Rich anymore. "I'm so worried about you."

"I'm fine." I thread my fingers through her hair and guide her mouth back to mine. "In fact, with you right here, I'm fucking fantastic."

Chapter
TWENTY

TEAGAN

"I guess we pushed the Mehndi party back for nothing." Saanvi tosses her phone on the bed and frowns. "Sabrina missed her red-eye, and she's not going to be here until dinner."

Mom frowns, and I can tell she wants to rant about my cousin breaking too many promises, and maybe even give Saanvi a lecture about how she told her Sabrina shouldn't be a bridesmaid for this very reason. Our original schedule had us getting the traditional henna designs on our hands and feet yesterday, but Sabrina needed to stay at home another day for a story about some famous parrot, which was adopted by a country music couple, so we pushed it back.

Instead of giving her an "I told you so," Mom lifts her chin and shrugs. "Her loss."

We're all gathering in Saanvi's suite for her Mehndi party. My second cousin on my Dad's side, Pari, is a henna artist, and she'll use a special paste to paint designs on the hands and feet of the bridal party. Well, everyone except Sabrina, it seems.

"I'm sure she's sorry," I say lamely. I don't really mean it. Sabrina's pretty self-centered and wouldn't show up on time to meet the Pope if there was nothing in it for her.

Saanvi waves a hand. "I don't want to talk about her. Let's talk about something happy."

"Carter seems like a very nice man," Mom says, turning to me.

That is something happy, indeed. "He really is, Mom. You don't need to worry about that."

Saanvi winks at me from across the room where she's admiring the designs on Liam's mother's wrists. Pari has already completed her designs on the mothers of the bride and groom and has begun work on McKenna's designs. She'll do Saanvi's designs last.

"I do worry, of course," Mom says, pulling my attention back to the topic at hand. She studies me, and I can tell from the look in her eyes that she's trying to decide how much to say. "It worries me that you felt you had to keep the relationship a secret—not once but twice."

My brows shoot up. *Twice.* Someone's been talking to Rich.

"How healthy can a relationship be if the woman is keeping it a secret from her family?"

"Mom . . ."

"Enough of that," Saanvi says, waving her hands and saving me from having to come up with an explanation. "Their relationship is no secret now, so let it go. I've talked to him a lot the last couple of days, and I, for one, really like him."

"I do too," Mom says. "But Rich said you two acted quite serious when he met Carter last year, and yet you never told us about him then. And he seems wonderful, Teagan, but I keep wondering how wonderful he could really be if you've been here before and it didn't work."

"I'm sorry, Mom, but I don't tell you about every guy I date." I hate this lie. It makes me feel like such crap. But more than that, I hate the implication that Carter must not be good enough for me.

Saanvi studies me. "Do you love him?"

I open my mouth and close it again. "He's been my friend for a long time." I'm not sure how I feel about him. I loved him as a friend before we started all of this and have been attracted to him as a woman since the day we met. These days together have made those feelings tangle into a complicated knot I can't make sense of.

"You're afraid to love him," Saanvi says softly. "He told me why."

"Why?" Mom asks, her brow furrowing.

Saanvi squeezes my wrist. "Because of Heath, Mama. Carter has a dangerous job, and she's scared to lose him like she lost Heath."

I turn up my hand and let my little sister lace her fingers with mine. "That was why I didn't want to get involved at first," I admit. "But now . . ." *Now I don't care about that.* Now I want Carter. Even if I had to go through the same heartache again, I'd want him.

"Oh, Teagan." Mom sinks to the floor in front of us and puts her hands on my knees. "I am so sorry that still haunts you, but you cannot let this fear keep you from the person you love." She smiles and slowly shakes her head. "It's always scary to give your heart to someone—no matter their job—but far worse than that fear is living a life without the person you love. If you push him away again and something happens to him at work, do you think it'll hurt any less?"

"No," I whisper. "I don't."

She nods sagely and squeezes my free hand. "Then I think you have your answer."

Then I smile, realizing Mom is talking me into a relationship with Carter, talking me into giving him my heart—despite Rich's attempts to make her worry about our relationship. "Thanks, Mom."

CARTER

"I'm glad you're here, Carter," Marta says, grabbing me by the arm and pulling me into her house. "That boy is in a funk, and there's nothing I can do to get him out."

"Is he taking his meds?"

"Yes, but he's not talking. Not to me, not to his friends. He's not even playing that dumb online survival game he likes so much."

My chest goes tight. "You should have called."

"Oh no, you're busy with your wedding, aren't you? Isaiah

told me your girlfriend's family is in town, and I didn't want to bother you again after you two were kind enough to come over here Wednesday."

"I could've gotten away sooner." I should've come over yesterday. I could have made it work—slipped out between the brewery tour and the bachelor party, or even stopped by in the morning.

Marta puts a hand on my arm, warm and soothing. "He's fine. A grump but not in any danger. Carter . . ." She hesitates a beat. "Do you remember what you asked me a couple of months ago? Before this mess with Isaiah's accident?"

I draw in a deep breath. I asked her if she thought Isaiah would like to live with me. Marta's age makes it hard for her to keep up with him. If he lived with me, it would take a weight off her shoulders. But she'd been offended by the offer. "I'm sorry about that. I didn't mean any harm, and I shouldn't have overstepped."

She frowns. "I know you didn't. But I've thought about it, and I think that might be the best for my grandson. If the offer's still on the table and you're sure, I think we should let him decide." Her hands shake as she wrings them together. "But only if he understands that I only want what will make him happy."

"Of course," I say softly. "I'll talk to him."

She hobbles into the kitchen, and I head to Isaiah's room. His door's closed, and I'm surprised when he answers my knock right away.

"Hey, bud. How are you feeling?"

He tilts his head to the side, looking over my shoulder. "Where's Teagan?"

"Oh, *that's* why you let me in so fast. I get it. You only put up with me so you can get closer to my girlfriend."

He shrugs. "Can you blame me?"

"She had to meet her mom and the other bridesmaids to get their wedding henna done."

He wrinkles his nose. "What's that?"

"You know, the designs on the hands and feet?"

"Oh, right." He nods. "I bet she'll look hot with that."

I grunt and sink into the couch. "I'm pretty sure she's doing it for the sake of tradition and her cultural heritage, and not to look hot."

He rolls his eyes. "Whatever."

"Marta says you've had a rough couple of days," I say gently.

"I've been taking my meds. I'm fine."

Life isn't about going through the motions, bud. I look around the room, imagining what it would be like to have him live with me. I was having a good day when I brought it up with Marta, but on my bad days, I've been ashamed of myself for the suggestion. I had no right. And then all the shit with the viral picture happened, and every person who called me a hero reminded me how much I've failed this kid. I can't fix it by moving him in with me and trying to be some sort of guardian.

And yet . . . after talking to Teagan last night, I feel a little lighter. Nothing's changed. My grief for my friend and my guilt surrounding everything that happened that night is all still there, but maybe this heaviness isn't going to last forever.

"What is it?" Isaiah asks. "Is something wrong?"

I draw in a deep breath. "Marta's worried about you."

"She's my grandma. She worries. It's pretty much her job description."

"Of course. She'll always worry, and she'll always try to make it better if she thinks you're unhappy."

"No one in my position would be happy right now." He exhales heavily. "No one around me is even happy. I'm in the *way*, Carter. Especially now." He waves both hands to the clunky cast that goes all the way up to the top of his thigh.

"I've never thought of you like that. And neither has your grandmother. In fact . . ." I blow out a breath and realize I'm *nervous*. This kid means the world to me, and I don't want to fuck this up. I know I can't fix what's broken, but if my relationship with him can give him something solid, I'm going to try. "A few months ago, I asked Marta if she'd consider letting you move in with me."

He straightens. "You did? Why didn't she tell me?"

"She didn't want to let you go. She loves you, and she'd just lost her son." I shrug. "It actually hurt her feelings that I'd even asked."

"It's not about her," he says, and there's so much excitement—*hope*—in his eyes that my chest swells. "I'm not used to living with Grandma. I love her, but she doesn't know what it's like to be a guy. And she lost a son, but I lost a *dad*, and she doesn't know what that's like either. But you get it."

"She'll let you move in with me if that's what you want. She loves you and wants what's best for you."

"But what about you? You don't have kids but you're suddenly gonna have to take care of me?"

I scoff. "Oh, hell no. You're far too old to be taken care of. I mean, I'd have rules and you'd have chores, but don't get it in your head that life at my place would be like a vacation, because I'm not about that."

He laughs, but his bright eyes dim and he leans back, his gaze locking on his lap.

"But I would like to have you there. If that's where you want to be. I have the room, and I love you. You're pretty much my fifth brother, like it or not."

"That's cool of you, Carter," he mumbles, but I can see the change in his posture—the way his expression went from hopeful and excited to withdrawn again. "You don't have to be my friend just because you were there that night, you know," he says, his voice softer than I've ever heard it. "It's not your fault he died, so it's not your job to take his place."

My heart is a stone dropping into my stomach. "I don't want to take your dad's place. I couldn't, and I wouldn't try." I swallow hard. *It's not your fault he died.* "I won't pretend I don't feel guilty that we lost him. That's there, but it has nothing to do with me wanting to be here for you."

He nods, still not meeting my gaze, and that stone in my gut turns into an ache.

"You can think about it. There's no rush to decide."

"Are you going to marry Teagan?"

The question catches me off guard and I laugh. "Hell, it's a little early for plans like that."

"But . . . ?"

"But if that's how it turned out, I'd consider myself luckier than I deserve."

After swinging by my house to get the mail, I go to Jackson Brews to grab lunch. This morning's conversation with Isaiah left me raw but hopeful. I have no doubt the arrangement would bring up a hundred complications I haven't even considered yet, but I know that it'd be worth it. If he doesn't want to live with me, that's fine, but I want him to know he's welcome. I want him to understand he might have lost his father, but he has a family beyond his grandmother.

"How's Operation Fake Boyfriend?" Jake asks, one brow cocked.

"I've moved on to Operation Make Her Mine," I say, pushing my plate away. For once, I'm stopping because I'm full and not because of my lack of appetite.

Jake grins. "I approve."

"I thought you might." I trail my thumb through the condensation on my water glass. "She has secrets."

"Don't we all?"

I nod. "Sure. I only hope she'll eventually trust me with hers."

My phone buzzes by my arm, clattering against the bar top—once, twice, three times. I grin as I grab it, expecting a text from Teagan and hoping for a picture. Or a few pictures. It's just after noon, and she thought she'd be done with the henna party by now. We don't have anything scheduled until the rehearsal and dinner tonight, and I've spent my morning preoccupied with the idea of spending the afternoon in bed with her. Maybe she could try on the lingerie her sister bought her and then spend some time getting her to let me slowly peel it off.

I unlock my phone, but my smile falls away when I realize it *is* a picture, but it's not from Teagan. Sabrina has sent me a picture of her *panties*—colorful scraps of lace and silk spread out across a stark white duvet.

> *Sabrina: Which of these is the sexiest? Asking for a friend who wants to look her best when she returns to your family's bar tonight.*
> *Sabrina: If your answer is NONE, then I can tell my friend that too.*
> *Sabrina: Or maybe I should model them to give you a better idea?*

"Fuck," I mutter. "She can't take a hint."

"Myla?" he asks.

"No, that journalist from last month. Remember the one who didn't tell me she was in town to do a story on me until *after* I took her to bed?"

Jake's eyes are wide. "I don't think you told me about that. If you'll recall, you haven't been Captain Shares-a-Lot lately." He extends a hand, palm up, for my phone. "Luckily, you've turned over a new leaf, and your brother Jake is here to help you clean up your messes."

I give it to him, and he frowns at the screen before looking back at me. "Mind if I scroll through the history?"

I grimace. "What ever happened to boundaries?"

"Oh, so it's *that* kind of history. In that case, I'm good." He hands back the phone. "Was the story she did bad?"

I drag a hand through my hair. "No, it was more of the same. She described my house like I *invited* her in to do her little investigative report, but she really wasn't saying anything everyone else didn't already say."

"You're saying it *wasn't* an exposé about how Carter the puppy hero takes home different women every night?"

I wince. "Was I really that bad?"

He lifts a shoulder in a halfhearted shrug. "Only you really know the answer to that."

I think this over for a minute. We both know that, speaking literally, I was never a *different woman every night* guy. The real question is whether my actions were as despicable as Jake made them out to be the day we fought in Brayden's backyard. Truth be told, I wouldn't judge anyone for having a couple of regular bedroom partners or for taking home a woman from time to time—assuming everything's consensual and the limitations of the relationships are clear. But maybe what upset Jake so much was that I wasn't being true to myself. Before the warehouse fire, I always wanted more. And after? After, I didn't dare want anything beyond any given moment. Because I didn't believe I deserved it. Teagan makes me want more, though.

He watches me as I type out a reply. "What are you saying?"

"That my girlfriend and I have plans all weekend, but that I hope she enjoys her visit to Jackson Harbor."

"Think that'll do the trick?" he asks, clearly unconvinced.

"Does it really matter? By the time I'm done doing wedding stuff with Teagan, she'll be gone again."

"Cross your fingers she doesn't see you and throw herself at you in front of Teagan's family."

I groan. That hadn't even occurred to me.

Chapter
TWENTY-ONE

TEAGAN

I grin when I see the door to my suite cracked. *Carter.*

I haven't gotten to spend time alone with him all day. The henna party spilled over into the afternoon—well worth it for the beautiful work Pari did, and the joy on Saanvi's face when she looked at the final product—and then Saanvi wanted all of us to go with her to the Jackson Brews Banquet Center to check on how the room was coming along for the reception. Now it's after two, and I'm already dead on my feet. We didn't sleep enough last night, and I need a nap, but if I have to choose between a little sleep and being ravished by my fake boyfriend, I already know which I'll choose.

Carter gives me butterflies, and I can't wait to be back in his arms. I need to figure out where we stand—where *I* stand. I guess he's made it clear what he wants. He wants more. He wants the real thing. And I think I do too.

I've never talked to anyone about what happened with Rich after Heath died. Never. I was always so convinced I'd sound insane—Rich convinced me of that. But once I started telling Carter, it all spilled out of me. Carter didn't make me feel crazy or try to convince me I was overreacting. He listened and made me feel safe. Understood. I didn't realize how much I needed that. So now I need to decide if what's happening between us might actually become something real. Or if maybe it is already.

I push into the room and shut the door behind me.

"Carter?" The lights are off, but candlelight flickers ahead, the flames seeming to dance to Dave Matthews' "The Space Between" from the bedside stereo. The song brings back memories, but I shove them away. Carter's trying to be sweet. He has no way of knowing that I associate this song with Rich, or that Rich would always make sure it played any time we were at a bar or party together after Heath died—a little reminder that was like a razor blade running across the open wound of my grief.

"Carter?" I call again. Did he set the stage for seduction and *leave*? He's a firefighter—would he really walk away from burning candles?

When I step farther into the room, my phone buzzes, and I wonder if it's Carter explaining that he had to run out. Instead, I have a text from the same number that sent me that awful picture. *Rich.*

> Unknown Number: *You always made me jump through such hoops for your attention, but I know this night's been on your mind as much as it's been on mine.*

My stomach free-falls before surging violently back up into my throat. Candles flicker all around the bed, and on the center of the mattress there's a single red rose and a bottle of Swagger from Paradise Springs winery. The bourbon-barrel-aged wine used to be my favorite, but there's only one person alive who'd know that or know that it and this song would all bring back memories of a night better left forgotten.

I'm tense all night.

The rehearsal dinner is served in the gardens behind the Hayhurst mansion. It's so beautiful out here that I understand why Saanvi initially hoped to do her reception in this spot. However, destination wedding or not, the guest list grew too large, and the ballroom at Jackson Brews Banquet Center was the obvious location. I reassured her that Molly would do a beautiful job making the reception everything Saanvi's dreamed of, but there is something magical about these gardens in the moonlight.

Strings of fairy lights twinkle above the tables, and a jazz quartet plays from their spot in the gazebo. We've enjoyed four delicious courses with wine pairings, and conversation flows easily as we wait for dessert. The night's grown chilly, and the staff brought out big outdoor heaters to sit on the edges of the cobblestone patio, allowing us to be comfortable in our dresses and still enjoy the starry autumn night sky.

Everything's beautiful, and I'm surrounded by my family.

I should be happy.

Instead, I feel like there's a weight on my chest too heavy to let me take in a deep breath.

Before Carter returned to our suite this afternoon, I turned off the music and blew out the candles, throwing them in the trash with the wine and the rose. When that still left me feeling jumpy, I ran the bin to housekeeping and asked them to empty it. I needed to physically distance myself from the evidence that Rich had been in our room—from the reminders that he holds a secret of mine.

I'd desperately wanted alone time with Carter before the rehearsal, but the scene Rich set changed all of that—changed my whole mood to the point where I practically avoided Carter for the short time we were alone together. When I saw Rich before dinner, I was torn between wanting to hide and wanting to scream at him. I did neither. I'm stuck, and he knows it.

He smiled and looked me over like a lover would. I wanted to claw those eyes out.

From his devoted-boyfriend post beside me, Carter didn't miss a thing. The meal started with him flashing me knowing smiles and touching my hand and bare shoulder at any given opportunity. But I couldn't focus on him and spent my time watching the faces around us and bracing for Rich to drop a bomb on my life. The more I withdrew from Carter's touches, the more I failed to return his sweet gestures, the less he tried. We spent the last two courses silent beside each other, like a couple of strangers.

Carter frowns in Rich's direction. I'm guessing he's clued in to who's responsible for this shift between us. "Is everything okay?"

The waiter leans between us to serve dessert, and I smile at him and wait for him to serve Carter before I reply. "Everything's fine. Why?"

He shakes his head, but I can tell he wants to push the issue.

As I poke at my lemon torte, my phone buzzes with a text.

I pull it from my purse and flinch. It's from Rich. *Shit.* I need to block this damn new number. Should I do it now or wait until the weekend is over? If I block him now will he do worse than harass me with old pictures?

Before I can decide, I read the text.

> *I learned some interesting things about Carter today. We need to talk. My room. Tonight. Eleven. Only tell Carter if you want him to see my photo collection.*

I shove my phone back into my purse before Carter sees.

My gaze drifts to Rich as everyone finishes their dessert. What does he think he knows? He catches me looking and winks, his grin suggesting lovers' secrets and quiet promises.

I hate him so much.

Carter touches my wrist, and I jump. "Are you sure you're okay?" he asks softly.

"Yeah." I force a smile. "Fine. A little chilly." He starts to shrug out of his coat, but I put a hand on his arm. "Don't. I'm fine."

He studies me for a long beat before lifting a hand to my face and cupping my jaw. "Don't shut me out, okay? You don't have to do this alone."

The words rock me so hard that my throat goes thick, and I have to swallow back tears. *I feel so damn alone.*

I don't want to lie to Carter. But I don't want him to know the truth, either. *There's the rub.*

"Carter!" Liam calls from the opposite side of the patio. "Come here. I want you to meet my cousin."

Carter nods at him then searches my face one more time before pulling away.

I can't sit still anymore, so I'm happy to follow everyone's lead and leave the table. I weave through the small crowd and step into the dim sitting area just off the patio where vines climb white trellises up the side of a gazebo.

Carter's words echo in my head. *"You don't have to do this alone."* But don't I? What's the alternative? What would Carter think of me if he saw those pictures? If he knew what I did?

I'm not left alone with my thoughts for long before my sister joins me. "Are you and Carter fighting?"

I shake my head. "We're fine. Why?"

"You looked distant all through dinner. I thought maybe he said something that upset you." She bumps my shoulder with hers. "Let me know if you need me to beat him up."

I snort. "That wouldn't be a fair fight."

"Hey, I can hold my own."

I laugh. "Oh, I know you can. It wouldn't be fair because Carter wouldn't fight back."

She sighs and watches him talk to her fiancé across the patio before turning back to me. "You're really okay?"

The words are right there on my tongue: *I hate that Rich is here. He ruined my whole life, and I'll never be able to escape him as long as he's welcome with our family.*

My sister would tell him to leave right now if I asked her. And then she would corner me for an explanation I can't give.

Before I can decide on a response to her question, Saanvi stiffens and folds her arms. "Look who's finally here."

I follow her gaze to the bustle of the aunts' excited squeals as Sabrina steps onto the patio. My cousin is as striking as ever with her long red hair and perfect ivory skin. I was so jealous of her when we were growing up. She was the classic American beauty that adolescent me longed to be. It took me until I was in college to see the beauty of my olive skin, dark hair, and dramatic curves.

Those insecurities slammed back into me full force when Health cheated on me with her. It was just once. One drunken blow job. The first domino of many that turned my happy little life into a disaster I needed to run from.

Sabrina doles out hugs to our relatives before spotting Saanvi and rushing toward us with open arms. "Saanvi! I thought I'd never get here."

Sighing, my sister hugs our cousin. "That makes two of us."

"I'm so sorry I missed the rehearsal. And the henna!" Sabrina steps back and takes one of Saanvi's hands in hers, investigating it in the dim light. "Oh, it's beautiful."

"Thank you," Saanvi says, and I can feel the tension drain from her. She's never been able to stay mad at Sabrina for long. "Pari said she can come to your room tonight to do your hands if you want."

Sabrina presses her palm to her chest. "She'd do that for me? That would be wonderful." She smiles at me, but I can't help but notice that she doesn't offer me a hug. "Teagan, it's so good to see you."

"You too." We're both lying, and we know it. I already feel an ache in my gut at the sight of the cousin. She's never forgiven me for what she saw in Heath's bedroom that day more than four years ago, and I've never had the courage to explain. I let her believe the worst of me because the truth made me feel even dirtier than the lie.

"How'd the rehearsal go?" she asks, her gaze swinging back to Saanvi.

"Smoothly, considering we were missing a bridesmaid," Saanvi says, but there's no bitterness in her voice. "Teagan's boyfriend stood in as you while we ran through the ceremony and figured out where everyone will stand."

My gaze drifts to Carter again. His antics at the rehearsal gave me my only genuine smiles of the whole afternoon. Carter made us all laugh, pretending to hold a bouquet and lifting his imaginary skirts as he walked up and down the church steps.

"I didn't know you had a *boyfriend*," Sabrina says, smacking my arm lightly. "Do tell!"

I shrug. "We've been dating a couple of months. His name is Carter Jackson." I nod across the patio to the man in question. He's engrossed in one of my dad's stories and doesn't notice us.

"And he's a *dream*," Saanvi says. "You should see how he looks at her. It's something out of a fairytale."

Something shifts in Sabrina's expression as she takes Carter in.

Saanvi squeezes Sabrina's shoulder. "I need to go rescue Liam. If I had to guess by the way she keeps gesturing to his butt, I'd say Aunt Tammy is giving him her fiber lecture. I'm glad you made it safely. We'll talk later."

She rushes over to Liam, who's looking mildly horrified as our mother's sister speaks. I can't hear their conversation over the music, but I catch the words *bowels* and *roughage*, and I know Saanvi's mission is indeed dire.

"I didn't realize you were dating Carter Jackson," Sabrina says.

"Well . . ." I swallow. "We were friends first, so we kept it quiet for a while. We didn't want everyone's expectations weighing on us. You know?"

She worries her bottom lip between her teeth as she stares at him. "I guess that makes sense." Crossing her arms, she rubs her hands over her bare shoulders. "And to think I believed this would be the weekend you finally got back together with Rich." She meets my gaze, and there's something hard and bitter in those icy blue eyes.

"Rich and I are over *for good*."

"Hmm. We'll see."

I want to rail at her for judging me for what she *thinks* I did to Heath when Heath cheated on me with *her*. *Hypocrite much, Sabrina?* But she never believed she did anything wrong with Heath. He'd told her about a fight we were having, and she assumed we were breaking up. The truth is that Heath was drunk, and she saw an opportunity to get him back. She believed what she wanted to believe. I bite the inside of my cheek and push down the old anger—at her, at Heath.

"How long did you say you and Carter have been together?" she asks.

"Casually for a while, I guess, but we've gotten serious the last two months." I swallow the bitter taste the lie leaves in my mouth. I'm not close to Sabrina, but she's the person here who would most enjoy catching me in this lie. I guess that's what I signed up for by asking Carter to pretend to be my boyfriend.

"Did Carter ever . . . mention me?"

I frown. I didn't expect *that*. "You and Carter know each other?"

Her porcelain-perfect cheeks flush bright red. "We don't *know* each other. Not well, at least. I came to town and interviewed him." She clears her throat and dodges my gaze. "After the whole puppy-rescue thing?"

She came to Jackson Harbor and didn't even tell me she was here. Of course. Because she still doesn't like me after . . . everything. I try not to let it sting, but it does. "Did you tell him you were my cousin?"

She shrugs. "Your name never came up."

I lift my chin. "I guess you had no way of knowing he and I were close friends."

"And more," she says softly. "Apparently."

For the first time, Carter tears his attention away from my father and looks across the patio, spotting us. There's heat in his eyes when he grins at me, his eyes dragging over my dress in a way that suggests how he plans to peel it off me later. Then his gaze shifts to Sabrina, and he does a double take and pales.

I don't blame him. He wants the attention from the puppy incident to die down, and now he's going to be right next to a story-hungry journalist for the rest of the weekend.

"You know, I'm feeling a little jet-lagged," Sabrina says. "I think I'll go say goodnight to the happy couple and see about getting Pari to do my henna in the morning so I can tuck in early." Her throat bobs. "I want to be at my best for Saanvi's big day tomorrow."

I nod. I've had enough awkward small talk anyway. I'm ready to sneak away with Carter, apologize for my mood at dinner, and have him hold me until I forget that Rich was in our room earlier. Instead I have to figure out how to get to Rich's room tonight without Carter knowing. "Okay, sure. It was good to see you."

"You too." Her gaze lands on Carter again, but this time I see something like longing in her eyes.

He's mine, bitch. I swallow the hateful words, and when she brings her gaze back to me, I simply smile. "Sleep well."

Chapter
TWENTY-TWO

CARTER

I can't tear my eyes off the redhead as she walks away from Teagan and heads into the building. *Sabrina the journalist and the journalist bridesmaid are the same fucking person.* If I hadn't been so preoccupied by Teagan and the shit with Rich, maybe the thought would have occurred to me. It should have.

I'm so fucked.

Frantically, I look to Teagan. I need to get her alone so we can figure out what the hell we're supposed to do. I stare her down, trying to get her attention, but she's busy staring at her phone. Seems like she's been busy staring at anything but me all night. I hate it. It's like she's already pushing me away, and I have to remind myself over and over again not to cling to that which was never mine.

"You're coming out with us tonight, right, Carter?" Liam asks.

"Of course he is," Trevor says, slinging an arm around my shoulders. "Guys gotta stick together."

"I don't know. I was hoping to turn in early with my girl."

Trevor waves away my objection. "You get to see her all the time. When's the next time we'll all get to go out again? Probably not until you and Teagan tie the knot."

I swallow at the image his words flash into my mind and the feeling that it's beyond my reach. Teagan in white, wearing my ring, promising to be mine. *Don't think about it.*

"Just for a couple of drinks," Liam says, grinning. "Come on. You can make sure we order the best beers. We're counting on you."

My phone buzzes. *Teagan.* But once again it's not, and when I see the text, my stomach sinks.

Sabrina: Does she know we slept together?

I darken the screen before the curious eyes around me can read it. I feel this whole charade falling apart. *Fuck, fuck, fuck.* I need to talk to Teagan so we can figure out a plan. She's already pushing me away. What happens when she finds out I had a one-night stand with her cousin? Will she shut down, stop this between us before we even get a real chance to start? Should we tell Sabrina the truth to keep this from imploding on us? Tell her Teagan and I weren't exclusive back when Sabrina came to town? At the very least, we need to get our stories straight.

"What do you say?" Liam asks. "Join us?"

I slide my phone back into my pocket as it buzzes again, just as Rich returns to the party and takes Teagan by the arm. My whole body goes into battle mode.

Don't fucking touch her.

"Everything okay, Carter?" Liam asks.

"Yeah. I think so. I'll be right back."

"Carter," Rich calls when he spots me walking toward them. He waves me over. "Just the man I want to see."

I watch Teagan's posture beside this man she loathes, a study in casual grace. Is she trying to pretend that he doesn't bother her for the sake of the rest of the party? I know she doesn't want anything to do with Rich—or so she says—but then, she couldn't keep her eyes off him tonight. What's that about? And why has she kept me at an arm's length all afternoon? Did something happen between them?

"What did you think of the gift I left you two earlier?" He beams, bright eyes and a wide smile, as if he's truly our friend.

"What gift?"

Rich looks at Teagan and cocks a brow before looking back at me, confused. "You haven't been to your room?"

I fold my arms. I don't know what the fuck he's talking about, but I have a feeling that if I admit that, it'll be some giant *gotcha*. "Did you need something, Rich?"

He shakes his head slowly. "You two are really something. I'm starting to figure out what that something is." He smacks me on the back—harder than necessary. "Are you going out tonight? You should be there for Teagan's future brother-in-law. That's what Teagan's boyfriend would do, right?"

I try to catch Teagan's eye to get some sort of feel from her about how I'm supposed to handle all of this, but she's still staring at the ground. Did she tell him this is all fake? Why won't she look me in the eye?

Dammit. I need to talk to her. Alone. I need to tell her about Sabrina so we can decide how to deal with it. *Together.* Our lies are crumbling beneath our feet, and with them, the fragile beginnings of this thing between us.

I touch her wrist gently. "I don't need to go out. I'll stay with you."

She shakes her head, still avoiding my eyes. "Liam wants you there. You should go with him. I'll be with Saanvi most of the night anyway."

I touch her one last time, not wanting to let go but knowing she's right—*Rich* is right. I should go with Liam. Teagan and I can talk later. She'll do her thing with the bride and I'll have a couple of drinks with the groom and groomsmen. We can talk when we both get back to the room.

Two hours later, and I have to admit that I'm procrastinating. I'm nervous about the conversation I need to have with Teagan, and hanging out with the guys is the perfect excuse to avoid it.

Rich declined the invitation to join us, so at least I don't have to deal with his shit, and hanging out with Liam is no hardship. Honestly, if this guy lived in Jackson Harbor, I could see us being good friends. He'd fit in great with my family, and so would Saanvi. But I know my decision to have a third beer is less about enjoying the company of Liam and his groomsmen and more about avoiding a conversation about Sabrina. Am I making a bigger deal of this than it is? Will Teagan hold it against me when I tell her I slept with her cousin?

You know how you aren't sure you want to be with me for real because you're afraid I'll break your heart? Well, hey, I might have a head start on that.

I vacillate between telling myself that it doesn't matter—Teagan and I weren't together, pretend or otherwise, when I slept with Sabrina—and trying to figure out how I can keep the truth from Teagan altogether.

All in all, I'm enjoying the safe little bubble of Jackson Brews, until Sabrina walks in the door and I wish I were anywhere else.

I half expect her to march up to our table and start chewing me out, but I guess I should have given her more credit. She catches my eye from her spot at the bar and nods toward the door before heading back out the way she came in.

"Are you okay?" Liam asks, frowning at me. He turns around, scanning the room. "You look like you saw a ghost."

I paste on a smile. "That last beer hit me pretty hard. I'll be right back." I head toward the bathroom, waiting until the last second before changing direction and heading to the door.

When the doors close behind me, Sabrina waves me over from her spot in the alley.

Cringing, I reluctantly follow. The last time I was in this alley with her . . . well, she wanted me to fuck her against the building, and I was *barely* sober enough to realize that was a terrible idea and I should take her home instead.

I keep to the street side of the alley, not anxious to slip into the shadows with a woman who continued to text me after I told her I had a girlfriend. "Hey," I say softly.

"Hey." She takes a step toward me and scans my face. "How are you?"

I shrug. *Been better.*

"I feel like a bitch for being persistent with the texts. I didn't realize it was serious." She bites her lip. "And I definitely didn't realize it was Teagan. I haven't told her about our night together. And if I had to guess from the look of terror in your eyes right now, neither have you."

I swallow. I want to tell myself that she's misreading me, but I do feel guilty—whether that's rational or not. I feel guilty for sleeping with Sabrina to begin with, guilty for not making Teagan talk to me before I left tonight, and guilty for the lies I'm about to tell a woman I had in my bed less than a month ago. What can I do but continue to play the part of the boyfriend, even if it makes me look like a jackass?

"Did you know I was her cousin when you slept with me?" she asks.

I drag a hand through my hair. "No. You didn't mention it, and your last name isn't Chopra. It's . . ." *Fuck.* I have no idea. Did she even tell me her last name? No wonder Jake read me the riot act. I don't even know who that asshole was.

Sabrina lets out a small squeak. "Cruise."

Right. Sabrina Cruise. I remember her byline under the damn article she published. "I didn't know you were related."

"Does she know you were sleeping around?" When I open my mouth, she holds up a hand. "Do you two have an . . . agreement or something? I'm not judging. I just need to know what kind of mess I've walked into."

Her question makes me think of that weird conversation I

had with Rich in the dining room this morning. What was it he said? That Teagan made sure she did what she needed to stay satisfied?

What happened in her old life to give these people an impression of her that is so completely different than the woman I know?

"It's not like that," I say. I don't think Teagan would ask me to play the part of her boyfriend and then have me tell her family we have an open relationship.

Sabrina grips her little red purse in both hands, her knuckles white. "So she *doesn't* know?"

"I don't want to hurt her." As soon as the words are out, I realize they're true. Teagan would be hurt if she knew I slept with Sabrina. I'm afraid I'll lose her completely if I tell her the truth about Sabrina before I figure out what scared her off this afternoon.

"And I don't want her to hurt you."

I frown. This seems like an odd time for her to worry about my heart, given that she thinks I betrayed Teagan.

Sabrina sighs. "What a mess."

"I'm really sorry. That night with you . . ." Telling a woman I took home that she was a *mistake* feels like a jackass thing to do, even if it's true, so I don't let myself finish that sentence. "I'm sorry."

She blows out a breath. "No big deal. I mean, you two can't be too serious, right? So we keep it under wraps, and in a week or two it won't matter."

"Teagan's my girlfriend." *And I'm fucking praying I'll still be able to say that next week.*

Sabrina snorts. "Sure. For now."

The words are worse than a knee to my nuts. "I'll tell her about what happened with us, but let me . . ." I turn away, watching as my brother Ethan pushes out of the bar with his wife Nic. Arm in arm, they look so damn happy. I want that, and I know exactly who I want it with. I've known since that day I pulled her into my arms at the lake. I take a step into the shadows so they can't see me, waiting until they pass before I speak again. "Let me find the right time to tell her. She has enough going on this weekend, and I don't want to ruin it."

"So you know she's meeting Rich tonight?"

My stomach sinks. "Why? Did he need something?"

Sabrina laughs, a low, sardonic chuckle. "Oh, bless your heart, Carter. Didn't you wonder why Rich didn't join the guys? And Teagan conveniently had a 'stomachache' when Saanvi and the others left for the martini bar. If you really think Rich and Teagan are alone in that big mansion together and *not* banging each other's brains out, then you don't know her nearly as well as you think you do."

What *the fuck* with all of her family thinking they belong together? "Sabrina, listen, I think you're hurt and maybe a little jealous, and throwing around some pretty gross assumptions."

"Oh, hell yes, I'm jealous. I'm always jealous of Teagan because she gets *everything* she wants and then she throws it away." She blows out a breath. "I know what I'm talking about when it comes to Tea and Rich. I know better than *anyone.*" She laughs again. "I'm guessing she didn't tell you all the details about their history, did she?"

I stiffen. I don't like this conversation, but worse is this dread crawling up my throat. Teagan wouldn't meet my eyes tonight, and she was trying to get rid of me. I thought she wanted some distance after an intense night and morning together. Is she really meeting with him? "I know they were together again after Heath died. She told me."

The corner of her mouth twists smugly. "*After*." She steps forward, shaking her head. "Yes, they were together after. But not again. *Still*."

I scowl. "What?"

"There are enough of us who know the truth about her relationship with Heath. It wasn't as perfect as she lets on. She wasn't as faithful as she'd have everyone believe, and neither was he. She'll deny it, but I know. Rich knows."

She's jealous. Hurt and upset. "I don't want to have this conversation with you. Teagan can tell me whatever I need to know."

"But why would she?" She shrugs. "Fine. Go back to the mansion and ask her about it. I suggest checking Rich's room if she's not in yours."

My stomach curdles at the idea, but no. Teagan wouldn't sleep with Rich. He terrifies her. She asked me here to be a buffer between them. She even warned me that he'd try to get in my head. I wonder if she knows her cousin is just as bad. "Why do you hate her so much? You and I had *one* night. Why be so terrible to her?"

"You're a nice guy, Carter. And I think that night, part of you already knew you and Teagan wouldn't last. Otherwise, you would've never taken another woman home." She draws in a ragged breath. "I'm pissed you didn't tell me you had a girlfriend.

You're not off the hook for that—I've been the other woman before, and I never would have cast me in that role again if I'd known."

"You sent me pictures of your underwear after I told you I have a girlfriend."

"I didn't think it was *serious.*"

Bullshit. I clench my teeth so tight my jaw clicks.

"But despite that," she says, her voice softer now, "I still believe you deserve better than a woman who will always end up back in Rich Nasser's bed."

Chapter
TWENTY-THREE

TEAGAN

I knock on Rich's door at 10:59. I can't risk being late. Can't risk him punishing me by sending those pictures to Carter—pictures of me in Heath's bed. With Rich. Pictures of a night that has haunted me since it happened.

Rich pulls the door open. He's shirtless, his jeans slung low on his hips. I can't deny he has a beautiful body. He's strong and built from long hours at the gym and a strict bodybuilder's diet. I'm in the same black dress I wore to dinner, and he looks me over slowly—*so* slowly that I want to take a hot shower and scrub away every inch of skin his eyes touch. "You've done such a good job avoiding me the last few years, I didn't think you'd show." He pulls the door wider. "Come on in."

"I'd rather not."

He arches a brow. "I thought we already established that the ball's in my court now. I'm done chasing you, Teagan."

If only that were really true. "Fine, but keep the door open."

His nostrils flare, and his eyes flash with anger. "Have I ever—*ever*—forced myself on you?"

I lift my chin. "Door. Open."

"Sure. If you want everyone who passes by to hear what I know, it's your call."

Everyone who passes by. There's no one in the halls right now. Everyone's out celebrating and probably will be for a couple more hours. Even my parents are staying out late to take advantage of the time with all their best friends in one place, and he knows it. That's why he suggested this time to meet.

Ignoring the warning bells blaring in my head, I step into the room. "What do you want?"

"You." He shrugs. As if it's so simple. As if he's asking for a glass of water. "That's all I've ever wanted."

"Too bad. I'm with Carter."

He chuckles, shoving his hands into his pockets and nudging those jeans lower. "But you're not. Not really."

My stomach plummets. "What are you talking about?"

He turns into the room, and his message is clear. He has the power, and I'm going to have to follow him inside if I want to know more.

I take a deep breath and walk down the short hall and into the room, leaving the door wide open behind me. *I can do this.*

He sits on the edge of the bed, propping himself on his arms behind him. "Was this really all for me? Did I commit some terrible offense that made you so desperate to be rid of me that you'd create a fake relationship?"

My muscles lock up. *He can't know.* "There's nothing fake about me and Carter."

"I've been doing a little detective work." He laughs. "Not that it was hard. A town this size, and everyone is dying to talk. And the guys at Carter's station? Well, let's just say they shouldn't be trusted with any state secrets." His grin is slow and vicious. "One of two things is happening here, Teagan. Either Carter is playing you, or you two are only pretending to be together."

I will the emotion to stay off my face, but I don't know if it works. It's hard not to give away the surge of my stomach to my throat. I screwed this up. Rich knows our lie, and now I can't even think straight. "You don't know what you're talking about."

"I'll be honest—I was fishing a little earlier. I knew about Myla and the redheaded nurse, but neither would talk to me to confirm anything. But then when Sabrina came to my room crying, I knew, I *knew* you and Carter weren't for real. I mean, it seems he has a thing for redheads."

What? "What about Sabrina?" I think I might throw up on my shoes.

"Sabrina came to town to do a story a month ago."

"I know she did." I swallow back bile. It's all coming together, and I feel like I've been punched in the gut. Sabrina's confusion about how long Carter and I have been dating, her nosing around about the status of our relationship. *He slept with her.*

And because Carter and I were supposedly dating then, she thinks he cheated on me. It's not fair that I feel hurt. We *weren't* together. We weren't even pretending to be.

"This is excellent. She didn't think you knew, and it looks like she was right." Rich lazily scratches his bare stomach. "And even though your boyfriend's fake as fuck, you hate the idea that she slept with Carter. You and your cousin are something. Still fighting over men after all these years."

Rich is a liar and manipulator. Don't fall for it. "This is ridiculous. You know nothing about me and Carter. You can't stand the idea that we're together—can't stand that there's no way you can worm yourself back into my bed—so you're throwing out conspiracy theories."

He stands and steps toward me. "So you're okay with the fact that your boyfriend has fucked at least three other women in the last month."

"We started as friends. He stopped seeing them when we got serious."

He cocks a brow and takes a step closer. "But he never told you about Sabrina?"

I shrug. "It doesn't matter." This is my fault. I knew Carter wanted to talk to me earlier, and I ignored all the signals because I was too afraid of missing this meeting and Rich punishing me by sharing those pictures. "Will you please delete those pictures? That's all I want from you."

"How badly do you want that?" With a flick of his wrist, he releases the button on his jeans. "What would you do for it?"

My nostrils flare, my fists clenching at my sides. "Cut off your dick? Sure, Rich. Let me grab a knife from the kitchen. I'll be right back."

He chuckles softly, completely unfazed by my threat. "God, I've missed that mouth of yours. And I know you've missed mine too. I remember how much you liked it."

"*Fuck. You.* If I wanted you, I knew where to find you. Anyone else would've caught on by now."

"You *did* want me." His jaw ticks. "You wanted me so badly you let me take you in his bed. You wanted me when you were still wearing your funeral dress."

My eyes burn, but I'll be damned if I let him see me cry. "*Don't* throw that in my face."

"I wouldn't. Not when I'm the only one who understands your guilt, and the only one who really knows you don't deserve to feel that way. You and I both know you'd have done anything to make him happy. You proved it, and it's not your fault he didn't know himself better." He lifts a hand and drops it before he touches my face. "But it's been years, and I'm tired of seeing you—"

"Hey, Rich, have you seen . . ." Carter steps into the room, and I spring away from Rich. As if I've done something wrong. As if I have something to be ashamed of. "Teagan," he says softly, meeting my gaze for only a beat before his eyes dart around the room, taking in the scene. The two wine glasses on the desk I didn't notice before. Rich's bare chest and unbuttoned jeans. Carter's Adam's apple bobs. "Sorry. The door was wide open."

"Told you we should close it," Rich says, smirking at me. "I'm sorry, Carter. Teagan and I were talking. Memories, you know. There are some things only our oldest friends understand."

"Right." Carter takes a step back. "I'm going to the room, Teagan. See you later." He doesn't even spare me a final look over his shoulder as he strides away, pulling the door shut with a harsh *clunk* behind him.

"Fuck," I say, rushing after him.

"Teagan—"

I spin on Rich. "Don't. I'm sorry about everything that happened. I'm sorry I ever made you believe we were meant for each other. I'm sorry I let Heath push me into something I didn't want. But mostly, I'm sorry you don't understand how fucking controlling and manipulative you are. We're *never* getting back together, and if you don't move the fuck on, I'll file a restraining order. I don't care if that means you plaster the internet with those pictures and tell everyone what a whore I am. I'm done with you. *Done.*"

I race out the door and run to the opposite end of the hall and up the stairs to our suite, unlocking the door and shutting it softly behind me. It's too quiet in here, and the silence rings in my ears.

Carter is sitting on the couch, his head buried in his hands.

"When you walked in . . . it wasn't what it looked like." My voice is shaking, and when he lifts his head and levels that weary gaze on me, everything else seems insignificant. I don't care about Rich or my parents or the pictures. I want to make him stop looking at me like that.

"That's good," Carter says, his voice rough, "because it looked pretty damn bad."

"I don't *want* him."

"Because you don't want anyone, right? Sure, you date and pretend you're looking for that special someone, but you'll never let any of them get too close. You never wanted *me* to get too close. If I did, I might have seen that you were a little broken inside, like the rest of us."

I gape at him, anger slashing through me. "You're going to accuse me of hiding my feelings? What about you, Carter? What about the way you've been sleeping around to avoid your pain and guilt? You can't pretend that's not a coping mechanism. Not with me. I lived that shit."

Exhaustion lines his face as he shakes his head. "I showed you my ugly insides. But I don't do lies, Teagan. Not with the people who matter to me. Not with you. If you don't want your parents to know what happened between you and Rich all those years ago, then fine. Don't tell them. But don't hide behind me one second and arrange to meet him in private the next."

I can't catch my breath. I keep trying, but I can't seem to force air into my lungs. "What do you mean, what *happened* between me and Rich? I told you."

"Did you? Everything?" He huffs and drags a hand through his hair. "I talked to Sabrina tonight. She said you weren't faithful to Heath."

Of course Sabrina said something. After all these years, I knew she'd be the one. "She doesn't know anything."

"Really?" He grunts out a laugh, but his face twists into a nasty sneer. *At me. He's sneering at me.* I want to hate him for that sneer. To walk away. But part of me will always believe I deserve to be seen the way he sees me right now. "Did you cheat on Heath with Rich?"

Even when I know they're coming, the words are a blow to my gut. "No," I say between clenched teeth. "I never cheated on Heath."

"So you've told me everything? Shown me all *your* ugly insides?" He stares at me, and when I don't answer, he nods. "Exactly. You have no plans on opening up about what's really between you and Rich. But why would you? This is just pretend.

You and me? This is over the second your family leaves town."

"I never said that."

"I offered you more. I told you what I want. You didn't say no, but where I come from, when a woman doesn't say yes, you take it as a fucking *no*."

My chest shudders as I pull in a breath. *This hurts.* "And what about you? You got all this from *Sabrina*? Did you fuck her tonight too?"

Those dark chocolate eyes go cold. "You know I wouldn't."

"I know you *did*. Last month when she was here, you fucked her. You want to know why I keep pulling away?" I ask, folding my arms. "*That's* why. Because no matter how attracted I am to you, no matter how good we are in bed together . . . I'm not interested in being one of your days of the week."

"Jesus, Teagan. You know I want more than that."

I know he does—*I do*. I knew the objection was bullshit the second it came out of my mouth. "I can't." God, this hurts, and I know I'm making it worse, but I'm so scared. I feel my heart breaking again—breaking like it did when Heath accused me of wanting Rich more than him, accused me of doing what he asked and liking it *too much*, breaking like it did when the chief of police came to the door hours after our worst fight and told me Heath was dead. I can't love someone like that again. "I'm sorry, Carter, but I can't." He stands and steps toward me, but I'm already backing out of the room. "I'm going to stay with Saanvi tonight. I understand if you want to leave."

"I'll go to the wedding. I'll pretend we're whatever you want me to pretend to be."

I swallow hard. The tears are coming, and once they start, I'll be a mess. "You don't have to."

"I'll be there," he says. "I made you a promise."

You made me fall in love with you.

I step into the hall and pull the door shut behind me.

Chapter
TWENTY-FOUR

CARTER

Teagan didn't come back last night. Three different times, I headed toward Saanvi's suite and made myself turn around. We were both angry. Hurt.

I still don't know what to believe about her and Rich, but it looked bad. She was in his room, inches from him, and he was half-naked with his pants unbuttoned. If I'd found them like that in *our* room, I'd have assumed Rich had pushed his way in, would've tackled him to protect her. But that wasn't the case. She went to him. They planned that meeting and waited until everyone else was gone to have it.

There's more I need to know, but she'll never share it with me. I need to be okay with that. I need to be okay with letting her go. Even if it kills me.

I go down to breakfast, hoping I'll spot her there. I don't. I spend the whole meal checking my phone for a text from her every other minute, starting texts *to* her just as often and not letting myself send them.

After breakfast, I go back to the room and pack my things. Part of letting her go means giving her space. So after I've fulfilled my promise to her at the wedding and reception, I'll head home.

I take a long shower and shave. I'm still in a towel when my phone buzzes, and I snag it to see a text from Isaiah.

Isaiah: I can't move in with you.

I take a breath and frown at my phone. He *can't*, or he doesn't want to?

Me: Whatever you want. The offer stands if you change your mind.
Isaiah: I want to, but I can't.
Me: Why not?
Isaiah: Because it's my fault.
Me: You made a mistake, but you won't do it again.
Isaiah: Not the accident. Dad. It's my fault he's dead.

I brace myself on the bathroom vanity and stare at Isaiah's text. One emotion after another slams into me, too fast to identify. This poor kid. I don't know why he could possibly think that, but I understand the feeling all too well.

It's still early. I could go to Marta's and still be at the church in time for the wedding.

Me: I'm coming over. I'll be there in thirty.

Someone knocks on the door, and relief floods me. *Teagan.* It's like she knew I needed her right now.

"Did you forget your key?" I call, tightening the towel around my waist.

If she answers, I don't hear it over the sound of the maid vacuuming in the hall. I unlock the door. I'm so relieved to have her close that I'm actually smiling—even if this is a mess, even if I don't know how we're going to fix this, I just want to see her. I want to tell her what Isaiah said, want to explain that no matter what happens between us, she'll always be precious to me.

When I yank the door open, my smile falls away. It's Sabrina when I expected Teagan. *Theme of the fucking weekend.*

"Sabrina. What do you need?" Dread curdles in my stomach as I scan the hall for Teagan. She didn't come. She won't. After our fight, she probably doesn't want to see my face.

Maybe I should have gone home last night.

Sabrina steps into the room and looks me over with a small, sad smile. "I was hoping we could talk again."

Shit. Shit, shit, shit. "I can't right now. I need to run out for a bit."

"Please." The word rips out of her like a sob. "Please, Carter?"

I told Isaiah thirty minutes. I can talk to Sabrina for a few before I head that way. "Let me get dressed, and then we can go down and get coffee together or something." I turn to the bathroom.

"Wait."

I stop and face her. "What?"

"I'm going to lose my nerve, so let me say this, okay?"

Nodding slowly, I fold my arms. "Okay."

She draws in a ragged breath. "You're a good guy, Carter. You aren't a cheater." I wait, unsure how to respond, and she laughs. "Though I guess you kind of are . . ." Turning, she starts to pace the room. "I've thought about that night we had together so many times. I felt something special, and I think you felt it too. If you hadn't, you wouldn't have taken me home with you."

"Sabrina . . ."

She stops pacing in front of the bed and stares at the rumpled sheets. What does she see there? Are the rumpled sheets proof enough of what's between Teagan and me, or does she know that Teagan stayed with her sister last night?

When she turns back to me, there are tears in her eyes. "I like you a lot, Carter, and you deserve better than Teagan."

I almost laugh. "I think you have that backward."

"Heath deserved better than her too, but the moment he spotted her, it was like I didn't exist anymore. And look what she did to him."

I replay her words in my head. "You were with Heath?"

"We were . . . dating. Until he dropped me for her." She shakes her head. "I told him he deserved better, and he didn't listen. I'm telling you the same thing. Maybe you made a mistake with me, but that's because we have a connection. Just like Teagan has a connection with Rich that will always lead her back to him."

"Sabrina, you don't really want me."

"I do." She steps closer to me and places her palm flat against my bare chest. "I want you to choose me."

"No." Christ, I feel bad for this woman. The desperation in

her eyes has nothing to do with me and her, and everything to do with her personal demons. "You want to be chosen over Teagan. That's not the same thing."

"Do you love her or something?"

"Yeah." I swallow hard as the truth slams into me. I should tell Teagan before I tell Sabrina, but here I am. I won't deny it. "Not *or something*. I'm in love with her." My throat burns. *I am.* I fucking love a woman who's pushing me away because I'm a mess.

Dad. It's my fault he's dead.

Maybe we're all a mess.

Sabrina blinks away. "You weren't in love with her when you took me to bed."

"That doesn't change how I feel now."

Hurt washes over her face before she stomps toward the door. "Don't say I didn't warn you."

TEAGAN

I knock on the door first. It's ridiculous, I guess. I mean, it's my room too, but after our fight last night—after the things I said—I feel like he deserves some privacy. So I knock, and when he doesn't respond, I knock again.

I was grateful that Saanvi was nearly drunk upon returning to her suite last night. She was giggly and chatty and completely oblivious to the fact that I was one wrong word away from falling apart. I slept like hell, wondering if I'd ruined everything between me and Carter, wondering if we ever stood a chance to begin with.

"Carter?" *No answer.*

I use my key and squeeze my eyes shut at what awaits me inside. His suitcase is packed and sitting by the door. He's ready to leave, and I can't blame him one bit.

I pull out my phone and open the text stream between us to tell him it's okay. To tell him I understand if he wants to go, and I appreciate all that he did. But our most recent texts stare back at me from the night he showed up at my house and made me dinner.

> *Carter: You home?*
> *Me: In my pajamas and curled up with a book. I'm trying to enjoy the calm before the chaos tomorrow.*
> *Carter: Want to come to the door?*

I close my eyes, remembering that night. Was that only four days ago? It feels like a lifetime has passed since he sat across from me and made me laugh with his stupid pet names. I tap to start a new message, but I can't do it. I can't bring myself to ask him to stay, because I'm not sure I deserve it. But I can't bring myself to tell him he should go either.

CARTER

I could count the number of times I've seen Isaiah cry on one hand, but I'm not sure I've ever seen him cry like this. When I push into his bedroom, he's sitting in silence, curled on his side—as much as a linebacker teen with a thigh-to-foot cast can curl—tears rolling onto his pillow.

I sit on the couch beside the bed and run through a dozen things I can say. None of them are right.

Before I can figure anything out, he says, "It's my fault he's dead," and my heart breaks for him all over again.

"Isaiah, it's normal to feel like that, but—"

"You aren't hearing me. It's *my fault.*" He rolls to his back and stares at his ceiling. "I'm the reason he went back in there—the reason he broke the rules and got himself killed."

I shake my head. "I don't understand. Why would you think that?"

"Because I was there. He caught me hanging out there a few nights before the fire. It's where a bunch of us would go to smoke." When I lift a brow in question, he sighs. "Weed, Carter. But as far as Dad was concerned, we might as well have been smoking crack or some shit. We used to smoke in Rafe's basement, but his mom said she could smell it, and we'd all heard rumors that people would hang out at the warehouse to drink and smoke and screw.

"The night of the fire, Dad had the neighbor check to make sure I was home like I was supposed to be. Only I wasn't. I was at the warehouse. About an hour before all hell broke loose, he'd texted me. *Get the fuck home.*" He releases a long breath and shakes his head. "I ignored the text. I was being a punk and was pissed at him for trying to control me. I wasn't about to admit to anything or let him tell me what to do."

I rest my elbows on my knees. *That's* why Max was so insistent about there being kids inside. He thought his son was there.

"I was there when the fire started," Isaiah says, his voice low and distant. "We couldn't get downstairs. By the time we realized the building was on fire, it was too bad. We crawled out through a second-story window and jumped down onto one of the rusted-out old cars in the back. The fire trucks were already there, but we hid. We didn't want anyone to know where we'd been because we'd get in trouble, so we ran into the forest. Everyone else scattered—headed home or wherever—but I couldn't make myself leave. I saw Dad go in. I was so scared, but I told myself this was his job. He wouldn't do anything stupid. I stood watching through the trees and waited for him to come back out." He pushes himself up and grimaces as he scoots back to lean against his headboard. When he turns to me, tears stream down his cheeks. "Only he never did."

I reach for his hand and squeeze. He doesn't pull away. "Your dad made his own decisions that night. He was *trained*. He knew the dangers, and it wasn't the first time he took risks when he was told to pull out."

"I wanted to blame you, but I couldn't, and the guilt ate at me. It's my fault."

"No more than it's mine." I draw in a long, deep breath. "Every day since it happened, I've blamed myself."

He shakes his head. "What were you supposed to do? Drag him out? If you'd gone back in and tried, you'd be dead too."

"I know. And for more days than I want to admit, I wished for that. Thought it would be easier to live with than this failure. But I'm glad I didn't, because I couldn't have saved him from the fire, but I can be here for you." I squeeze Isaiah's hand hard, and he surprises me when he squeezes mine in return, and I feel the shift in both of us—from guilt to true grief—like a presence in the room.

Maybe we both blamed ourselves because that was easier than accepting that Max is gone. He's never coming back, no matter how unfair that feels. And maybe now, together, we can finally let him go.

Chapter
TWENTY-FIVE

TEAGAN

He came. Carter came to the wedding. I almost cried with relief when I saw him seated in the pew behind my mother, but I kept it together. Of course he came. He's Carter Jackson, and I can count on him.

I'm so lost in my thoughts that the hour-long ceremony passes in a blur, and before I know it, Saanvi and Liam are kissing and everyone's cheering as they head back down the aisle. The bridal party follows, and we take our places for the receiving line.

Sabrina nudges me when I stand too close to her. "Back off, would you?" She's been shitty with me all morning, and I've ignored her. I do the same now. I wish we could both let go of the past, but she'll probably always hate me for what happened with Heath.

The next fifteen minutes are a blur of greetings and

handshakes as everyone makes their way through the receiving line. I wait and wait for Carter to come through, but he doesn't. I spot him across the church vestibule, talking to Liam's dad. He looks somber, and when I catch his eye, he nods solemnly and gives me a subdued smile before following the rest of the guests out of the church.

I try not to read too much into that, but I can't help it, and all through the pictures, I analyze that half-smile from a hundred different angles. Is he still mad at me? Does he want to talk? Or is he just biding his time until the weekend is over and he can get away from this mess?

Valarie claps her hands. "Okay, everyone! I need the bridal party to go out front. The limo will take you to the reception while the bride and groom finish pictures."

I go to my sister and pull her into a tight hug. "I'm so happy for you."

Saanvi squeezes me tightly. "Not as happy as I am for you. Good things are happening between you and Carter. He's the one for you. I know it."

My eyes burn with the tears that have been threatening all day. I hurt Carter, and if I'd been honest with myself, I would've realized I was pushing him away because I was scared. Because I knew he'd be able to hurt me more than anyone else. In my desperate attempt to save my heart, I broke his.

And he showed up anyway.

He's playing the good boyfriend, even though I've proven to be a shitty friend.

When Saanvi pulls back, she cocks her head to the side and smiles at me. "Don't get in your own way, okay?"

"I'm afraid it might be too late for that," I whisper, and to my dismay, a tear slips free.

She squeezes my wrist. "We'll talk. As soon as all the formal stuff is done, we'll sneak away in the limo and talk it out."

"No. Absolutely not." I shake my head. "Saanvi, it's your wedding day. I'm *fine*."

She sweeps away my hot tears. "You're my sister, and I want to be there when you need me."

I kiss her cheek. "You always have been. I'll see you at the reception."

Liam and Saanvi follow the photographer for more pictures, and I head outside with the rest of the bridal party. I'm the last to pile into the limo and have to take the only open seat—beside Sabrina. She pulls away from me and sneers.

"What's wrong with you?" I ask.

She rolls her eyes. "Nothing. I'm just having a shit day."

When Rich climbs in after me, I balk. This limo is for the bridal party. "What are you doing here?"

"I asked him to stick around," Sabrina says, flashing me a look that dares me to defy his right to be here. "For me."

Rich winks at me from the seat opposite us. The groomsmen dig into the mini fridge and pull out bottles of champagne. Rich grabs one. "Here we go," he says, popping the cork. The champagne bubbles over the side, and he hands the bottle to me. "Your favorite champagne, if I recall."

I take it and look around. "Where are the glasses?"

"Come on, Teagan," Rich says. "What happened to the girl who could chug half a bottle of wine in one go?"

She grew up? But I smile and drink from the bottle before

passing it on to Sabrina. She tilts it upright, and the guys chant, "Chug, chug, chug!"

"That's what I'm talking about," Rich says, grinning at her.

The ride to the reception is blissfully short, but somehow the bridal party has drained four bottles of champagne by the time we pull up to the Jackson Brews Banquet Center. I'm worried how much of that Sabrina's responsible for.

She's a grown woman. She makes her own decisions.

The group is considerably louder and less coordinated than before as we file into the reception. While the rest of them make a beeline for the bar, I search for Molly to give her the update on the bride and groom's arrival. I find her on the dance floor, chatting with the band.

"Hey there!" she says when she sees me. "You look gorgeous. The henna is so detailed!"

I smile. "Thank you. You should see the bride."

"Oh, I can't wait." Molly's smile is genuine, and something tugs in my chest—an opportunity lost. A different life, down a different path, where Molly my friend would have become Molly my sister-in-law.

"How's everything going here?" I ask.

"Smoothly. The waitstaff will circulate with hors d'oeuvres in"—she checks her watch—"two minutes. And the bar is open." She grins when she spots the rest of the bridal party already gathered there. "As your friends have already discovered."

"Thank you for everything, Molly. Today means so much to Saanvi, and I'm so proud to have you lead the charge in giving her the magical celebration she deserves."

"You're welcome." She frowns and studies me. "But why . . .?"

"What?"

"Why do you seem so sad?"

I swallow, and again my eyes fill with hot tears. When this day is over, I'm going to let myself have the longest cry ever. And then I'm going to beg Carter to forgive me and explain that I'm insecure and jealous, and so scared to be hurt again. I'm going to tell him that I want us to try to be together. For real.

"Is this about Carter?"

"What did my brother do now?" Brayden asks from behind me.

I spin around to face the eldest Jackson brother. He's in a dress shirt and tie, his sleeves rolled up to his elbows. Knowing Brayden, he's probably been working most of the day. "Nothing." I force a smile, even knowing my friends can see right through it. "Carter's a prince."

Brayden snorts. "Now I really don't believe you."

"Are you talking about me again?" Carter asks.

I'm so relieved to see him walking toward me that I almost melt into a puddle. "I was telling Brayden that you're a prince."

"Of course I am." He wraps one arm around my waist—for show or because he wants to touch me? "Do you need anything?" he asks softly, studying my face in that way of his that makes me feel like I'm precious.

I shake my head. "I'm fine."

He brushes his knuckles down the side of my face and gives a shaky smile. "You look amazing. Just . . . stunning."

Even as my heart swells, I try to tamp it down. I can't let myself want him too badly. We have so much to figure out.

Molly grabs Brayden's arm and backs away. "You know where

to find us if you need anything," she says before pulling Brayden back to the kitchen with her and leaving us alone.

"Thank you," I tell Carter. "You're stunning too."

He laughs, but I wasn't making a joke. Carter in a suit is a sight to see. His broad shoulders fill it out perfectly, and there's something about seeing him like this that makes me want to wrap his tie around my hand and drag him down to kiss me.

"The pictures went okay?" he asks.

I nod. "Yeah. They were easy." I press a hand to my stomach. I haven't eaten all day, and the champagne I had in the car is starting to go to my head. "Are *you* okay?"

He looks out the long bank of windows that face the lake and nods. "I will be."

Between me and a chance with Carter is a gaping hole where my courage should be. If I want him, I'm going to have to find it. "We should talk."

I almost expect him to evade, but he pulls me into his arms and presses a kiss to the top of my head. "I'd like that."

I don't get to say more, because Valarie appears. "Teagan, could you get the bridal party to take their seats, please? The bride and groom will be arriving soon."

"Later," Carter says, scanning my face.

I nod and force myself to take a deep breath. I haven't lost him. "Later."

"If I could have your attention, please?" I use both hands to hold the microphone, trying to hide my trembling. We've made it through dinner and to the part of the evening I've been dreading since Saanvi asked me to be her maid of honor—my speech. As everyone turns their attention to me, I remember why I hated my public speaking class so much.

"I'm Teagan, Saanvi's big sister. Public speaking has never been my thing, but I couldn't be more honored to be able to stand by her side while she begins her life with a man who makes her so happy." I smile, the words coming easily now. "Liam, you've married a woman who's always believed in happily-ever-after and who deserves one of her own more than anyone I know. Please keep sweeping her off her feet. Keep making her smile like she's smiling today. And Saanvi, don't be afraid to tell him if you need something. I remember when you were three years old and insisted on tying your shoes yourself. You'd make such a mess of the strings that no one could get them unknotted. It's okay to ask for help, and as you go through life, if there are times that your marriage is a little tougher than others, it's okay to tell this guy what you need. He's promised me that he'll do everything in his power to give it to you, and I believe him."

Sabrina stands up and reaches for the mic. I clear my throat and discreetly turn away to finish my speech. "I consider myself lucky to be able to say—"

Sabrina grabs the mic out of my hand. "I'm sorry, everyone, but I have to add something."

Saanvi and I look at each other, but my sister laughs softly, so I take a step back to let Sabrina say her piece. Unlike me, she *likes* this stuff.

"I want you to know how lucky you are," Sabrina says,

swaying slightly as she smiles at Saanvi. "You two deserve each other. And you know who else deserves each other? Carter and Teagan."

I feel the blood drain from my face. *What is she doing?*

Sabrina turns her smile on me now, but it isn't a happy smile. It's the expression of a woman gone mad. "It took me some time to realize it, Teagan, but you two deserve each other, and I'm glad you're together. After all, you're both cheaters."

Everyone gasps, and I feel my dinner surge in my stomach. "Sabrina, stop."

"I've walked around all this time with your dirty little secret." She points a pink, manicured nail at me but addresses the crowd. "She slept with Rich while she was with Heath. Did you know that?"

Another wave of gasps ripples through the room. While no one in Jackson Harbor knew about Heath before this week, nearly everyone in this room does.

"Sabrina," Saanvi says from her seat. "Please, stop this."

"Oh, you guys didn't know?" Sabrina asks, squeaking. "It was crazy. I walked in on them one morning. She was with Rich in Heath's bed." She shrugs. "You can't blame Rich. He's always been clear about how he feels about her, but Teagan did *just enough* to lead him on so he could never get over her, even while keeping Heath to herself."

Liam pushes out of his chair. "That's enough." He reaches for the mic, but Sabrina scrambles away before he can take it.

"I'm not done!" She's crying and swipes angrily at her tears. "And now Teagan is with Carter, who's supposedly in love with her even though he slept with me four weeks ago."

Murmurs rise from the crowd, and heads turn in every direction, as if they can't decide whether to look at me, Sabrina, or Carter. Carter's staring at me. I can handle the questions in his eyes. What I can't handle is the hurt, the betrayal.

"In my defense," Sabrina says, "I didn't know she and Carter were together then. I came to town to do a story on him. We had a couple of drinks and went to his place . . . You know the rest of the story. I was an idiot, but now that I've had a chance to think about it, I'm glad you two are together. Because you deserve each other."

Mom yanks the microphone out of Sabrina's hand. "That's *enough.*"

I try to catch Mom's eye, but she doesn't even look at me. I'm shaking and speechless and horrified. Every set of eyes on me feels like an accusation, a guilty verdict. Is this really happening? It feels like a bad dream—like someone else's drama on TV.

Saanvi looks between me and Sabrina and shakes her head. "I'm sorry," she says softly.

She's apologizing to *me.* The decisions *I* made brought us here. I ruined her wedding, but still she's the one whispering the apology. Two little words, delivered with love, and I don't deserve them.

I shake my head furiously. "Don't. Don't apologize."

Tears roll down her cheeks, and her husband leans forward and kisses her shoulder before saying something in her ear.

She nods.

Everyone at Carter's table is staring at him. He's stony-faced, his jaw hard. Seeing that steely façade of his in place is worse than the hurt I saw there last night.

"It's not Carter's fault," I blurt. I can't bear to have everyone here think he's a cheater. He shouldn't be punished for doing *me* a favor. I don't have a mic, but the whole crowd goes quiet to listen to me. "When Sabrina came to town a few weeks ago, he had every right to do whatever he wanted with her. We weren't a couple then." Murmurs of confusion fill the room. I draw in a breath. "I asked Carter to pretend to be my boyfriend so I wouldn't have to come to this wedding alone."

At the sound of a sob, I turn away from the guests to see my sister staring at me, tears rolling down her cheeks. "I'm sorry, Saanvi."

She shakes her head. "How could you? How could you lie to me?"

I catch sight of Rich down at the other end of the room. He folds his arms and leans back against the wall. Is this what he wanted? For everyone to find out what we did? For everyone to believe I cheated on the man I loved?

"I couldn't handle the idea of being close to Rich. You invited him to stay with us, and I didn't feel . . . safe."

Mom blanches. "Teagan, *really*?"

"He scares me, Mom. He was so controlling when we were together. Didn't you see it? He told me what to wear, who I could be friends with, what parties I could go to. I loved him, and I had no idea how bad it was until I got away. When I went to college, I escaped him and that control, and I was so glad. But when I came home, he'd become like a son to you. I was forced to accept him back into my life. When I started dating Heath, I thought it'd be okay. If I was dating his friend he'd have to let me go, but he still found ways to manipulate me. To make Heath doubt me.

And then when Heath died . . ." I squeeze my eyes shut. I don't want to tell this story. Not here. Not now. "Please, don't choose him over me."

"I would never," Mom whispers. "Oh, Teagan, why didn't you say something?"

A sob lodges in my throat. *Courage.* "I was afraid you wouldn't believe me. I was afraid you'd let him convince you I was crazy."

"You're my *daughter*," she says, intensity vibrating through every whispered word. "We might not agree on everything, but I will always choose you."

She pulls me into a hug—so tight and comforting that I regret every minute I didn't trust her to take my side.

When she releases me, I scan the crowd to find Carter. *He's gone.*

I turn to my sister. "I'm so sorry, Saanvi. You have no idea how sorry. For all of this." Then I run from the reception, feeling every single pair of eyes on me as I chase after the man Sabrina has proven I don't deserve.

Chapter
TWENTY-SIX

TEAGAN

I'm somehow not surprised to find Carter in the empty office by Levi's. I can't believe it was only a week ago that we were tangled up together in here. It feels like decades have passed. Now, instead of two adults blurring the lines of their friendship for the first time, we're two people who've shared a bed, secrets, and passion.

He's sitting on the floor in the dark, arms folded on his knees. Through the light streaming in from the hallway, I can make out his grim expression, his tie askew, top button undone.

"I'm sorry," I say as I step into the room. I grimace at how empty the words sound. My own words to Heath echo back to me. *"Sorry isn't enough. Sorry doesn't erase your actions."*

"I specifically asked you," he says. "I *asked you* if you cheated on Heath with him. You said no."

"Because I *didn't* cheat." A sob tears from my throat.

"And yet Sabrina walked in on you two in Heath's bed. Was she lying about that? Was she wrong about what she saw?" I've never heard his voice so raw, so full of pain.

I squeeze my eyes shut. "She isn't lying, but she doesn't understand what happened."

"I'm guessing only you, Rich, and Heath know that. Because I certainly don't see you trying to tell *me* the whole story." He drags a hand through his thick hair, making a mess of it. "I'm done, Teagan."

Oh God. After all this time. I thought I could run from the truth. That I'd be safe from it. But now Carter's walking away.

"I don't like being lied to, and I'm shit at lying. So maybe I should've never agreed to this." He pushes off the floor and past me. Leaving. *Leaving.* He stops in the doorway, gripping the frame. "I believed you when you said you were scared of Rich, but you waited until I wasn't around and met with him. I believed you when you said you didn't cheat on Heath, but you don't deny what Sabrina saw. You aren't who I thought you were. If you're not someone I can believe, I don't know how to do this."

CARTER

"**S**top."

I squeeze the doorframe harder. I need to get the fuck out of here. Looking at her hurts too much.

She takes my shoulder and turns me to face her. "You want the truth?"

I want you. *But I want you to want me enough to show me your whole self. Ugly insides and all.* But I'm too raw to put that out there, and I already know there are parts of herself she's not willing to share. So instead I ask, "Whose truth?"

She shakes her head. "Isn't there only one?"

I wanted to tell her about Isaiah. I wanted to tell her how good it feels to know I'm doing something for him. I wanted to kiss and make up and start something real. And instead I've found myself in the middle of a disaster created by years of omission, lies, and . . . God knows what else. "This has all happened really fast, Teagan." I swallow hard. "Last week, I didn't want to be close to anyone, and then this week . . . It's been a lot. For both of us. I think it's a good idea if we both figure out our own shit before we try to figure out if we can work together."

She opens her mouth, then closes it again. "Okay. I understand. I'm sorry. For everything."

Walking away is hard, but what's harder is seeing Rich right outside the back door, his smirking face all the proof I need that he was waiting there for me. "If you don't believe Sabrina, I have the proof right here." He grins and waves his phone at me. "Do you have any idea how hot it is to have a woman want you so much she lets you take her in her boyfriend's bed while he *watches*?"

I catch a glimpse of the photo on the screen—bare flesh and hands, Teagan's dark hair. I pull my gaze away and my arm back. Maybe I should be a bigger man, but throwing the punch *isn't* hard, and the flare of pain as my fist connects with Rich's jaw is the best thing I've felt in a long time.

TEAGAN

I don't know how long I sit on the floor alone in that dark office. I thought the tears would come when Carter walked away, or when I looked out to the parking lot and watched him drive off. They didn't. I feel too empty to cry. Too shell-shocked from the last twenty-four hours. I can't cry, but I can't return to the reception either. All I wanted was to make it through this weekend while staying safe from Rich and keeping my secrets from my family. And I failed. I failed and ruined Saanvi's wedding in the process.

There's a knock on the open door. "Someone wants to talk to you," Molly says softly.

I look up and see a beautiful bride step into the room in her white lace dress. "Saanvi?"

"Would you two like to talk in my office?" Molly asks. "It might be more comfortable."

Saanvi shakes her head. "No. We're fine." She hoists up her skirt and lowers herself to the floor in front of me, then smiles up at Molly. "Could you close the door, please?"

Molly nods and does as she was asked, and when the door clicks closed, my sister and I are left sitting on the floor, face to face in nothing but the light from the street lamps outside the window.

"Rich and Sabrina left," she says softly. "Mom asked Rich to leave, and Sabrina threw a fit and went with him."

I take a breath, trying to imagine my mom, who loves Rich so much, asking him to leave her daughter's wedding.

"I will always choose you."

I should have given her more credit.

I swallow. "Saanvi, I'm so sorry about all of this. I ruined your wedding day."

"To be fair, Sabrina's the one who gave the drunken revenge speech." She smiles, actually *smiles* at me, as if she's more worried about cheering me up than the mess my drama made of her special day. "Did Carter leave?"

I nod. I'm shaking. "He didn't let me explain." I swallow. "And I'm afraid that even if I make him listen, he still won't want me."

"Explain to me." She takes both of my hands in hers and squeezes hard. "Tell me everything."

I take a deep breath, and for the first time, I tell someone the *whole* story.

Chapter
TWENTY-SEVEN

CARTER

Teagan: Are you home?
Me: Yeah.
Teagan: Will you let me in?

I stare at my phone for a long time before heading to the door to unlock it. It's after midnight, and Teagan is at my house. I almost don't trust myself. I'm afraid I'll say fuck everything and pull her into my arms before either of us knows if that's really what's best. Just because it's what I want right now doesn't mean it's what I need.

When I pull open the door, my breath hitches at the sight of her in the soft glow of my porch light. She's changed out of her bridesmaid dress and into a pair of jeans and a Jackson Brews T-shirt. Her face is scrubbed free of makeup, and her hair is tied into a sloppy bun on top of her head.

And she looks so fucking beautiful like this—so much like the woman I've been falling for slowly over the last four years that I'm not sure I *do* have the willpower to keep my distance.

"I know I'm the last person you want to see right now," she says. She's so wrong about that. She's the only person I want to see right now. "But you accused me of lying to you, so now you have to listen."

I close my eyes for a beat, then pull the door wide. "Come on in."

"I was in love with Heath. *Desperately* in love with him." She crosses into the living room and stares out the window. I hate how hard I have to fight the instinct to hold her. I want to tell her it doesn't matter. I want to beg her not to say a word and to forget about everything so we can be together. But I know I'll hate myself later. And our relationship would be doomed from the start. "I would've done anything for him. We say that about people we love like it's a good thing—as if ignoring our own instincts and fears is commendable. I thought it was. I thought it proved how much I loved him. I didn't understand that giving him that kind of control over me would be the end of us."

I sit on the couch, needing the distance. I'm not sure what to say, but she seems content to carry on without my input.

"We told each other everything. Our secrets, our hopes and dreams, and our fantasies. I told you he was a bit of a player before we got together, and one of his *days of the week*, as I called them, was Sabrina. We'd been living together a couple of months when Heath came home late and confessed he'd gotten a blow job from her. A relapse, he called it." She closes her eyes and shakes her head, as if she has to fight to keep the memory from taking her under. "He had the perfect solution, though, so it was going to be fine."

"A solution?" Sounds like a load of shit to me.

"If I slept with someone else, we'd be even and could start over."

I sit back. "What? That's *insane.*"

She laughs, low and a little jaded. "I know, right? I told him that would only be throwing gas on the fire. It would make things worse, but he said he'd be there, he'd be part of it, and it would be good—for both of us. I thought he was nuts, but he pushed for weeks. Eventually, he admitted it wasn't about evening the score between us. He was turned on by the idea of sharing me with someone—of *watching* me with another man."

I swallow. I know some guys are into that, but I've never understood it. Maybe it's unenlightened or some base caveman instinct to possess, to claim a woman as my own, but when I have Teagan in my arms, there's not a single cell in my body that wants to share her with anyone else. But if they were both into it . . . "Did you like the idea?"

"No. But once he'd admitted it was a fantasy, I thought that would be the end of it. I thought it was just something he wanted to talk about to get turned on. It didn't mean we were going to act on it. There's a difference between talking about a fantasy and actually wanting it to happen. Heath would whisper in my ear when we were . . . intimate. Describing it turned him on. He'd tell me he wanted to watch someone else go down on me, told me I was so beautiful to him that he just . . . He wanted to watch.

"I don't think there's anything shameful about fantasies,

or even this particular fantasy. But this fantasy was his. His descriptions only turned me on because I knew how much they turned him on. And it was safe—just his imagination, just *talking.*"

I lean forward, propping my elbows on my knees and swallowing back my nausea. My stomach clenches as I realize where this is going.

"*Do you have any idea how hot it is to have a woman want you so much she lets you take her in her boyfriend's bed while he watches?*"

Holy shit. She didn't sleep with Rich because she wanted to. She did it because Heath wanted her to. "Did Heath . . . make you?"

She looks me in the eye for the first time since she walked in the door. "I like to think he'd have backed off if I'd said no that night, but . . ." She squeezes her eyes shut and takes a deep breath, as if she's trying to brace herself for what comes next. "He and Rich were such good friends, but Rich and I had a history. It never occurred to me that Heath might be thinking of him— *planning* something with him. One night, Rich was over. The three of us were drinking bottle after bottle of my favorite wine, and they were killing me in poker. I was too naïve to realize what was happening. I went to use the restroom, and Heath caught me in the hallway on my way back."

"Shit." God, I don't know what else to say. I'm sorry I only took one swing at Rich. He deserved much worse.

She wanders toward the chair opposite me and traces the seams. "Heath was so turned on. I don't think he'd ever kissed me as deeply or passionately as he did that night. Rich was right around the corner, and Heath put his hand between my legs. He touched me until I was nearly undone. Then he started whispering his fantasies again, but now instead of this nameless, faceless third party, he used a name. He talked about the way *Rich* was looking at me. About how hot it made him to think about watching me with his best friend.

"He knew I was nervous. Even drunk, I was scared. But I loved Heath, and I thought if you loved someone, you tried to make them happy. He stroked me through my panties and kissed my neck until I was too turned on to care about anything but my own release. When he led me out of the hallway, I thought maybe that was it. Maybe he thought it was hot to talk about it with his friend so close. But we walked back into the living room, and he looked Rich right in the eye, smiled, and told him I was . . . wet. Ready."

Her voice shakes with . . . shame? Embarrassment? It kills me, and I want to roar my anger on her behalf, but I stay quiet, understanding that she needs to tell it all.

"I should've said no right then. If I had, everything would've been different. There was part of me—some warning siren going off in my head that said this couldn't end well—but I blamed it on my conservative upbringing and told myself to relax. To try to enjoy it. I *loved* the way Heath was looking at me. I'd never seen so much hunger in his eyes or felt so desired. Heath held my hand and kissed my neck when Rich started touching me."

She shakes her head. "Heath took pictures of the whole thing. I focused on that to get through it—focused on him watching, on him being so turned on—and then I passed out afterward. To make matters worse, Sabrina came by the next morning after

Heath left for work. Rich and I were still in bed together. I was still half drunk. She flipped on the lights, and I closed my eyes against the bright light, but Rich barked at her to get the fuck out." She swallows and wipes her cheeks again. "I didn't even try to jump out of bed. I froze while Sabrina stared at us. She was so disgusted, and I didn't know what to do. I was so ashamed of what I'd done that I didn't ever tell her the truth about what she saw that morning. And when she told Heath what she walked in on, he didn't tell her either. I was never sure whether to be grateful or upset about that."

"Why was she even there?"

"I think Rich had texted her that morning. They were friends, and he said he couldn't make their meeting or something." She shakes her head, and her brow creases as if she's still trying to make sense of what happened that day. "I suspect that he alluded to being in bed with me. I think he wanted her to see us there together."

"Just like he wanted her to tell me last night that you two would be in his room." I nod. Teagan had warned me that he was manipulative, but I don't think I had any idea. Guilt roars through me. She warned me, but I was duped anyway.

She closes her eyes. "Something like that."

"What happened . . . after? Did Heath try to make you do it again?"

"No." She grips the back of the chair, her knuckles whitening. "The thing about fantasies is that sometimes people don't understand that something they like to think about isn't actually something they should act on. Not all desires need to be lived, and some fantasies are better left to the imagination. But Heath didn't understand that. He thought he knew what he wanted, but he didn't. And after that night, he was different. *We* were different. He was possessive, unlike he'd ever been. If I even looked in another man's direction too long, he'd snap at me. He'd accuse me of wanting the fantasy all the time, say he knew he wasn't enough for me anymore, say I'd enjoyed Rich more than I ever enjoyed him. I told him that I'd done it for him." Her voice cracks, and tears stream down her face. "He didn't believe me. It's like he forgot that it was all his idea, *his* fantasy. It didn't take long for me to figure out we were better off not talking about it at all. But he'd taken those fucking pictures of me in bed with Rich, and he refused to delete them."

"Jesus. None of that was your fault."

She swipes at her tears. "Rich was different too. It wasn't uncommon for me to find myself hanging out with Heath and his friends, but any time Rich caught me alone, he'd whisper suggestive things in my ear. He'd say he could tell what I was thinking and knew I wanted him. When I told him I didn't, he'd laugh and remind me that he'd gotten me off, that he'd been inside me. It kind of fucks with your head when someone tells you with such confidence that they know you better than you know yourself. He'd touched me, and I'd *let him*.

"Heath was struggling with what we'd done—what he'd asked me to do. Heath was struggling, but Rich . . . Rich was *obsessed*. He'd text me dirty pictures of couples and little snippets of his memories from that night. I was so afraid Heath would see and be jealous that I'd delete the messages, but Heath saw one come through. The day he died, before he left for work, he saw a dirty message Rich sent, and he went off the handle. Told me that if I wanted to be with Rich, to fucking leave and do it." She draws in a ragged breath. "That was the last conversation we had, and the next thing I knew, I was burying him. Sometimes I think I only slept with Rich after the funeral to punish myself. Or maybe even to punish Heath for putting me through all of it."

I stand and cross the room, but she keeps her gaze on the back of the chair until I touch her arm. "It wasn't your fault."

When she lifts her face, the tears I see streaming down her cheeks break my heart. "For years, I hated myself. It's not like Rich raped me or Heath forced me. I let it happen. I let Rich touch me while Heath watched. I didn't stop it. And I never told anyone because I felt so dirty. Not dirty because of what we did—I don't have any issue with people who want to watch their partners or who want to share. It works for some. But for me, the ugliness I associate with the memory wasn't about what we did or even about how Heath responded. I felt dirty because I'd let them make a decision that should've been mine."

I cup her face in my hands and wipe away her tears with my thumbs. "I'm sorry you were cornered into it."

She looks into my eyes for a long time, as if she's looking for answers, before asking, "Do you remember what you said last night?"

I shake my head. We both said a lot last night. Maybe too much. "What?"

"You said that if a woman doesn't say yes, you take it as a no. I've spent years blaming myself for not saying no. I still have to own that. I *should have* said no. I needed to use my voice, but maybe Heath should've had more respect for the fact that I never said yes."

I throw all my plans to keep my distance out the window and pull her into my arms. I cradle her against my chest and stroke her hair as she cries for a choice she was never given. But maybe she's crying for more than that. Maybe these are tears for the man she never got to say goodbye to. Maybe these are also tears for *Carter and Teagan*, for the damage one man's recklessness four years ago did to something young and promising between us. If it hadn't been for Heath, Teagan wouldn't have worked so hard to push me away. But if it hadn't been for him, she may have never moved here.

I hold her tighter, letting her cry, letting myself relish the comfort of her presence. I hold her the way I held Max's hand after they turned off the machines. I knew he was gone but I didn't want to let go.

I don't know how long we stand there, but when she pulls away, she's no longer shaking and she stands a little taller, as if the weight's been lifted off those beautiful shoulders. Does she have any idea how strong she is?

"Thank you for listening to me," she says softly, stepping back. "I'm sorry I didn't have the courage to tell you before."

I reach for her, then force myself to put my hands back at my sides. "Thank you for trusting me with your story."

She tucks her hands into her pockets. "I should go." It's on the tip of my tongue to invite her to stay when she says, "You're right. We both need to figure our shit out before we have any business trying to figure *us* out."

"Teagan, please . . ."

"Don't." Pain flashes over her features, and I hate that I played any part in putting it there. "Don't make this harder."

Swallowing, I nod. I knew this was coming, but it doesn't change the fact that it breaks something inside me, makes the words *I love you* sit like rocks in my gut. "Let me know if you need anything?"

She rises onto her toes and kisses my cheek. "I think you've already given me more than I deserve."

Chapter
TWENTY-EIGHT

TEAGAN

"This emergency girls' night is called to order," Shay says, lifting her beer.

"Hear, hear!" Ellie taps her glass to Shay's.

I grin at my friends. "Thank you, ladies. I'm grateful for you."

Shay, Molly, Ellie, Nic, and I are all gathered into the booth at the back of Jackson Brews. Ava's at home with Lauren, who has a nasty little baby cold, but I'm glad the rest of them found a way to meet up with me. Girls' nights have become a rare exception rather than a rule over the last year or so. Everyone's so busy.

"So," Ellie says, folding her arms and leaning forward. "What's the emergency? Teagan, are you pregnant?"

All the eyes at the table go wide and turn to me.

Shay visibly brightens. "Do I finally have an excuse to kick Carter's ass for this whole 'we both need space' shit?"

Nic presses her hands to her mouth, and tears spill onto her cheeks in the space of a heartbeat. "You're pregnant?"

"Oh my God." I shake my head. These women are *way* too used to drama if they jump to such extreme assumptions. "This is how rumors get started."

"Who's pregnant?" Jake asks, stepping up to our table with a notepad in hand. He follows the gaze of everyone at the table to me and takes a half step back. "Holy shit. Does Carter know?"

"Stop. This womb is vacant, and I'm planning to keep it that way for a while yet." I can't help it. I laugh.

In addition to giving Carter space the last two weeks, I've been giving myself some space. I've needed it. I carried around an ugly secret for more than four years, and now that it's off my chest, I've actually been able to spend some time figuring out who I am.

"What about your stomach?" Jake asks, wielding his notepad. "Any plans to have new tenants there?"

Nic frowns. "That metaphor is weird. And not at all appetizing."

"Yeah," Jake says. "The second I heard myself say it, I regretted it."

"Jake," Ellie says, leaning forward on her elbows to get a better look at Shay's brother. "Levi said he heard that Easton Connor is looking for a vacation home in Jackson Harbor. If he needs a real-estate agent, *please* put in a good word for me."

Shay's eyes go wide. "What? Easton . . . *What?*"

"Who's Easton Connor?" I ask, then the familiar name clicks into place in my mind. There are Connor jerseys all over town. The guy is Jackson Harbor's single claim to NFL fame. "Easton

Connor, the *quarterback*?"

"Yeah," Ellie says. "He grew up here, and now he's looking for a vacation home or something."

"Why?" Shay says, looking between Ellie and Jake. "He doesn't have any family here anymore. He . . . *Why*?"

Jake frowns. "Why not? It's not like he can't afford it."

Ellie clears her throat. "The favor?"

He shrugs. "Easton and I haven't really kept in touch. He was better friends with Carter than with me. Ask him." He taps his notepad. "So, what can I get you ladies?"

"Goat balls," Nic says.

"And cheese fries," Ellie adds.

Molly and I exchange a look. These girls can eat anything and still fit into their clothes. "Jake," I say.

He rolls his eyes. "Fine. Grilled chicken on lettuce for you two and my sister, but don't you dare tell anyone I'm serving that crap here. Or everyone's going to order it and then they'll stop coming because it's *not good food*."

"Thank you, Jake," Molly and I say in unison as he walks away, but Shay doesn't say a word. She still looks shell-shocked by the football player news.

I nudge her. "You okay?"

"Sure." She draws the corners of her mouth up, but I know her too well to call it a smile. "Why?"

"Is there something between you and Easton Connor?" I ask softly.

"What?" Nic squeaks.

Apparently not softly enough.

"No," Shay growls. "There's nothing between us. He was my

brothers' childhood buddy and a pain in my ass for years. That's *it.*"

"Methinks the lady doth protest too much," Ellie says, earning a scowl from Shay.

"Carter could have at least warned me about this," Shay grumbles.

"He and Carter are friends?" I ask. I don't know if I'm bothered by the fact that Carter never told me about his friendship with a future NFL Hall of Famer or impressed that he didn't brag about it.

"I don't think Easton's friends with anyone around here anymore," Molly says, and the look she exchanges with Shay is heavy with meaning. There's definitely a story here that I'm missing out on.

Ellie talks about the mansions she's dying to show the quarterback, and the girls—all but Shay, that is—talk about what they know about his personal life and what it might be like to have him live part of the year in Jackson Harbor.

Jake returns with our food and leaves again before Ellie remembers that she was giving me the third degree about what's happening with Carter.

"So you're not pregnant," Ellie says. "But have you and Carter reunited yet?"

"We're still giving each other space."

"I can respect that," Ellie says, but Shay grunts and pokes at her salad. She's definitely team Just Get Back Together Already. Honestly, I'm coming around to that side too, even if I know this time is for the best. *I miss him.*

"Cool, cool," Molly says. "What, exactly, are you doing in that space?"

Figuring myself out? Trying to believe I'm worthy of him?

I had a long talk with Mom and Dad before they left town. I didn't tell them everything, but I explained Rich's manipulative behavior after Heath's death, explained how I left because it felt like the only way to escape him. Mom was devastated that she didn't see it, and Dad was upset that I didn't tell them. We talked and talked some more, and by the time they went home two days after the wedding, I felt closer to them than I have in years.

In a way, I think I've done more grieving for Heath in the last two weeks than I did in all the years before. I couldn't fully let him go until I forgave him, and I couldn't forgive him until I forgave myself.

I heard through the grapevine—a.k.a. Shay—that Carter's been spending all of his time finishing his renovations on the attic so Isaiah can move in with him. I was happy to hear it, even if it made me a little sad to know I was unaware of such a major change happening in his life.

The girls all stare at me, and I realize I never answered Molly's question. "It all started in such a messy, unintentional way. I want us both to be sure."

"And are you sure?" Nic asks.

I swallow hard, but the emotion surges through me—the *ache* of wanting something that's so close but not yet in my grasp. "So sure."

"Oh, I see what's happening," Ellie says, sitting back and studying me.

"What?" Shay asks. "Because, honestly, I don't get it."

"She thinks *Carter* isn't sure," Ellie says, reading me way too well.

Shay snorts. "Well, *that's* ridiculous. He's practically lovesick. I thought you were punishing him, but if this is you waiting to make sure he really wants you, you're wasting your time."

Ellie nods. "He's been working out with his brothers again. Did you know that?"

I straighten. I didn't know that, but it's a sign that he's getting back to his life as it was before the warehouse fire. "That's good."

"Do you remember that Levi and I took a month apart after everything with Colton?" Ellie asks, and everyone at the table leans in. We were all around for the days before Colton's arrest and after they released him. They were hard days. "This morning at the gym, Carter asked Levi how he did it. Carter said he doesn't *want* to wait anymore, but he doesn't want to rush you either."

My throat is thick. "He really said that?"

Ellie's eyes are bright as she nods. "Yes, and Levi told me that he told him that it was hard but worth it. Levi said that he had to wait for a signal from me that I was ready."

Shay arches a brow. "So you're saying we need to flash the Carter Bat-Signal in the sky?"

Ellie and Molly look at each other and burst into laughter.

"Something like that," Ellie says.

Nic beams and nods. "I love it. And Isaiah is staying at his grandma's tonight."

"Are you thinking what I'm thinking?" Molly asks Nic, who nods enthusiastically.

"What am I missing?" I ask.

Shay sighs. "I think they're going to dress you sexy and send you over to seduce my brother."

"The Carter Bat-Signal," Ellie says, as if that explains

everything.

"It would be the sign he's waiting for," Molly says, grinning.

"Oh." I bite my lip. "Yeah, I could be up for that."

"Sustenance first," Molly says, winking at me and pointing to my salad. "You'll need it."

CARTER

When I answer the door and see Teagan for the first time in two weeks, I'm shirtless, sweaty, and covered in drywall dust. She looks me over, her gaze snagging on my bare chest and then my toolbelt. I'm a mess, but she's . . . perfect. She's wearing a red dress that hugs her from its high neckline all the way down to the hem beneath her knees, and with it, those sexy heels with the ribbons that wrap around her ankles.

"Nice shoes," I say.

"Thanks. Nice tat."

My breath stalls in my lungs as she reaches out and wipes the white dust off the new lotus tattoo on my left pec. "Thanks."

She keeps her hand there as she lifts her gaze to mine. "Is it okay that I'm here?"

Every second I've been away from her has killed me. I've kept myself from calling her at least thirty times. Deleted dozens of half-composed texts. And now she's here, and nothing else matters. "Yes." I sound breathless.

"I wanted to know your take on the KonMari method for girlfriends."

Confused, I frown. "What's that?"

She swallows. "Remember, I decided I didn't care if Liam was good enough for my sister as long as he makes her happy?"

I nod carefully. "Right. I remember now."

"I am not good enough for you, Carter."

"Tea—"

She presses her fingers to my lips. "I will never be that perfect girl you were looking for. But I'm hoping that, just maybe, your life is better with me in it."

I wrap my hand around her wrist and pull her fingers from my mouth. "I don't want perfect. I want you."

"I want you, too," she whispers. "So badly."

Hell yes. "Is it okay that I'm going to get drywall dust all over that sexy dress?"

"Yes," she says, stepping closer. "I'm here to be ravished, if you couldn't tell. That is, if you can manage to ravish me."

"Is that a challenge, Teagan?"

She shrugs, biting back a smile. "Maybe."

"I can't back down from a good challenge." I pull her into my arms and lower my mouth to hers, but she stops me with another finger to my lips.

"You should know something."

I growl against her finger. "Can it wait until after I kiss you?"

"No." She trembles in my arms. "I love you. I think maybe I even loved you before you pretended to be my boyfriend. I think maybe I've loved you all along, and maybe that's why I wouldn't give you a chance. I was too scared."

My heart races. *Best. Night. Ever.* "I love you too." Smiling, I catch her finger between my teeth before releasing it. "I was scared of that too—after losing Max, I was scared of loving anyone. But at some point, loving you became a good kind of scary."

She nods. "Exactly."

"I've missed you, pinkie toe."

She laughs against my lips, then melts into me. "Shut up and kiss me, kidney stone."

Epilogue

TEAGAN
SIX MONTHS LATER...

"They couldn't have asked for better weather. Today is going to be perfect," I tell Carter as I straighten his tie.

The last six months have been incredible. Date nights with Carter, evenings helping Isaiah with his homework, Sundays at Brayden's having brunch with the family. Today will be the cherry on top.

It's a beautiful spring day, and we're all gathered at the Jackson family cabin for Molly and Brayden's wedding. The bride and groom insisted on a small event—or as small as anything can be when it involves the whole Jackson clan. We'll all gather in front of the lake at sunset to listen to them say their vows and then have a barbecue on the back patio and dance until the moon is high in the sky.

"I'm pretty sure it could've been raining buckets, and Brayden and Molly would still think it was the perfect day," Carter says.

"Is the groom nervous?"

"I think he's convinced she's going to realize she can do better than him and disappear."

I laugh. "I really doubt that. I think she's nervous, but not as nervous as the ring bearer. He's told me fourteen times that Brayden's going to be his dad."

"Only fourteen?" Carter asks. "Every time I've called him Noah this week, he's corrected me. 'It's Noah *Jackson*,'" Carter says, imitating the little boy's adorable voice.

"He knows where he belongs."

Carter pulls my hands off his tie and closes the distance between us, wrapping his arms around my waist and slowly lowering his forehead to mine. "I can't blame him for being excited about it. It's a good feeling, knowing where you belong, knowing who you can call family."

"Can't argue with that." I loop my arms behind his neck and melt into him.

"Get a room," Isaiah calls from behind me, and I grin, as grateful to the Jacksons for pulling the teen into the fold as I am for their willingness to include me.

"Can you go find something else to do for a while?" Carter asks Isaiah, and I hear the kid chuckle and the sound of his steps.

"You didn't have to do that," I say, even as I curl into him.

"I wanted to ask you a question in private," he says in my ear.

"What's that?"

He clears his throat. "Today's all about family. About making those who are family in our hearts family in name."

That is such a freaking sweet way to look at it. "I love that."

He's quiet for a beat and I feel him go tense. Is he . . . nervous? "So what about you? Would you want to be a Jackson?"

I pull back to look in his eyes, sure I'm misunderstanding what I think I heard and hoping beyond hope anyway. "What?"

Carter grins and shakes his head. "You look amazing in that dress, but I keep thinking you'd look even better wearing a ring." He digs a hand in his pocket and comes out with a black box. "My ring."

Oh my God. "Carter . . ."

"You've been an honorary Jackson for a long time, Teagan, but I'm ready to scratch the 'honorary' from that title altogether." He drops to one knee and opens the box to show a sparkling diamond. "I love you. You saved me from the darkness, and I'd be grateful to you every day for that alone, but then you became part of my life. You brighten every day that I get to spend with you and bring me more joy than anyone else I've ever known. I'm the luckiest guy in the world to call you my girl, but I'd rather call you my wife. Marry me?"

"Yes." I drop to the ground in front of him and offer him my shaking hand. He slides the ring on, and I wrap my arms around his neck. "I love you so much."

He lowers his mouth to mine and his kiss is long, lingering, and full of promise. When he breaks the kiss, his smile is radiant. "I can't wait to do this for the rest of our lives."

The End

Thank you for reading *Crazy for Your Love*, book five in The Boys of Jackson Harbor series. I hope you'll check out Shay Jackson's happily-ever-after in *If It's Only Love*, coming September 2019! If you'd like to receive an email when I release a new book, please sign up for my newsletter on my website. I hope you enjoyed this book and will consider leaving a review. Thank you for reading. It's an honor!

Acknowledgments

A huge thank-you goes out to everyone who helped make this story into more than a mess of words on the page. Most of all, a big thanks to my incredible family. Brian, you are my absolute favorite human. Thank you for believing in me, for listening to me, and for being the calm to my constant storm. Date nights forever! To my kids, Jack and Mary, you are so freaking cool, and I'm so proud of you both. I'm the luckiest mama ever! Thank you for inspiring me to be my very best. To my sister Kim, thank you for coming up with the Jackson Brews slogan. I love it so much I had to put it on T-shirts (and, okay, that part was your idea too). Of course, to my mom, dad, brothers, sisters, in-laws, aunts, uncles, various cousins, and cousins-in-law, thank you for cheering me on—each in your own way. On all days, but especially the heavy ones, I'm grateful for my tribe.

I'm lucky enough to have a life full of amazing friends. Thanks to my writing friends who sprint with me and talk me off the ledge when the book looks like a disaster. To my BFF, Mira Lyn Kelly, who does more than her fair share of hand-holding, hair-stroking, and pep-talking, my eternal gratitude. To my CrossFit friends who have just accepted that sometimes I disappear for a few months but don't hold it against me, thank you.

To everyone who provided me feedback on this story along the way—especially Heather Carver, Samantha Leighton, Tina Allen, Lisa Kuhne, Dina Littner, Nancy Miller, and Janice Owen—you're all awesome. A huge, special thanks to Chanpreet Singh, who was my sensitivity reader for Teagan's story and held my hand through some of the cultural elements in this book. I'm grateful to my source at the Terre Haute Fire Department for answering my protocol questions. Any errors are my own. I appreciate you all so much!

I have the *best* editorial team. It truly takes a village. Lauren Clarke and Rhonda Merwarth, thank you for the insightful line and content edits. You push me to be a better writer and make my stories the best they can be. Thanks to Arran McNicol at Editing720 for proofreading. I've worked hard to put together this team, and I'm proud of it!

Thank you to the people who helped me package this book and promote it. Sarah Eirew took the gorgeous cover photo and did the design and branding for the whole series. A shout-out to Lisa Kuhne for stepping up and promising to put out any release-day fires since I'll be on an international flight the day Teagan and Carter are released into the wild. Nina and Social Butterfly PR, thank you so much for all your work! I love working with you and your awesome assistants! To all of the bloggers, bookstagrammers, readers, and reviewers who help spread the word about my books, I am humbled by the time you take out of your busy lives for my stories. My gratitude will never be enough, but it is sincere. You're the best.

To my agent, Dan Mandel, for believing in me and always believing the best is yet to come. Thanks to you and Stefanie Diaz for getting my books into the hands of readers all over the world. Thank you for being part of my team.

Finally, the biggest, loudest, most necessary thank-you to my fans. Because of you, I'm living my dream. I couldn't do it without you. You're the coolest, smartest, best readers in the world. I appreciate each and every one of you!

XOXO,
Lexi

Contact

I love hearing from readers. Find me on my Facebook page at www.facebook.com/lexiryanauthor, follow me on Twitter and Instagram @writerlexiryan, shoot me an email at writerlexiryan@gmail.com, or find me on my website: www.lexiryan.com.

Made in the USA
Monee, IL
11 September 2024

65408499R00187